K. L. HAWKER

CHASING LIGHT

A DREAM KEEPER NOVEL

CHASING LIGHT

This is a work of fiction. The characters and events portrayed in this novel are fictitious. Any
similarities to real people, living or dead, business establishments, events or locales is entirely coincidental and not intended by the author.

Chasing Light / K.L. Hawker
ISBN: 978-1-7753011-1-0

Written by K.L. Hawker
www.klhawker.com

Cover Design by Design for Writers
www.designforwriters.com

Published by Pages & Stages Publishing
www.pagesandstages.com

For those who struggle with depression . . .

For getting out of bed even though you don't want to.
For learning how to breathe through the pain.
For finding the strength to carry on.
This book is for you.

I believe in you.
Keep chasing your light.

"Do not follow where the path may lead.
Go instead where there is no path and leave a trail."
~ Ralph Waldo Emerson

K. L. HAWKER

CHASING LIGHT

A DREAM KEEPER NOVEL

PROLOGUE

Sleeping Beauty

~ LUKE ~

EACH BREATH SHE took was gratifying to watch. Air slipped in and out of her mouth as her chest rose and fell in rhythm, and this meant that she was alive. Sure, it had been nearly a week since her near-death battle with the beast, but every time I closed my eyes, I was right there again, watching her die while I could do nothing about it.

I shuddered, pushed the thought from my mind, and focused again on her breath. The only thing sweeter than watching her sleep was watching her wake. She would inhale one big breath as if fueling her lungs with the oxygen needed to open her eyes, then her eyebrows would twitch, she'd open her mouth and slide her tongue across her lips, and finally, her lashes would lift and I would get lost, once again, in the brightness of her yellow-speckled eyes.

Maddy thought it was weird that I watched Sarah sleep, and she would tease me every time she came in to check on her. But I didn't care. When you come this close to losing your soul mate, you don't care how crazy you look by vowing to never leave her vulnerable again.

Drew, on the other hand, understood my plight. If it wasn't me sitting here next to her bed day in and day out, it would be him. He still checked in on us far more than he had to, but who was I to argue? This was his world. His house. And he still loved her—that was obvious. I was just grateful he didn't make too much of an issue about my refusal to leave her side. It wouldn't have changed anything, of course, but it was nice to finally feel his support instead of his suffering.

Drew rapped his knuckles on the bedroom door. "How was her night?" He leaned against the doorway, his eyes softening as they landed on her.

"She slept for most of it," I replied. "Woke up a few times in a cold sweat."

"Did she say anything this time?"

"Not really." Maybe this meant she was improving. Maybe she wasn't recreating the battle with the beast over and over in her head while she slept. I winced. We could prevent her from dreaming, but we couldn't prevent her from remembering.

Drew was deep in thought too, and I felt his concern. He cleared his throat. "Can I talk to you for a minute?"

"Sure. What's up?"

He jerked his head toward the living room. "Out here?"

"Uh, sure." I stood up and went to the door as Drew led the way into the living room. I took another look back into the bedroom, and fought the strong urge to stay within eyesight of her.

"She'll be fine," Drew said. "I promise. It'll only take a minute."

Even so, I could only make myself stand a couple feet from the bedroom. Her breathing was heavy enough that I could still hear it from this distance. Drew rolled his eyes, but didn't argue.

"Sarah listens to you," he started. "More than she listens to me."

I watched him carefully. This was a fact, it wasn't a question, and he was right. She found it hard to trust Drew ever since she discovered the truth about the dream worlds and that he had been keeping her from them, and of course, after she discovered that Drew's alliance with me meant that I had to stay away from Sarah.

"What did you want me to tell her?" I asked.

"Yelram isn't worth it."

"What?"

"Saving Yelram is not worth the risk."

"Why?"

"Luke, you know why." He began pacing the floor. "Let's say for a minute that no one dies while trying to find the key, which, for the record, will be near impossible. Leah hid it from keepers with powers and strengths. You can sure as hell bet that it won't be a walk in the park. So then we find the key, and by some miracle everyone is still alive, then we have to go to Yelram. You and I both know that Yelram won't be like any other world we've ever seen. Monsters and beasts have been trapped in there for nearly two decades. They've multiplied by now, they've destroyed everything, and they've claimed the world as their own. We will have to take the world back—four of us against who knows how many of them. Each of them as strong and vicious as the beast that just nearly killed us."

I hung my head. I hated being reminded of what Sarah would have to go through to win back her world. For me, the mission promised adventure and excitement, but when I thought about Sarah going through it too, it scared the hell out of me.

"Have you talked to Maddy about this?" I asked.

"I thought I'd try my luck with you first."

"Drew, man, you know I'd do anything to keep her safe—"

"I know, which is why I came to you."

"But more than that, I want her to be happy."

"She won't be happy if she's dead, Luke."

"She won't be happy if we keep her locked up."

Drew shook his head. "I don't get you sometimes, man. I mean, I know you love her. I know watching her almost die nearly killed you, so why won't you just convince her to forget about Yelram and live here on Earth where she's safe?"

"I can't do that to her, Drew."

"Luke, if you don't, you know the chances of her

surviving are—"

"Why don't *you* convince her then?" I didn't want him to finish that sentence.

"Without either you or Maddy on my side, I haven't a hope in hell of convincing her of anything."

That was true. "I don't think she'll listen, Drew. She's quite adamant that this is what she was born to do. That this is her purpose."

"Just can you try?" His eyes pleaded with mine, begging me to side with him on this. He loved her. He would do anything for her. Of course I understood why, but it still frustrated me to realize I wasn't the only one in love with Sarah.

"If Sarah wants to go, I'll support her," I said, returning to the bedroom door. "But if you're able to convince her to back off, then I'll support that, too."

Drew grabbed his keys off the coffee table and headed for the front door.

"Where are you going?"

"Maddy." He left without another word.

Would Maddy be receptive? She was eager for another adventure too, I could see it in her eyes every time she came around, but would her concern for Sarah, and her own memories of the battle with the beast, make her an easy sell? I couldn't decide what I hoped for.

Sarah pulled in a deep breath and I returned to her side so that I wouldn't miss the way her eyebrows moved, her lips parted, and her eyes slowly opened.

CHAPTER 1

The Awakening

~ SARAH ~

"HEY THERE, SLEEPING beauty."

It was how I woke every morning and after every nap—he'd be holding my hand and running his thumb along my fingers, then my eyes would find his, and he'd whisper his sweet words. A girl could get used to this. Although, I was mildly discouraged that, after nearly a week, I still wasn't able to be out of bed for more than an hour or two before I felt exhausted again.

I stretched and smiled. "Good morning," I moaned as his lips touched my forehead.

"How was your nap?"

I licked my lips and he had a straw at my mouth before I could answer. I swallowed a couple of mouthfuls and slowly sat up. "Good, I think. . . . Was it?"

"Yeah," he said, but he busied himself with setting the cup back on the nightstand so that his eyes didn't have to lie to me too.

"Did I say anything?"

"Not much," he lied again.

"Luke, I'm only going to say this one time. You are not Drew. You do not need to lie to protect me. We are a team now."

He brought his face to mine and I melted in his deep blue eyes. "You said you hated me," he said, cringing as the words left his lips.

I gasped. "What?"

"While you were sleeping. I know you didn't mean it, but that's what you said."

"I don't use that word!" I argued, offended that he would even suggest that such a strong word came from my mouth.

He shook his head. "Maybe you said 'ate.' I guess it could've been that."

"Maybe," I said, recalling my battle with the beast and how that same beast had eaten my mother. I shuddered at the thought.

"Come on," Luke said, helping me off the bed. "It's beautiful outside. I think we should go sit on the back deck for a bit and get some sun on you."

I nodded, happy to have his arms around me and to be heading out into the sun which I hadn't seen in nearly a week.

I could barely see through my eyelashes as I made my

way across Drew's deck, squinting through the brightness. As soon as I sat down, I heard Lucia bark from somewhere inside, and then her little claws scratching across the floor as she raced through the house toward the back door.

"Hey, baby," I said as she leaped into my arms. She licked my face repeatedly and I didn't have the heart to tell her to stop. "Where have you been?" I asked her, although my question was meant for Luke. "Why haven't I seen her before now?"

"She's been busy with Drew's dad," Luke answered. "Drew thought it best to keep her away for a bit. He didn't want her jumping on you and ripping open any wounds."

That reminded me that my belly where Lucia was standing, was incredibly tender. "Okay. That's enough, girl." I pulled her down and relaxed as soon as all paws were on the floor. "Good girl. Mama's not feeling the best today. We'll play soon, baby. I promise."

"Are you thirsty? Want a slushy or something?"

"I'd love just a glass of water with lemon," I said.

"Sure." Luke stood and then put one arm under my legs and the other around my back. "Ready? . . . Up." He hoisted me into his arms.

"What . . . are you doing?" I laughed.

"Getting us drinks."

"Why are you carrying me?"

"Because I didn't want to tire you out."

"No, I mean, why am I not still sitting in my chair? Why do I have to come with you?" *Not that I mind being in your arms. At all.*

"I just . . . I guess I just didn't want to leave you."

Then it occurred to me—every single second that I had been awake since the battle, Luke had been with me. Had he never left my side?

"No," he said. "And I don't plan to."

I smiled. "A girl could get used to this."

He gently placed me down next to the counter. "She's going to have to because this guy isn't leaving her again."

There was a knock at the front door and then it creaked open. "Hello!" Maddy called.

"We're in the kitchen," I called back.

"Hey, sunshine!" she said, tossing her bag onto the floor by the kitchen table. "You're looking good today."

"Why, thank you." I curtsied and checked my outfit at the same time. Pajamas. Lovely. "Why are you all dolled up?"

Luke handed Maddy two glasses of water and then put his arm around me while holding another glass and led us back out into the sun.

"I had a meeting with the dean of admissions at Dalhousie," Maddy mumbled. "So, it's good that you're sitting outside now. Feeling better?"

"Wait," I said, dismissing her change of subject. "Why would you meet with the dean? I thought you decided to take a year off?"

"I did," she said. "But since I don't technically have a plan for travel, my parents wanted me to consider going to university."

"But you *do* have a plan for travel. We have to find

Yelram's key, and who knows how long that will take."

Maddy didn't answer. I wanted to know what she was thinking, but restrained myself from reading her too much.

"Are you having second thoughts? Do you not want to go anymore?"

She shook her head. "It's not that. I just . . ." Maddy plopped her fingers into the glass and swished them around until she had the lemon, she squeezed the juice from it into her glass, and then dropped the peel back into the water.

"What is it?" I asked, my eyes bouncing back and forth between hers.

"Sarah," Maddy began, "I think . . . I mean, don't you think we should reconsider this quest for the key?"

"What? Where is this coming from?" I asked suspiciously. If it had been Drew making the suggestion, I could understand it, but coming from Maddy—my eager warrior sidekick—it was messing with logic.

"I mean, suppose we find the key." She paused and her eyes bore into mine while images of beasts and fire and blood flashed through my mind. She was doing this. She had opened her mind and let herself think of all these things so I would see them, too. "And suppose we're able to open the gate to Yelram . . ."

"Yeah?" I said, prodding her to get to the point.

"Then what? What do you think Yelram will be like? Do you expect it to be like Earth? Or Etak? Or even Nitsua?"

"What are you saying, Maddy?"

"It's going to be worse, Sarah. Much worse. It's been unmanned for almost twenty years, overrun by beasts and monsters that have multiplied by now, and—"

"You've been talking to Drew," I said, realizing that this sounded exactly like something Drew would say.

"Maybe," she admitted, knowing there wasn't any point in lying to me. Not when I could manipulate her mind.

"Luke?" I said, turning my narrowed eyes to him since he hadn't yet intervened.

Luke cleared his throat. "Well, I can't say she's wrong. Yelram will no doubt be much worse than we've seen."

"But?"

"There's . . . there's no but," he finished.

Shocked at their sudden reluctance to help me fulfill my destiny, I stood and fought the dizziness that was threatening to knock me over. "But what if we succeed, huh? What if we're able to take back Yelram? The worlds will be balanced and Earth will be stronger."

Luke wasn't making eye contact now. I knew he had an internal struggle to work out.

"I mean I'm obviously not going to force you guys to risk your lives for me, but I'm doing this regardless. I can do it alone. That doesn't scare me. What scares me is *not* trying."

"You're not doing it alone," Luke said. "Obviously I'll be going with you."

My heart swelled at this. All I ever wanted was for him to be with me. Always. And now he was here, and not leaving my side. I reached for his hand and he squeezed mine, then brought it to his lips and kissed my fingers.

"I'm going too," Maddy said. "Just don't tell Drew I gave up so easily."

"Ah-ha! So he *did* send you here to talk to me!" I wasn't surprised, but a little irritated.

"He just worries about you," Maddy said.

Luke was standing now too, and his arms were on my waist. "You need to sit down."

My legs were trembling from the weight of my upper body. I collapsed in the chair and closed my eyes, believing that this would allow my body to recharge faster.

"Why?" I asked. "Why am I still so weak?"

"The beast was created with dark magic," Luke answered. "Dark magic can't be healed by keepers."

"Luckily, most of your injuries were a result of being thrown into that concrete fountain and slammed against trees," Maddy added as Luke's grip tightened on my hand. "So Drew was able to heal those wounds, but not the poison that the beast injected." Maddy's face tightened as she looked away.

"So what does that mean?" I pressed. "Will I be like this forever?"

Maddy's eyes flashed to Luke's, and their concern was more than I could handle.

"Are you serious?" My tiny outburst caused my chest to burn and I bent over in pain.

Luke was kneeling in front of me when I re-opened my eyes. "Drink this," he said as he tilted my head back and poured a dark purple liquid down my throat. Slowly, a numbness transferred through my veins and took over my body.

"What is that?"

"An elixir. It helps numb the pain."

"But how will I get better? *When?*" I asked.

Luke shook his head. "I don't know. We're trying to find a cure."

"Who is?"

"Drew and I. And Eli and Trinity, keepers of the light worlds."

I scoffed. "What? Ella didn't want to help?" But Luke didn't find it as funny. "So then what next? *Is* there a cure?"

"The elixir will help the pain—"

"I know. You said that. But I don't want a quick fix. I want a cure."

"Trinity and Eli are working on something that could give you more of a long term . . ."

"Cure?"

"Solution."

My chest was rising and falling faster now. "I want a *cure!*" I shouted.

"We all do, Sarah," Maddy interjected. "Trust me."

"Is this why Drew doesn't want me to search for the key? He's afraid my body won't be able to handle it?"

"We all thought . . . or *hoped* you'd be better by now," Maddy said.

"It's only been three days!"

"Six," Maddy said. "You've been awake for three

days, but you were in a coma for three days before that. And you're not getting any better!" Maddy's rage matched mine. "And some might say you're getting worse!"

It took a few seconds to respond. *Who might think I'm getting worse?*

"I mean, you look okay to me, but Trinity said, you know, that the deterioration process is slow, and it starts with your . . . soul."

"What?"

"Maddy," Luke interrupted, "I think she's heard enough."

"No," I shouted. "Please don't keep things from me. I need to know the truth."

"I'm not keeping things from you, Sarah. It's just that we don't know for sure what's going on, and there's no point in worrying you when you need to focus on recovering." Luke stood up. "This has already been too much excitement for one day. Come on, we're going back to bed."

It should've been the words that melted me into his arms, but instead, I refused to stand. They just finished telling me that I was slowly dying and there was no known cure. How was I supposed to take this news lightly and just go lie down and have a nap?

Suddenly, the air around Maddy whooshed, causing her hair to whip around her face, and Drew appeared next to her.

"You scared me!" she reprimanded, slapping him on the arm.

"Sorry," he said, but there wasn't a sign of a grin as I had expected.

"What is it?" I demanded, searching his frantic mind for an answer.

"Luke," Drew said, his eyes wide with panic, "we need to talk."

Luke was on his feet and the two went into the house before I could make sense of Drew's jumbled thoughts. This was the first time Luke had left me alone since I first woke up. This had to be big. Maddy felt it too. She slowly came to me and knelt in front of my chair.

"Come on," she said quietly as she helped me up. Together, we walked to the patio door, listening for their hushed voices as we went.

"Say something," I heard Drew say.

"This can't be right," Luke answered.

"But it is," Drew countered. "I saw it with my own eyes."

"But *how*?"

"That's what I'd like to know."

"It doesn't make any sense. We killed it."

"I know."

"And you're sure it was alive?"

"Alive and thriving. Hungry as hell."

A gasp slipped from Maddy's lips, which silenced the two at once.

"Sarah?" Luke said.

I stepped into the house, holding my arms tightly around my waist where the beast's claws had ripped apart my flesh.

Maddy followed. "Is the beast still alive?" she asked, but I already knew the answer.

Luke nodded. "Apparently we never killed it."

"That's impossible," Maddy said. "We all saw it. It was dead. It wasn't breathing. You drove an effing sword into its head for crying out loud! If that won't kill a beast, what the hell will?"

In an effort to calm her, I put my arm on Maddy's, but also because the room was starting to spin. The beast was still alive. I nearly died—and I still likely could—and it was all for nothing.

"Sarah?" Drew said, coming quickly to my side. "Are you okay?"

I shook him off. "I'm fine." I sat down in a chair next to the table as eloquently as I could, but it didn't go unnoticed by Luke. He watched my every move, assessing my strength—mental and physical.

"Luke and I will have to go back," Drew announced. "We'll have to trap it so it won't be a threat to Sarah or anyone else." His eyes flickered to Maddy's. "Right now it's close to where we left it. We should go soon, though, so we don't lose it."

Luke was quiet as he continued to watch me. What was he thinking? I so badly wanted to get into his mind, but it was closed off. A fortress.

I'll be fine, I thought, but he just blinked, as if he hadn't heard my thought, but I knew he had.

"She'll be fine," Maddy reassured him. "I won't leave her side. I promise."

Our eyes were still locked, but then he unfroze and

moved quickly toward me. He picked me up and covered me with his arms. And as he held me there, he opened his mind to me.

I love you. I've always loved you. I've never stopped loving you. His voice echoed in my head as if he was speaking right into my ear.

Come back to me, I thought.

Nothing in any of the seven worlds could ever keep me away from you again, and then his lips were on mine, and I tasted the need that drove them to me.

"We have to go," Drew said after what seemed like only seconds. I didn't want to let him go. I wanted to stay in his arms, where I belonged, forever.

Our bodies separated, slowly and with angst, and then I reached for his lips one last time, leaving him with a small reminder of what he had to come home to.

Drew was at his side next and put his hand on Luke's shoulder. "Take us to Etak."

And then they were gone.

CHAPTER 2

Mother's Message

~ SARAH ~

"HERE," MADDY SAID as she put her arm around my back and pulled me into a chair, "you should sit down."

"No." I tried to resist, but she was strong. Or I was weak.

"They'll be fine," she assured me. "Luke can't die in his own world. Remember?"

I didn't respond. Sure, it would be near impossible to kill him, given his strength and healing abilities . . . but it wasn't impossible.

"And Drew . . . well, Drew's too arrogant to die young." She laughed, but I knew it was only said to make me smile.

"How do you think they'll trap it?" I asked.

"They'll figure it out," Maddy said, and I could tell she'd rather not think about it.

"Maddy, what did you mean when you said that the deterioration process starts with my soul?"

"That's just what Trinity said."

"I know, but what does it mean?"

"I . . . apparently the way it works is that the poison infects your soul, turning you from good to evil, meanwhile it's already crippling your body, and . . ."

"And?"

"The transition could . . . kill you."

My breath caught.

"But Trinity and Eli are making an elixir now that slows down the body deterioration process, and may even stop it."

"But what good will that do if my soul can't be changed? I'll end up as evil as Ella!"

Maddy didn't say anything.

"How long is this supposed to take?" I asked. "The soul change?"

"She didn't know."

"I mean, I *feel* fine."

"And you look great," Maddy added, encouragingly.

"Will you tell me if you think I'm turning . . . you know . . . evil?"

"Sure," Maddy said, but her eyes didn't meet mine.

"What is it? What aren't you saying?"

"I guess, you know, sometimes you snap at us. You're kind of cranky." She looked down at her hands. "But that could just be because you're tired," she added quickly.

"No," I said, "you're right. I have been short-tempered lately. Irritated. I've noticed it too." I straightened up. "Okay, I'm going to make a real effort to combat the negativity with positive thoughts. Whenever I get a cranky feeling or negative thought, I'm going to counteract it with a positive one."

"Sounds good." Maddy paused, then opened her mouth to say something, but closed it again as if thinking better of it.

"Say it," I pressed.

She shook her head. "Your key. Do you think . . .?"

I shrugged before she found the words she was digging for. She wanted to know if I believed my mother wanted me to find it. And I did believe it.

"I think so too," Maddy said.

"But she hasn't left me any clues."

Maddy was quiet while I played with a nagging thought at the edge of my memory. Eli had said something strange to me when we rescued him in Nitsua's dungeon. It had been something about my mother and now that I had her journal, I desperately searched for his voice inside my memory. Finally, I found it.

Your mother was an incredibly smart woman. I could hear the keeper's voice, faint but sure. *She was clever with words.* This part was louder and I straightened in my seat. *Remember that.*

"What is it?" Maddy pressed.

"Eli told me that my mother was clever with words, and that she was an incredibly smart woman."

Maddy furrowed her brow as she thought. "Maybe that was our first clue. If she was clever with words, then maybe there is a hidden message in the journal. I say we read it again." Her eyes lit with curiosity.

I smiled and nodded. "Okay."

Maddy's face brightened. "I'll go get it. I'll be right back." She disappeared from the kitchen into Drew's room where the journal was tucked away for safe keeping.

When she was gone, I pulled myself up and pushed through the aching pain in my bones as I made my way outside, stopping only when my feet felt the softness of the grass beneath them, and my face was turned toward the warmth of the sun.

I sat down and ran my fingers through the long blades of grass, trying not to think of Luke and Drew and what they may be facing at that moment.

A few seconds later, Maddy hastily plopped herself down next to me. She held out my mother's journal, and I hesitantly took it.

"You sure you're ready for this?" she asked.

I nodded, although I wasn't sure. If anyone could solve a riddle or word puzzle, it was Maddy. That thought both excited and unnerved me. What if Maddy figured it out? What would happen once we found Yelram's key? *My* key. What then?

Maddy touched my arm, and when our eyes met, my anxieties melted. No matter what happened next, I had Maddy by my side. We were in this together.

I took a deep breath, opened the cover, and laid the

book in the grass in front of us.

My Dearest Sarah,

If you're reading this, life is unfolding as it should. I will be gone, but you are alive and well, and that is what matters. I hope you can still feel my love because there is nothing in all of the seven worlds that has ever been loved more than you. From the moment you were conceived, I have known the greatest love in the world. You. You are filled with life and light, my love. I hope you always feel that.

1

"I don't see anything there, do you?" I scanned the page one more time, searching for any hidden messages or odd words that could be interpreted as a clue.

By now you know about the dream worlds. I wish I could be there to travel with you, as there is nothing more exciting and more thrilling than to navigate those worlds. I've always been fascinated with the worlds and their ancestry, in particular, the keepers' last names. And when it came time to name you, I didn't want you to take your father's last name, or mine, but instead, we chose "Marley" for you—a variety of Yelram, if you haven't yet discovered.

2

"She talks about the keepers' last names," Maddy began. "There must be more to that. Because that part doesn't make much sense otherwise."

"Do you remember any of the keepers' last names?" I asked.

"Maybe?" Maddy scrunched up her face. "I'll have to think about it."

"Can you grab a pen?" I flipped to the back of the journal and tore a piece of paper from the binding.

Maddy jumped up and ran inside, returning a minute later with a pen.

I wrote down the seven worlds: Earth, Etak, Yelram, Nitsua, Nevaeh, Lorendale, and Leviathan. Next to Etak, I scrawled "Luke Anderson," and then underlined "Anderson." Beside Earth, I wrote "Drew Spencer," and underlined "Spencer."

"Eli Snow for Lorendale," Maddy remembered, excitedly.

I nodded as I jotted it down. "And Ella Ingram for Nitsua," I said, a sour taste on my tongue.

"Trinity is Nevaeh's keeper," Maddy said. "But do you remember her last name?"

"Everlast!" I recalled as I quickly wrote it down. "And King Jefferson for Yelram."

"Yeah, but she says right here"—Maddy stuck her finger in the middle of the page—"that they chose 'Marley' for you instead of using your father's last name. Maybe that means Marley should be the name for Yelram."

"Okay, it's an option," I agreed.

"So we just need Leviathan's."

"Victor something," I said, but I couldn't remember the last name.

Suddenly, a gust of wind whipped at our faces and Drew appeared, frantic, a few feet away.

"Sarah!" he called when he found us sitting on the grass. His body glistened with sweat and his eyes were wide with worry. He clenched a knife in one hand as he hurried to my side. "Stay still."

He brought the blade to my arm and sliced a long, deep cut. It stung and burned all at the same time, but I didn't scream, protest, or demand a reason. I just focused on my quickening breath and erratic heartbeat as he ripped off his shirt and sopped up my blood with it.

"I'm sorry," he said, breathless.

"Where's Luke?" I heard myself ask as Drew squeezed more blood from my arm, causing my head to feel light. "What's happening?"

"He didn't want to use your blood, but he's in a rough way right now so I don't have a choice."

"What's wrong with him?!"

"He'll be fine!" Drew said, but his grip was tightening on my arm.

"That's enough!" Maddy said. "She's not well enough to take that much blood."

Drew agreed, then laid his hand on my wound, healing the opening.

"What's Leviathan's keeper's name?" Maddy blurted while Drew healed.

"Victor Haigh," Drew answered, and before he was finished with my arm, he took his key and quickly said, "Take me to Etak."

Horrified, I watched the place where Drew's body vanished.

Maddy's hand touched mine. "Are you okay?" she asked softly.

I nodded as I tried to find my voice, but to no gain.

She helped me to the ground and my eyes rested on my arm, stained and sticky with blood. It no longer hurt, but the redness was a sickening reminder that Luke was "in a rough way," and both he and Drew were risking their lives battling a beast that only wanted my blood.

And what did "in a rough way" mean, anyway? Was he *dying*?

Maddy pulled me to my feet and we crossed the lawn, made our way up the back steps, and into the kitchen.

She took a damp cloth and washed the blood from my arm as I watched, helpless, paralyzed with grief and fear. I couldn't speak. I couldn't think. I didn't want to think or know what was happening in Etak right at that moment. Would Luke be okay? Would Drew's blood-soaked shirt be enough to trap the beast? Or would it just enrage it more?

"They'll be fine," Maddy said softly.

My eyes stung with the reality that she was just guessing, and the probability of her being right was not in our favour.

When Maddy was finished cleaning, and all that was remaining was a faint red line, Maddy said, "How about we read the last page of the letter?"

I knew what she was trying to do. Distract me. Distract herself, too. If we had something to keep our minds occupied, we wouldn't have to spend each moment creating terrifying scenarios about what could be happening to Luke and Drew.

I took the journal from her trembling hands, and with my own unsure fingers, I flipped to the third page. Using a weak voice that I hardly recognized, I read the final page:

You are the one chosen to rescue the people from harm or danger. My darling Sarah, I believe that you will liberate the worlds. I know you will go on the quest to fulfill your destiny, and I trust that you will follow the path that I have laid out for you, my darling. Hear my voice in your head as you go, I will be singing to you softly as I always do.

Your Loving Mother

"She underlined the first sentence," Maddy said. "'You are the one chosen to rescue the people from harm or danger.'"

My mouth was dry. If I was chosen to rescue people

from harm or danger, why couldn't I help Drew and Luke? I was the reason they were there, fighting for their lives.

"Sarah, don't think about it. There's nothing we can do. They'll come back. I promise."

I nodded.

"You should go lie down."

Maddy led us to the living room and sat me down on the couch where I immediately curled up with a pillow to my chest. Maddy took the journal and the piece of paper with the keeper names and began studying it.

"Okay, this is good," she said. "We have all the last names. Now, I just need a pair of scissors."

She hurried off into the kitchen and I heard her rummaging through drawers. "Okay, got them." She was back in the living room and snipping away at the paper before I could ask what she was doing.

"Let's play Scrabble," she said as she spread out the seven square pieces of paper onto the coffee table.

"Huh?" I tried to sit up but my head was splitting and I could only prop myself up part way. Maddy slid the pieces of paper across the table so that I could get a better look.

"Okay, so these are the *first* letters of the *last* names of the keepers. A for Luke Anderson, S for Drew Spencer, another S for Eli Snow, E for Trinity Everlast, I for that crazy bitch, H for Victor Haigh, and M for Sarah Marley."

The seven letters representing the keepers' last names were in a line in front of me—A, S, S, E, I, H, M.

"Alright, so I'm literally an expert at Scrabble, so this

shouldn't be too hard."

She was moving the letters around, jotting down words on the paper, and rearranging them again before I could read the found words. After a few minutes, she set down her pen and looked at her list of words.

"Okay, so there is only one word that uses all seven letters if we use the M, but there are lots of other words that use five or six letters, and those words make a little more sense. Like Ashes, for example. Maybe she hid the key in ashes in Leviathan. Or—"

"What's the word that uses all seven letters?"

"Messiah," she said, then paused. "See? It doesn't explain where the key would be."

"Messiah," I repeated, and as the word left my lips, a look of recognition hit Maddy. She plucked my journal from the coffee table.

"What are you doing?"

"That weird underlined sentence," she said. "'You are the one chosen to rescue the people from harm or danger.'"

"Okay?"

"Isn't that the definition of a Messiah? We learned about it in History. Someone who liberates or rescues a group of people. Look it up. Where's your phone?"

I was searching the word before she finished. Maddy took the phone from my hands, too excited to wait, she mumbled through a few definitions, then read, "'A messiah is a person who is expected to save or liberate people from a very bad situation.' Bam!"

I laughed. "Well done, Detective Maddy."

She was smiling broadly. "Okay, so we cracked the first part of the code, but now what?"

"She also says that she knows I will go on the quest to fulfill my destiny, and that she trusts that I will follow the path that she's laid out for me." I looked up from the journal. "Maybe this is the map for the quest. Maybe there's more than one clue, and she hid a clue in each of the worlds." I pointed to the letters—M-E-S-S-I-A-H.

Maddy ripped another page from the journal and began jotting down the letters and making some notes. A minute later, she laid down her pen and looked up with a brightness in her eyes that wasn't there a moment ago.

"If this is right," she began, excitedly, "then the clues can be found in this order: Yelram, Nevaeh, Lorendale or Earth, then Earth or Lorendale, Nitsua, Etak, and then Leviathan."

M	Sarah _Marley_	Yelram
E	Trinity _Everlast_	Nevaeh
S	Drew _Spencer_ / Eli _Snow_	Earth or Lorendale
S	_Spencer_ / _Snow_	Earth or Lorendale
I	Ella _Ingram_	Nitsua
A	Luke _Anderson_	Etak
H	Victor _Haigh_	Leviathan

Maddy sat back against the couch. "Yelram is first, but I think this journal is that first clue."

"Makes sense since I can't get into Yelram without a key. So then the next clue would be in Nevaeh. That's not so scary."

"Yeah," Maddy agreed. "We don't know what we're looking for, but hopefully it won't be too hard to find." She folded up the piece of paper and tucked it into the journal. "We'll run this by the guys when they get back."

When *would* they be back? It had been at least an hour. Why was it taking so long? Were they okay?

I rested my head on a pillow and closed my eyes, imagining that Luke and Drew would walk through the door any minute and everything would be fine.

Chapter 3

M is for Marley

~ Sarah ~

It was dark when the back door opened, waking me from an unintended nap. I jumped from the couch, dizziness stalling me for a minute, and met Drew and Luke in the kitchen. Maddy was already there.

Luke was covered in blood, and Drew was healing himself as we watched, dumbfounded and horrified.

"Are you okay? What happened? We've been so worried!" I went to Luke's side and carefully touched his chest.

"I'm fine," he assured me.

"He's lucky he's hard to kill in his own world. That's all I have to say about that," Drew said, flashing his eyes to Luke's for a split second as he finished healing himself.

"And what about you?" Maddy asked. "Are you going to be okay?"

"Oh yeah," Drew said.

"So what about the beast? Where is it?" I asked.

"We have it contained for now," Luke answered. "We had to build a new vault for it as the original was destroyed."

"Did my blood work?" I asked.

Luke nodded sharply while Drew said, "Did it ever!"

Maddy smacked Drew.

"Sorry." He looked down. "Yes, it worked. Thanks and sorry about that."

"I hadn't wanted him to do that," Luke said. "How are you?"

"I'm totally fine. I'm just glad I could help somehow."

Luke pulled me into his side. "I'm glad to be back."

"Me too." My heart swelled. "And guess what we did while you guys were gone?" I turned to Maddy excitedly.

"We found the first clue!" Maddy squealed.

Drew scowled and then walked past her and into the living room. Maddy gave me a look of worry. She knew she would be in trouble later.

"What do you mean *first* clue?" Luke asked as he walked me into the living room to join Drew.

"Well, we think that my mother hid a series of clues in each of the seven worlds."

"The seven worlds," Luke repeated. "As in you have to go to each of the worlds in order to find the key?" He didn't sound as excited or convinced.

"Yeah," Maddy said. "We should've known it would

be harder to find. She obviously wanted to ensure it couldn't be found by just anyone."

"There was a hidden message in the journal," I explained. "And when we took the first letter of all the keepers' last names, we found the word 'Messiah,' which coincided with another clue in her letter, and we think that the order of the letters is a map for the order of the worlds we need to visit to find the clues." I showed them the paper with the word 'Messiah' down the side and the keeper names and worlds next to it. "The first world is Yelram," I continued, "but we think the journal was the clue from that world. And the next is Nevaeh, and then it's either Lorendale or Earth."

"And then after Earth and Lorendale, we go to Nitsua, Etak, and Leviathan," finished Maddy.

"Hold it right there." Drew stood up. "First, that sounds a little farfetched to me. Messiah? Really?" He scoffed, and I felt a familiar, yet uncomfortable, burning sensation in my chest. "And second, are you two honestly suggesting that we go to the *dark* worlds to find these so-called *clues* that will lead us to find the key?"

"Yes," Maddy and I both answered.

"Not happening." Drew sat back down. "You're out of your mind if you think Sarah's in any condition to go to a dark world."

"Drew," I tried, "I'm *sure* this is how we need to find the key."

"Well then we don't find the key," he said, shrugging.

Luke sat down next to me on the couch. He took my hand. "There's got to be another way."

"There isn't," I said, taking my hand from his. "Maddy and I went through the journal a half dozen times and this is the only thing that—"

"Then go through it another half dozen times! And another if you have to!" shouted Drew. "Because we're *not* taking Sarah back to Nitsua . . . or *Leviathan*! Maddy, what the hell?!"

"What is your problem?" I said, and it came out louder and fiercer than I had intended, but it felt good. Really good.

"What is *my* problem?" he shouted, matching my temper. "Have you lost your freaking *mind*, Sarah? Think about this—you are asking us to take you to *Leviathan* so you can rummage around for a clue that *might* lead you to your key if you can figure out what it means. It's messed up, dangerous, and not worth the risk! Maddy, I thought you were on my side with this?"

"STOP IT!" I roared. A hot fire took over my body, pushing me to my feet.

"Babe." Luke reached for my hand again but I pulled away.

"Don't touch me!" I yelled. "None of you believe in me! None of you want me to be happy!"

"Sarah," Maddy tried, "we're just talking it through. That's all. We're just—"

"Shut-up!" I snapped.

"Sarah!" Drew warned. "You need to keep that dark side in check, you hear me?"

"Or *what*, Drew? You're gonna what? Hit me?"

"What? No!" he said, appalled.

"Screw you."

"Okay, that's enough." Luke stood up, hoisted me over his shoulder, and carried me out of the room.

"Put me down!" I yelled, but he didn't until we were alone in the backyard where he carefully set me down in a lawn chair.

"You done yet?" he asked, his arms crossed.

"Done what? Speaking my mind?"

"Sarah," —he crouched down in front of me—"this is not you talking right now."

I crossed my own arms and frowned.

"You need to fight it, babe. I know how it feels. It's like a deep-seeded frustration and it kind of feels good to let it out. I get it. I fight it all the time."

My eyes flickered to his.

"I fight it for you," he said. "Because I love you and I want to be good for you."

He loves me.

His hands were on my thighs now. "Babe, I know you're stronger than this. You have so much power in there. You just need to tap into it."

I shook my head. I only had anger right now. And anger made me powerful.

"I fell in love with you because you were the kindest, brightest soul I had ever met. You still are, and I won't leave your side while you're trying to fight this darkness. No matter what." He took my face in his hands. "Sarah, I love you. So much."

My lungs filled with the sweet air around us and I collapsed into his arms. The floodgates holding back my tears opened and I sobbed into his chest as he held me, slowly rubbing my back and kissing my head over and over. When I finished crying, and his shirt was soaked with my tears, I dried my eyes and looked into his.

"I'm so sorry," I whispered. "I don't deserve you."

"Now don't get all crazy on me," he chuckled. "It's me that will never deserve you, but let's just say for now that we both deserve each other. I know this isn't the real you."

"It just . . . it burns. It hurts, and the only way I can make it feel better is to . . . lash out. To—"

"To hate?"

The word stopped me dead.

"I know exactly what you're going through, Sarah. I feel it all the time. But someone once told me that you can't heal hurt with hate. And you know what? She was right." He brought my fingers to his lips. "Love is a much more powerful remedy."

I felt my body slowly relax, and I buried my face into his neck. I was the luckiest girl in the world. How did I deserve someone so patient, caring, and loving?

After several minutes in his arms, he led me back into the living room where Maddy and Drew were waiting quietly.

"I'm sorry," I said. "I'm sorry I've been so awful."

Drew waved it off as if it were nothing, while Maddy said, "If it gets worse than that, I might have to hit you."

"And I give you permission to," I laughed.

"No," Luke said, aiming his comment to Maddy, "you won't be hitting her. This isn't something that's easy for her to control. And combatting it with more hate and negativity will only make it worse."

"So how did you pull her out of it?" Maddy questioned.

"By reminding her of what love feels like." He sat down on the sofa and I followed. "I think we all need to have patience with her. It's not going to be easy, but I think if we can manage to get her to stop long enough to be able to remind her of what love is and how it's more powerful than hate, then we can bring her out of it easier."

"Which will help slow down the process, too, right?" Maddy asked.

Luke gave a quick nod and Drew looked down at the table. They didn't like talking about it around me, but I wasn't afraid. Sure it felt like I was terminally ill, but it was reality, and no one ever escaped reality by avoiding it.

AT LUKE'S SUGGESTION, I called home to let my parents know that I would be staying at Drew's for a little while longer. And as I expected, it wasn't necessary. They cared so little for me that they hardly even realized I was gone. I tried not to let it bother me, but after I hung up the phone, I felt the familiar burning sensation that caused my tongue to yearn for the taste of insults.

"I need a minute," I said as the heat built in my chest.

"I'll come—" Luke began.

"No," I said, cutting him off. "I just want to be by myself. I need to see if I can control this on my own."

I left the house and entered the bright backyard. Any other day, the warm, sunny day would've felt like a big hug, but today, the brightness annoyed my eyes. The grass was too stiff, the air too dry.

I paced the yard, trying to find the good in everything around me. It wasn't raining. It wasn't snowing. Those were good things, weren't they? But at least if it were raining, the sun wouldn't be punching my eyelids right now.

I shook my head, realizing that it was harder than I thought to control the negative thoughts. They just kept barrelling through my mind, drugging me with pleasure at each mean thought I had.

My parents were assholes. Why did I even have to call them my parents, anyway? They never wanted me. I was a pay check to them, and they couldn't wait until my birthday came so they could be rid of me. The feeling was mutual.

My hands were balled into fists, and my fingernails dug into my palms. My internal temperature was rising, and I knew I would explode if I didn't learn how to control these episodes.

"I am loved," I told myself. "I have friends who love me. They are my family."

You aren't lovable. If you were lovable, your foster parents would've adopted you. They would've loved you.

"No," I hissed. "They're incapable of love."

Incapable of loving you. That's not their problem. It's yours.

My breath was angry as it forced its way through my

nostrils.

And Drew doesn't love you anymore. He gave up fighting for you. Luke only pretends to love you so you can reopen your world and save his.

"Stop it!" I screamed, gripping the side of my head. I was kneeling on the ground now. "You're wrong! You're wrong!"

"Sarah?" It was Maddy and she had one hand on my back.

"Get away from me!" I screamed.

"No, Sarah, I won't." She smiled weakly. "I want to help you."

Look at her smirking at you. She finds amusement in your misery.

"Sarah, your foster parents aren't worth losing your soul over. Come back to the people that love you. We love you, Sarah." Drew and Luke were next to her now.

My whole chest was on fire. I knew if I screamed obscenities, told them how much I hated them, which I didn't, the fire would burn less. But I fought against it. I held my stare with Luke's as I fell to the ground in pain.

"It hurts!" I screamed, clutching my chest. "Make it stop! Please make it stop!"

Luke collected me in his arms and held my head to his chest. "I love you, Sarah. I love you with all of my heart." I heard the misery in his voice. "Can you feel my heart beating? That beats for you, Sarah. We all love you. You're not alone in this."

"Come on, Sarah," Drew urged. "The more you can build a resistance to it, the easier it will be next time."

Shut-up! I screamed inside my head. *You don't know how I feel right now! You have no idea!*

Maybe it was from the incredible pain, or the exhaustion from fighting it, but the edges of my vision slowly turned black and I felt myself losing consciousness.

Chapter 4

Tempers & Tantrums

~ Luke ~

I CARRIED SARAH to the sofa and gently placed her down. Drew brought a cold facecloth to wipe her face.

"She did good," Drew said as he took a seat next to Maddy, leaving me to tend to Sarah.

"You think?" Maddy said. "I wouldn't call passing out a good thing. And that was her second episode in less than an hour."

"But did you notice she didn't scream at anyone?" Drew pointed out. "She only passed out from the pain of holding it in. And given what she's had to deal with today, I'd say two episodes is pretty darn good."

"It'll get easier," I added softly as my fingers made their way down her soft cheek.

"Is Trinity done making that elixir that will heal her temporarily?" Maddy asked.

"It should be ready by tomorrow," Drew confirmed. "But it'll just work on her body." The darkening of her soul was something none of us could stop.

"Then we'll go to Nevaeh tomorrow, with Sarah, and get the elixir. And Sarah can find out then if her mother left a clue with Trinity."

Drew scowled at Maddy. "What's your plan, Maddy?" he snapped. "Are you trying to kill her sooner than necessary?"

"My *plan* is to make sure she lives a good life with the time she has left."

"We're not taking her to the dark worlds."

"Why not, Drew?" Maddy challenged. "If she's turning anyway, why not give her some hope and light before she does?"

"I totally agree," he said, "but taking her to the dark worlds will only fast-track the soul turning, and I don't know about you, but I like the sweet and kind Sarah better than the evil and rude Sarah."

My jaw hardened. I hated his depiction of the new Sarah, and by the look on Maddy's face, so did she.

"No," Drew said, standing up. "I don't like it. If she goes to Nevaeh, she'll get her hopes up and want to keep on going. We'll just be setting her up for disappointment."

"It's not your decision anymore, Drew," Maddy pointed out.

Drew's eyebrows raised. "So we just let Sarah make

her own decisions when she has no idea how serious her condition is?"

"She gets it," Maddy said. "Trust me. She knows she's dying."

"Drew's right," I said, finally adding something to the conversation. "We can't drag her through the dark worlds. She'll never survive."

"She's not going to survive anyway!" Maddy shouted. "Can't we just let her have this one thing?"

Drew shook his head.

Maddy sighed heavily. She wasn't winning this one. "Then *we'll* go to the dark worlds. The three of us." She looked at Sarah's unconscious body. "Or Drew and I will go and you can stay here with her. She won't be happy about it, but at least we'll be able to carry on her dream for her."

Maybe she was right. Maybe we could find the clues without Sarah. She wouldn't like it. She would hate it, in fact, but what choice did we have?

"We'll take her to Nevaeh," Drew finally said. "But only Nevaeh. We need to get the elixir from Trinity anyway, and it might do Sarah's soul some good to be in a light world."

Maddy smiled. "Thank you. You're right—this'll be good for her."

It was settled. Basically it didn't matter what they agreed on, if I didn't like it, it wasn't happening. Sarah was my responsibility now and I would be damned if I put her in harm's way. I swallowed hard. It was easy to feel this way while she was sleeping and helpless. But when she woke up, would I be able to stand up against her? I loved the way her eyes lit up when she talked about taking back her world. She wanted this more than anything. If she fought us on it, would I be able to stand strong? Or would I give her what she wanted because I loved her more than anything? The struggle in my mind was exhausting so I shut out the conflicting thoughts and instead brought my attention to Drew and Maddy's conversation.

"Was Caleb there?" Drew asked, a tense edge to his words that he was trying to cover with curiosity.

"He was."

"Did he say anything to you?"

"Apparently he and Holly weren't really together. He just said that to make me jealous."

"Nice." Drew rolled his eyes. "Did you tell him you and Luke weren't really together?"

"Yeah." Maddy looked down. "I know I don't owe him anything, but it didn't feel right to lie. And he came right out and asked how Luke and I were doing."

Drew nodded slowly. "So now what? Are you guys getting back together?"

"What? No!" she said, shaking her head. "I mean, he wants to, but I'm just . . . I'm just not ready for that . . . right now."

Drew brought his eyes back to Sarah, but there was a hardness to his stare that wasn't there before. Maddy seemed to notice, too. Was there something going on between them?

"So there's a party this weekend," Maddy said,

ignoring Drew's unexpected silence. "At the St. Mary's Boat Club and the pool will be open. There'll be a DJ, dance, food." She played with the string on her sweater. "I was thinking maybe . . . the four of us could go."

"I don't think that's a good idea," Drew said. "Sarah won't be in any condition to go."

Maddy paused. "What about you? We could still go. It'd be fun."

"No, thanks." He stood up. "We should probably get Sarah some food for when she wakes up."

Drew left the room, leaving Maddy to pick up her pride.

"Sorry about the party, Maddy," I said, although I knew Drew was right—Sarah would be in no condition to go.

Maddy shook her head. "No big deal. I may just go on my own."

Drew returned with a take-out menu in hand. "Go where?" he asked as he sat down and opened the menu.

"Nowhere," she said, a look of quiet defeat on her face.

"To the party," I said, deciding to push the subject and see if Drew really did care about her.

"The party at the Boat Club?" Drew questioned.

"Yeah," I continued, "just because the rest of us can't go doesn't mean she should miss out, too. Maybe she and Caleb can spend some time together and figure things out."

Maddy was frozen in her spot, a pink hue to her cheeks.

"Why would you even bother? He's not worth your time, Maddy." Drew opened the menu and pretended to scan it.

"Maybe not," I said, "but Caleb won't be the only guy there. Maybe she'll meet someone else." I winked at Maddy and her face brightened. She had a thing for Drew and she knew I just figured it out.

"We'll talk about it later," Drew said. "What do you guys want to order? It's Thai. Sarah's favourite."

We placed our order and watched Sarah sleep while we patiently waited for our food to arrive.

"She looks so peaceful when she sleeps," Maddy said.

"When she's not having cold sweats," Drew added.

"We should keep her away from situations that can bring her down," Maddy suggested.

"What? Like talking to her parents?" Drew said darkly.

"Yeah."

"Makes sense."

"So no more calls home," Maddy said half-heartedly.

CHAPTER 5

E is for Everlast

~ SARAH ~

"SO NO MORE calls home," I heard Maddy say as the heavy haze cleared from my head. I groaned.

"Shh," Drew said. "She's waking."

I pried my eyes open and found myself on Drew's sofa, my legs draped over Luke's lap. He had one hand in my hair and the other caressing my leg.

"Hey there, sleeping beauty," he said, a small smile forming at his lips.

"Ugh," I groaned. "How do you not hate me?"

"How about we agree not to use that word?"

I tried to nod my consent, but my head split with a pain that felt like I had smashed it off concrete.

"So, I've been thinking," I said as I took Luke's fingers

with mine. "I tend to be happier when you're around, so I figure you and I should, you know, stick together from here on out."

"Oh, Miss Marley, you don't have to worry about that. I don't plan on leaving your side ever again. Unless, you know, I absolutely have to." He was referring to the trapping of the beast and this made him look away for a second as he tried to hide his worry.

"Sarah," Drew said, interrupting my moment with Luke. "We did some talking while you were . . . sleeping." He grinned and I rolled my eyes. "And we've decided to take you to see Trinity."

"Really?" I said, looking from him to Luke.

Luke nodded. "If you're right and there's something there, we'll discuss it further then."

"No," Drew said. "I think what we agreed was that if they're right about having to go to the dark worlds too, then it's not happening," Drew said definitively. "You're not strong enough."

I stared at him, unsure whether I should argue or just be thankful that they had agreed to take me to Nevaeh.

"One step at a time," Luke said, winking at me.

"In the meantime," Maddy piped up, "we'll hang out here tonight and get some rest."

"You should go have a shower," I suggested to Luke. "I don't want you to leave me, but you still have a little blood on your face."

He looked reluctant to take my suggestion.

"I'll shower first," Drew said, rolling his eyes.

WHEN DREW RETURNED from his shower, the rest of us were eating dinner. We had considered waiting for him, but the delivery guy showed up almost as soon as Drew got in the shower, and our empty stomachs persuaded us to start without him.

"Aw, smells good," Drew said, diving right into his plate of chicken pad thai. "What'd I miss?"

"Just us stuffing our faces," Maddy laughed. "I was starving!" Maddy finished her last bite, took a big drink of water, and then fell back into her chair. "That was awesome."

Luke was done too, and watching me as I scraped the last of my food onto my fork. "How are you feeling?"

"I'm good," I answered. "Just tired."

"You just woke up," Maddy laughed, but then stopped when she realized what she had said.

"I know. I shouldn't be."

"No, you should get all the rest you can. It'll help."

"Can we just watch a movie tonight?" I suggested.

"Sure," Drew said. "Just please don't say a sappy romance movie." He cocked a grin, but he wasn't kidding.

"It really doesn't matter at all. You guys can pick. I just want to lie down." I squeezed Luke's hand. *With you.* He nodded and winked his consent.

AFTER LUKE SHOWERED, we spent the rest of the night on the couch together, watching a movie about cars and gang wars. I wasn't paying attention, I was only interested in the arms that were around me, the regular breaths from his mouth next to my ear, and the rising and falling of his strong chest against my back. I let the rhythm and security of this movement lull me into a state of complete bliss as I drifted off into a dreamless sleep.

A BRIGHT LIGHT creeping in from a crack in the living room curtains woke me as it attacked my eyes. I squinted and pulled my face away, realizing that it was now morning and I was still on the sofa. With Luke. I hadn't woken when the movie ended, or when Drew and Maddy went off to bed. Surely there would've been some talking going on. Could I have slept through all of it?

Luke's breath was heavy on the top of my head. He was still sleeping, and I didn't want to move for fear of waking him. I just wanted to stay like this forever, hearing him breathe in and out, feeling his heart beating against my back, and having his warm arms wrapped around me. Protecting me. This was heaven. This was love.

My eyes were soon heavy again, and I fought against the closing lids so that I could enjoy more time in this moment. I pulled Luke's hands in closer to me and he moaned his consent as he squeezed me firmly. And then he relaxed back into a heavy sleep, taking me with him.

THE NEXT TIME I woke, it was to a clatter of pots and pans in the kitchen. The curtains were drawn tight, forbidding the sun's entrance.

"Hey there, sleeping beauty," Luke whispered in my ear. "You slept well."

"Did I?" My voice cracked with the need to be exercised.

"You did."

I pulled his arms tight to me again and pressed my lips to his bicep. "How long have you been awake?"

"Oh, not long," he said. "Maybe two hours at most."

"What?" I froze, suddenly very self-conscious about the last two hours of my sleep.

"Yeah, it's okay, though. I've been enjoying every second of holding you."

"That's not possible," I said. "I was awake not that long ago and you were sound asleep."

"You think so?"

"Yeah, the curtains were open and the sun woke me up."

He chuckled. "Maddy closed the curtains when she got up almost two hours ago."

"What time is it?" I said.

"Just after ten."

"Oh man, I'm so sorry." I pushed myself up and he let me go.

"Don't apologize. You needed that rest. You didn't miss anything. Drew's just making breakfast now."

I rubbed the sleep from my eyes. "Well, it *was* nice, wasn't it?" I was referring to our snuggling the whole night, and he knew it too.

"It was." He sat up, pulled my hair back, and kissed my neck softly.

"I think that since I slept so well in your arms, then this should be our new routine," I said, smiling coyly.

"And how could I object to that? It seems to make the most sense." He grinned and I blushed.

"Look who's finally awake!" Maddy said as she came into the room. She had Lucia on a leash next to her and as soon as Lucia saw me, she pulled from Maddy's grasp. "Lucia, no! Sorry, Sarah! Be careful!"

"It's okay," I said, catching Lucia in my arms. She licked my face until I put her down. "Did you miss me, baby?" Her tail beat repeatedly against the coffee table. "Wanna come with me, girl?" I said as I gathered strength to stand up.

"Where are you going?" Luke asked as he helped me stand.

"I'm gonna go shower and get changed and stuff. Lucia can come with me."

"Okay. You sure you're okay?"

I nodded and took a step, but my leg buckled and I nearly fell onto Lucia. Luke caught my arm, and I tried to ignore the concerned look that Maddy was giving Luke.

"I'm fine," I said. "My leg's asleep. That's all."

I shook my leg and tried again when the tingling was gone. It still required great effort, but I didn't let on. Lucia stayed by my side as I slowly walked to the bathroom. Luke was only a step behind me too, trying to give me my independence, but ensuring he could help if I fell.

EVERY DROP OF water felt like a hot ember. My skin screamed with discomfort, and my muscles moaned with distress. But I held it together while I cleaned my body as quickly as I could.

It took great effort to turn the faucet off, and I rested my forearms against the wall while I regained my strength.

I gently pulled the curtain back and held onto the towel bar while I stepped out of the tub, but somehow I managed to slip, and I fell to the floor, cushioning my fall by landing on Lucia who seemed all too happy to be used as a cushion. She licked my face and whined as I tried to focus on the door ahead of me. My legs vibrated with agony and refused to work. No matter how hard I tried, I couldn't stand!

Then Lucia barked.

Quiet, girl, I thought, but saying it would require too much strength and in that moment, my body was using all of its strength to try to stand.

Lucia barked again, and again, and then pawed vigorously at the door.

"Sarah?" Luke knocked on the door twice. "Are you okay?"

No, I thought.

The door opened and Luke dropped his plate of breakfast and ran to me. "Drew!" he called over his shoulder as he wrapped me in a towel and picked me up from the floor. "We're going to have to leave sooner than planned."

MADDY HELPED ME get dressed while Luke paced the room, his back to us.

"Relax," Maddy said. "You're making us all nervous."

"Sorry," Luke said as he turned to us, then realizing I was still half-naked, he turned away again. "Sorry."

I tried to make a sound of laughter, but it came out sounding more like a grunt. "It's okay."

Using the bedpost as a crutch, I tried to hold myself up so that Maddy could finish pulling up my pants. I kept my lower lip between my teeth in an effort not to scream from the pain.

"She's ready," Maddy said, and Luke had me in his arms the next second. He carried me out of the room and into the living room where Drew was waiting.

Drew took my hand and Maddy's, then he said, "Take us to Nevaeh."

NEVAEH WAS A sunny and cheerful place and I felt comforted the moment we arrived. We stood in the middle of a large park with beautiful exotic trees, bright, colourful gardens, and a quiet river meandering through.

The picturesque park was surrounded by a large golden, wrought-iron fence with an impressive gate to our right. I had been here once before, with Drew, but only for a few seconds, and it already felt so much different being here this time.

"It's beautiful," Maddy gasped.

"Nevaeh's Garden of Love," Drew answered. "This is the only place you can port into."

Luke sat down on the bench, still holding me in his arms.

"Trinity will be here soon," Drew said. "She never keeps you waiting."

"How are you feeling?" Luke asked.

"It's nice here," I answered, ignoring his question. A family of ducks waddled past us and I kept my eyes on their bright, yellow feathers that ruffled in the breeze. This helped me ignore the throbbing in my legs.

Soon, the large golden gates clanged and then creaked as they slowly opened.

"Don't be afraid," a soft, soothing voice called. "It is just me."

She was tall, well poised, and was dressed in an elegant white gown that flowed from her body, moving naturally with the air.

"Welcome to Nevaeh," she said as she approached. "Drew, it's nice to see you again."

"Hi, Trinity," Drew said. "This is Maddy, and you know Luke." He turned to me. "And this is Sarah."

"Sarah," she said, taking my hands in hers. Her skin was softer than silk.

"It's nice to meet you. I've heard so many great things," I said.

"And I've heard many great things about you, as well." She smiled a warm smile. One that made me feel comfortable and calm.

"You're in a great deal of discomfort, Sarah," Trinity said as she touched my leg. "I think I have a remedy for that." She pulled out a small bottle and handed it to me. "If you drink this, you should see some results straight away."

I quickly opened the bottle and drank the contents, desperate for the pain to disappear. The liquid slid down my throat, tickling as it went, and then it was as though it flowed through my veins to every point and extremity in my body. I flexed my fingers and they felt brand new. My legs tingled and vibrated as the liquid made its way through every muscle. And then . . . I could stand.

"Thank you," I said as I embraced her.

"Do you have any more of that?" Luke asked.

"Yes," she said, "but only two bottles, so use it sparingly." She turned to me. "You should feel better for a few days now. But then you'll need to take another dose. It's just a temporary fix. In order to permanently heal both the body and soul, we will need all three ingredients."

"Wait," Luke interrupted. "What's this about three ingredients?"

"Are you saying there's a cure?" Drew added.

"Yes. Eli, keeper of Lorendale, believes he has found a cure," Trinity said. "It requires one ingredient from each of the light worlds. We need one more ingredient that can only be found in Yelram's Garden of Hope."

"Yelram," Drew repeated.

"Yes," she confirmed.

Drew sat back down on the bench. "And we can't get in there unless we find the key."

"I realize this is a challenge seeing as how the world is lost, but the elixir I will give you now will keep her body relatively healthy for a week or so. Unfortunately, we can't help or stop the transition of the soul without that third ingredient."

"I don't get it," I said as I watched Luke and Drew in

their sudden frustration. "This is a good thing, right? We didn't think there was a cure. Now we know there is, we just have to—"

"Die trying to find it," Drew finished, but it was under his breath and not meant for Trinity's ears.

"We don't have a choice now, do we?" I argued. "Well, I guess *I* don't have a choice. You do."

Drew lifted his head long enough to glare at me and then returned his gaze to the grass at his feet.

"Well, I, for one, think this is great news," Maddy chimed in. "This elixir will keep Sarah's body healthy for a week. We just have to find the key in the meantime."

"And then destroy the monsters in Yelram, while somehow finding this rare ingredient," Drew added, sarcastically.

Drew's negativity was annoying me so I turned to Luke who was watching me with a look of lost sadness. "What are you thinking?" I asked.

"I think we're in for one interesting journey." He smirked at me, but I saw the concern in his eyes.

"What?" Drew snapped.

"Drew," Luke began, "you don't know what it's like to fight the evil that relentlessly tries to take over your soul. It's not easy, and when I see Sarah in that much pain because of it, I'll do just about anything to take it away for her. If that means risking our lives to find the key, I'm all for it."

Drew closed his eyes and as he considered Luke's reasoning, the hardness in his face began to dissipate. "We'll take it a day at a time," Drew finally said. "And when it comes times to go to the dark worlds, Sarah stays on Earth while we go find the next clue."

Luke agreed, and I realized that I wasn't in the mood to argue. Of course I wanted to be the one to find my key, but I would cross that bridge when the time came.

"Well, it looks like you have your work cut out for you," Trinity said softly.

"Trinity," I began, "how did you know I would need this elixir?"

"Drew came to me a few days ago. I've been working on a cure for many years. I feared that you would one day face the beast, and I wanted to have a cure for you when that time came. I promised your mother."

"You . . . you knew my mother?"

"Of course." She smiled as she took my hands in hers. "Now, is there anything you need from me before you go?"

I swallowed. "I . . . do you have . . . something from my mother? A clue maybe?"

Her eyes sparkled. "Answer me this," she began. "The path is for who?"

I glanced to Maddy who was searching her memory for an answer to the riddle. She shook her head, apologetically, leaving me desperate to come up with the answer myself.

The path is for who? Who is the path for? Me? Is that too obvious?

"The Messiah," Luke said.

Trinity smiled, but kept her eyes on mine. She reached into the folds of her billowy dress and pulled out a small wooden box.

"What is this?" I asked as she offered it to me.

"Your mother knew this day would come." She looked at Luke, then Drew, and then Maddy. "I don't think she expected you to have such a following," she said with a grin, "but I am sure she would be pleased to know you are not alone."

"Thank you," I said, taking the box from her hands.

"It is my greatest pleasure, Sarah. Now,"—she reached into her dress again and pulled out two more vials of the elixir—"who can I entrust with these?"

"Me," Drew said as he reached for the vials, but Luke cut him off.

"I'll keep them," he said firmly, and his rebellion caught Drew off guard.

I didn't take notice of Drew's reaction as I was too interested in the box in my hands.

"Well, I see that you are in good hands, Sarah. I will leave you now to be on your journey. Take as much time as you need in the garden."

We all thanked her as she departed and headed toward the golden gates at the far end up of the garden.

When she was gone, I jumped off the bench and spun around. "Look!" I shouted. "I'm all better! I'm ready to go questing!"

Luke laughed and joined me in my excitement by picking me up and spinning me around.

"You're not all better," Drew said. "You're good for a few days. That's all."

"Nine days, to be exact," Luke pointed out, holding

up the other two vials.

"If it works," Drew grumbled.

"What is your problem, Drew?" Maddy snapped. "Why can't you be positive for once? You know you're not doing Sarah any favours by being so negative!"

Luke pulled me into his side, as if Drew's reaction might be something worth protecting me from. But Drew didn't react, he just closed his mouth and looked down.

Luke nodded toward the small box in my hands. "Do we open it now?"

I took a deep breath. "Or we could go home first?"

"No," Maddy interjected. "I think being in Nevaeh is good for your soul. We should soak up as much light as we can while we can."

Drew nodded. "She's right. We're in no rush to go home."

I ran my fingers across the top of the box—it was textured and worn, and had a strong smell of cedar. I carefully sat down on the grass and opened the lid. Drew stayed seated on the bench across from me while Maddy and Luke took a seat on the grass next to me.

Inside the box were three folded pages from my mother's journal, along with a small, polished green stone—an emerald. I carefully took the stone from the box and rubbed it between my fingers.

Next, I unfolded the pages and took a deep breath as I slowly read my mother's graceful handwriting that covered the page.

My Dearest Sarah,

Oh how I wish I could be on this journey with you. Please know that you are never alone, my sweet girl. My spirit is always with you. Now in order to release your next clue, you will need to give this gem to the right person at your next destination. The clue will only be released if you are the one to show this gem. If you give it to the wrong person at the wrong destination, the gem will burn and disappear.

1

"So if we give the emerald to the wrong person, it'll disappear and we can't move on," Luke repeated, as if reiterating the importance of being sure of our next destination.

"There were two options for where to go next," Maddy clarified. "S is the next letter, but both Eli Snow and Drew Spencer begin with S."

"Perfect," Drew said sarcastically.

So please, my girl, ensure you have thought this one through. If you need some help in deciding which path to take, please think back to whenever you were sick. I would always sing you a song to take the pain away.

Do you remember the words?

2

Do I remember the words? Seriously? How was I supposed to remember a song that she sang to me when I was *three years old?*

Confused, and slightly concerned that this might be the end of the line for me, I shuffled the pages and hurried to read the last page.

Yes, the key to remembering the song will lie in your memory of our moments together. The first line of the song goes like this:

When your dreams are gone, and night turns to day,
All your worries and fears will soon fly away.
And soon you will see your value and worth,
Dancing under the sun and on top of the _____.

Love,
Your Mother

"Earth!" Maddy shouted, excitedly. Drew and Luke nodded their agreement.

"Which would also explain the emerald," Drew added. "That's Earth's stone."

"Wait," I said as the words played through my head again, this time with music. And then I heard my mother's soft, melodic voice. I felt her hand on my forehead as she checked my temperature. I felt her breath on my cheek as she sang softly from her kneeling position next to my bed. I was burning with a fever and her voice soothed me. But she always made me laugh. "Why do you always sing the wrong words?" I would ask her, and my voice was small and cute and void of the r's. "To make you laugh," she would answer, "and sometimes to make you remember." And she continued to sing the song, "And soon you will see your value and worth, dancing under the sun and on top of the . . ."

"Snow," I finished aloud. I broke from my revelry and met eyes with Luke. "Under the sun and on top of the snow."

"That doesn't rhyme," Drew pointed out.

"She never wanted it to rhyme. She wanted me to remember."

"Are . . . you sure?" Maddy asked uneasily. "I mean, Earth makes the most sense here."

"We go to Lorendale next. Eli Snow's world. I am sure of it. I remember her singing it to me and I thought it was funny. We would laugh. She was different."

Luke took my hand. "Then we go to Lorendale."

CHAPTER 6

S is for Snow

~ SARAH ~

IT WAS SUNSET in Lorendale when we arrived in the middle of a snow-covered bridge that spanned a wild river filled with chunks of ice. Across the bridge, the snow was replaced with lush vegetation that covered hills and mountains as if leading into a jungle. The trees and grass were a bright green, and the flowers were healthy and plentiful. It made sense that Eli was a groundbender. The mountains painted in the distant sky were vast and rugged, and the ground on the riverbanks sloped neatly down to the water. It was a masterpiece, and I was suddenly excited to see Eli to tell him I thought so.

The last time I had seen Eli, we were rescuing him

from Nitsua's dungeons. He was in rough shape then, and I looked forward to seeing him in better condition.

"Are you feeling okay?" Luke asked, his breath tickling my ear.

"I'm perfect." I spun around and wrapped my arms around his neck, kissing him. I was so happy to share this adventure with him. To have him by my side, protecting me and caring for me.

Suddenly the air swirled triumphantly and a figure appeared on the bridge next to us. Maddy pulled a knife from her boot, but Eli just laughed.

"You won't be needing that here, my dear," he said.

"You scared me," she admitted.

Without any warning, I launched myself onto Eli, covering him with the most love-filled embrace that I could. Tears rushed to the surface and overflowed as I held him. He gently patted my back, assuring me he felt the love, too.

"Thank you," I sobbed. "Thank you for finding a cure. Thank you for caring."

"Is that what this is about?" he laughed, but he didn't let go of our embrace. "It is I who should be thanking you, young princess. You who saved my life only days ago. Have you forgotten?"

I shook my head. *How could I ever forget?* "You're okay?" I asked, pulling from him now and assessing his health. He was still old, but not as frail. He stood tall, and no longer hunched over in pain.

"I'm perfectly well," he said, dismissing my concern. "And I see you're doing quite well, too. The last I heard from Drew, you weren't doing so great. Have you taken the elixir?"

"Yes," I said, "I just took some. It has made a world of difference. Thank you."

"Eli," Luke began, "Trinity told us that you found a *cure* for Sarah's condition."

"Yes, I believe we have," he said, nodding slowly. "But the final ingredient lies within Yelram's borders, I'm afraid."

Luke glanced at Drew. "Yes, we heard," he said. "We're trying to find Sarah's key now."

"Unfortunately," I started, "my mother decided it was necessary to send me on quite the quest to find clues that will lead me to the key."

"That mother of yours was a smart woman."

An eruption of pride bubbled inside my chest. "Thank you," I said, and it sounded funny that I was thanking him for a compliment given about a woman I could hardly remember.

I stuck my hand into my pocket and pulled out the polished emerald. I closed my eyes, took a breath, and then displayed it for him. "Eli, do you have something for me from my mother?"

Eli looked curiously at the stone, then carefully touched it with one finger. I held my breath until I was sure it hadn't disappeared. Then his fingers wrapped around the gem and he smiled. "I do, princess."

Like Trinity, he only had to reach into his coat to retrieve the envelope that was meant for me. Had they kept the clues with them at all times? Or were they just expecting me today?

"I am proud of you, Sarah," Eli said. "And I know your mother would be, too." He lowered his head in a bow, which was only mildly uncomfortable to watch, then he turned to Luke and shook his hand. "Take good care of her, Luke. I know this must be hard for you, given your ancestry, but I can see that there is real love here, and I hope that it can break the chains of darkness that surround you."

"Thank you," Luke offered.

Eli turned to Drew and Maddy next. "This will be a challenging journey, I am sure. I don't know Leah's plans, but I do know she had the utmost faith in her daughter, and she was very concerned about the key falling into the wrong hands. I trust you will help Sarah attack the challenges that are sure to present themselves as she moves forward."

Both Drew and Maddy nodded and said, "We will."

And then, with a smile and nod, Eli vanished. He was gone only a few seconds before I opened the envelope, which contained more pages from the journal and a gold coin.

I carefully held the coin between my thumb and forefinger while gently rubbing it, perhaps expecting some sort of memory or magical moment to ensue. When nothing happened, I tucked it into my palm and unfolded the journal pages. My heart quickened as it always did when I saw the scrawl of her handwriting.

The others were quiet while I took a deep breath and began:

My Dearest Sarah,

I'm glad you remembered the song, and that it has led you to this next clue. You always ask me to sing songs to you, and you have such a gift for remembering all of the words. Whenever I pause, your face lights up and you happily sing the next words. I have faith that this will be the key to helping you through this difficult journey.

1

I could hear her voice in my head as I read each line, which filled my heart with a newfound sense of love. It felt odd, but I liked it. Almost like that numb, relaxing feeling you get when someone gently plays with your hair. Maybe it was the connection with the songs that helped bring her voice forward in my mind. Whatever it was, I savoured the sound of it—strong, yet soft.

Friendly, yet firm.

When her voice began to fade, I rotated the pages and started reading the next line, desperate to bring her back.

> *The next part of your journey won't be so easy, I'm afraid. There is only one way to open the clue there. I hope you'll realize that this has to be done in order for me to ensure that no one else is able to find this clue and survive to tell about it. This sacrifice is necessary, and I am sorry if it causes you pain.*
>
> 2

And just like that, the warm and fuzzy feeling was gone, replaced by a sickening sense of pre-grief.

"I don't like the sound of that," Luke admitted.

"Me, neither," Drew agreed.

Maddy was watching me, and I felt her concern for my safety, but I knew I would be fine. It was them I worried about.

Sarah, this is not something to take lightly. Do not be hungry for this clue. It will reveal itself in due time, but you must be patient. Present this coin to the keeper of this next world and he will tell you where you can find your next clue.

I'm sorry.

Your Loving Mother

I re-read the pages, which made little to no sense, but I loved them just the same. I loved how she wrote my name so regally, I loved that I could hear her voice when I read the words, I loved that she always drew a heart at the bottom of the last page, and I loved that these words were written for me.

"So we know the next world is Earth," Luke said after allowing me some more time with the pages. "Drew's father would've been keeper then."

"What do you think the rest of it means?" Maddy asked uneasily. "The part about a sacrifice?"

"I don't think it's going to make any sense until we find the clue. Let's go talk to Drew's dad," Luke finished. He took my hand while Drew took Maddy's. We ported out separately this time, knowing we would all end up at Drew's, and we would be safe.

"Take us to Earth," Luke said, and we were gone.

CHAPTER 7

S is for Spencer

~ SARAH ~

MR. SPENCER WAS in his workshop when we arrived. Lucia was curled up at his feet, and I watched her for a few seconds through the window before I pulled open the door. The moment she heard the handle, Lucia bolted toward us and leaped at me, kissing me profusely when I knelt to her level.

"Well, you're looking much better," Mr. Spencer said as the others filed through the door behind me.

"I feel much better," I replied as I held Lucia and soaked up her energy.

"She sure missed you," he said. "She's been whining for your return since you left."

My eyes stung with this thought. "I love you, girl," I

cried softly for only her ears. She let out a tiny cry, but it wasn't out of misery; she wanted me to know how much she loved me, too.

"Dad," Drew began, "Sarah's mother left something with you for Sarah."

Mr. Spencer nodded. "She did."

"Why have you never told me? Why would you keep something like this from us?"

"It wouldn't have helped you, son. I'm not physically able to tell you where the clue is until you give me the piece."

"The coin?"

Mr. Spencer nodded. "Because that was the terms of the enchantment agreement. I agreed to be enchanted to forget where the clue is until a certain piece was presented."

I handed him the gold coin. "Here," I said.

He took the coin and rotated it in his fingers. "Yes," he said. "Yes, this is the piece. I remember it well."

"So?" Luke prodded. "Where's the clue?"

"I . . ." He struggled with a memory as his brow furrowed. "I . . . wait a minute . . ."

"Dad?" Drew said, forcefully. "What's wrong?"

"I . . . don't remember."

"You're kidding me, right?!" Drew yelled.

"Wait now," Luke said, taking the coin from a bewildered Mr. Spencer. "If this gold coin was enchanted to reveal the secret location of the next clue once it touched your fingers, then there's no way it can't work."

"Explain this, then, Luke," Drew barked.

Luke turned to Drew. "Unless it wasn't Mr. Spencer that was charmed; it was Earth's keeper."

Drew shook his head, frustrated. "Who was my father!"

"Yes," Luke continued, "but he's not Earth's keeper now. The charm would have passed onto the next keeper." He held the coin out for Drew. "You."

Drew looked, somewhat anxiously, at the coin. "You think . . . me?"

"Yes," Mr. Spencer cut in. "Yes, it would make sense. That way, even if I died, the clue could still be found."

Drew slowly reached for the coin and the moment that it touched his fingertips, he gasped, pinched his eyes closed, and clutched the coin for all it was worth. It was several seconds before his eyes opened again.

"We need to bring this coin to the portal," he said, his chest rising and falling quickly.

"What did you see?" I urged.

His eyes found mine, and a mixture of sadness and excitement filled them. "You get your looks from her."

I gasped. "You saw my mother?"

He nodded.

"What did she look like?"

Drew's face brightened. "Beautiful. A slightly older version of you." His eyes followed the lines of my face, hair, arms.

Luke cleared his throat, causing Drew's eyes to come back to mine. "She gave you instructions to bring the coin to the portal?" Luke repeated, more as an interruption than as a question.

"Yes," Drew said, and his gaze fell to the floor. "We go to the portal and the clue will be revealed from there."

"What are we waiting for?" Maddy said. "Let's go get that clue."

I knelt down in front of Lucia. Her deep, brown eyes entered my soul, and I felt a trace of her misery. She worried I wouldn't come back.

"I promise you I will be back soon, Lucia." I kissed her furry head and then let Luke take my hand.

THE APPLE TREE wasn't far from Drew's house. I always wondered if that was intentional. Was a keeper able to choose the portal? Or did he choose to live here because this was where the portal had always been?

As we approached the meadow, Luke's hold tightened around my fingers. "What's wrong?" I asked.

He shook his head as if it were nothing, but I felt his worry. He, too, worried about my mother's warning in the last clue.

As we cautiously approached the great, old tree, something happened. The leaves rustled gently, shimmering in the now late afternoon light. The trunk seemed to come alive in vibrant waves of the bark. And then . . . the tree glowed.

"What's happening?" Maddy asked as we all paused in our advance, about twenty feet from the tree.

"I don't know," Drew said, his focus locked on the tree ahead. "I've never seen anything like it."

The coin in my hand was burning now and I nearly dropped it. Somehow I knew that bringing it closer to the tree would cool it down, so I didn't hesitate to quickly move forward.

"Sarah, wait," Luke cautioned, but I couldn't adhere. The moment I took my first steps, I knew it was in the right direction.

The tree glowed brighter with every step I took, and soon all of the apples hanging from the branches and bows were a brilliant red, reflecting the sun and sending a shower of sparkles through the air. It was beautiful and I had to resist reaching out to touch them, as my only mission right now was to get this coin to the tree.

When I reached the tree, Luke was right behind me. Drew and Maddy stayed back, Drew holding her in place as she evidently wanted to come, too. Rays of light erupted from every crease of the tree until finally it exploded in a shower of light and crystals that took to the sky.

And when the impressive display of light diminished, one red apple fell from a branch and landed on the ground next to me.

"The clue," Luke said as he bent to pick it up, but I intercepted his reach.

"I got it." I picked up the apple and rotated it in my fingers. "Do you think it's inside?"

Drew and Maddy had joined us now. Drew pulled a knife from his boot. "Cut it open and see?"

"Wait," I said, cradling the apple close to me, as if it needed protection. I reached into my pocket and pulled out the latest clue and read from the second page. "'There is only one way to open the clue . . . in order for me to ensure that no one else is able to find this clue and survive to tell about it. This sacrifice is necessary, and I am so sorry if it causes you pain.'"

"If you try to open it, you will die," Maddy guessed.

Everyone was silent for a minute while I quietly re-read my mother's twisted riddle. Then I said, "It sounds like it." I flipped to the next page and continued reading, "'Do not be hungry for this clue. It will reveal itself in due time, but you must be patient.'"

"That must mean the apple will eventually open on its own, in due time," Maddy deduced.

"But then why did it say that someone would need to die?" I wondered.

"Maybe it will lure its prey," Maddy said, shuddering. "Whoever takes a bite will die . . . and the clue will then be revealed."

Drew and Luke had been quiet up to this point, and when I looked up from the apple, I realized that they were exchanging a look that I didn't like.

"What are you thinking?" I asked. "Why haven't you said anything?"

Luke looked down at me and smiled. "I think you're right. I think someone needs to take a bite in order for you to be able to move forward. I think whoever does take a bite will die, and I think there is an element of temptation to it."

"Do you feel it?" Drew asked quietly.

"I do," Luke answered equally as low. "You?"

Drew nodded.

"Wait," Maddy said, holding her hand up to Drew.

"You feel tempted to eat the apple?"

"Just one bite," he said, licking his lips.

Maddy reached up and slapped him. "Well, don't you dare! You heard Sarah's mother! Whoever eats it will die!"

Drew touched his face where the redness from Maddy's slap was surely stinging. His eyes refocused and he shook his head. "Right," he said, then stealing a quick look at Luke, he added, "Maybe you should keep this one away from me and Luke."

"Are you not drawn to it?" Luke asked me.

"No," I answered. "Not at all."

"Me, neither," Maddy added. "So we'll keep watch until . . . it either opens on its own or someone takes a bite and opens it for us." She pointed a finger at Luke and then to Drew. "But *not* one of you two!"

EVEN THOUGH I knew it would be near impossible for Luke or Drew to steal the apple, I couldn't stop obsessively checking to ensure it was still tucked away safely in the bottom of my bag.

"You must be starving," Luke said as we walked up the front walk to Drew's house.

I shrugged. "Not really."

"You haven't eaten anything all day."

"Neither have you," I pointed out.

"I didn't say I wasn't hungry."

I smiled and nudged my shoulder into him. He stopped me on the steps and waited for Drew and Maddy to pass.

"I'll make spaghetti," Maddy said before she disappeared after Drew through the front door.

Once we were alone, Luke pushed the stray strands of hairs from my face and smiled. "I'm so proud of you."

I matched his adoring smile and slid my hands around his waist. "Why?"

"For being so brave," he said. "And for going after your dream."

I rested my head against his chest. "I couldn't do it without you. You're the only one who believes in me half the time."

His arms were around me and holding me securely. "I believe in you *all* the time. It's just sometimes I'm too afraid to lose you again to let you have free rein."

I closed my eyes and smiled, a tonic of love bubbling up inside me. "You won't lose me again," I whispered.

He tightened his hold, but didn't reply.

"Luke," I started, "will you . . . will you promise me something?"

"Anything."

"Will you promise me that you will never go back to Ella? I mean, you know, in case something happens to us, or to me—"

"Stop right there," he ordered. "First of all, Ella is nothing compared to you. After how she treated you, she'll never be more than an enemy to me. And second, nothing will ever happen to us. Sarah, you are the only girl I've ever loved, and I plan to spend the rest of my life by your side. Nothing will tear us apart ever again. I promise you that." He took my face in his hands. "And I don't care how nasty you get over these next few days, or weeks, or however long it takes for us to save your soul, I will not leave you, and you can't push me away."

My eyes were glistening with the salt of my tears, but there was no point in trying to hide it. He saw into my soul. He knew me.

"I wish I didn't hurt you," I said, referring to the uncontrollable urges to lash out at him.

"That's what the darkness does. It *needs* to destroy all love, and makes you attack the ones you care about most. But I promise you it won't destroy ours." He pressed his lips to mine and it sent shivers up my spine. I never wanted to leave his arms. This was where I belonged.

"Do you think we'll grow old together?" I asked into his lips.

"Baby, I'll be loving you 'till we're seventy."

I laughed. "Pretty sure you just quoted lyrics from a song there."

He laughed too. "Was hoping you wouldn't notice."

"Let me guess—my soul will never grow old because it's evergreen, right?"

"Old, maybe, but never dark."

"Speaking of which, I think the elixir worked on my soul a bit too, 'cause I feel better since taking it."

"I think you feel better because you just spent time soaking up some light in Nevaeh and Lorendale. I don't think it was the elixir. Trinity said the soul couldn't be cured without that ingredient from Yelram."

"Well, I'll keep telling myself it's the elixir. Maybe the placebo effect is working."

Luke laughed. "Yes, you keep telling yourself that, then."

After several minutes of bliss in Luke's arms, Lucia interrupted by bounding up the front walk and jumping at our legs.

"Hey, girl." Luke released me so he could greet Lucia. "Did you think I wasn't going to bring her home, did ya?"

I sat down on the step and let Lucia attack me with kisses.

"She misses you," Luke noticed.

"She does." I covered Lucia's face in kisses. "I feel so guilty for not being around for her anymore. I mean, what'll happen to her when we find the key?"

"What do you mean?"

"When we take back Yelram, I can't just leave her here. I have to take her with me."

Luke nodded. "I'm sure that's possible."

"I want to take her down to the waterfront tomorrow for a walk. Before we go to Nitsua."

"Sure. That sounds nice."

"You don't have to come," I said. "I mean, if you have business to take care of at home, I can take her on my own."

"No," Luke said, definitively. "I told you I have no intention of leaving you again."

"But Luke, you're going to have to eventually go back, aren't you?"

He looked away, avoiding my eyes.

"Of course I love having you with me, but what'll happen to Etak if you don't ever return?"

"Nothing," he said, but then paused before adding, "Drew is checking in on it for me."

"Which is cool and all, but your people need you, too, right?"

"Sarah, I'm helping you take back Yelram first. Then I'll worry about my world." And it was said with such finality that I knew better than to press the subject further.

We stayed on the front steps watching the sun slowly descend, Lucia between my legs, her head on my lap, and me between Luke's legs, his arms around me. It was the happiest I could ever remember being.

"Supper's ready," Maddy announced through the screen door, and I nearly jumped from start.

"Smells good," Luke said as he helped me up. "We'll be right in."

"Don't be fooled," I laughed quietly. "Smells can be deceiving; Maddy's not much of a cook."

"Heard that!" Maddy called from near the kitchen.

"She's got bat ears," Luke laughed.

"Heard that, too!"

CONTRARY TO MY prediction, dinner was delicious. Maybe Drew had helped her, or maybe I was just too hungry to care that the ground beef was crispy and we needed rolls to sop up the runny sauce. No one complained, though, and Maddy was very proud of herself for this achievement.

"I think we should all get an apartment together," she said as she cleared the table.

Drew just smiled and shook his head. "Where? Here or Etak?"

Maddy paused for a second before putting the dishes into the sink. "Yes, I suppose Luke's residency could pose a problem."

Luke narrowed his eyes out the window at a distant thought. I squeezed his leg under the table and winked when he looked at me, reassuring him that it didn't matter where we lived—we would find a way to be together.

"So for dessert," Maddy announced proudly as she opened the oven door. "I made a pie!"

Maddy slid the pie onto the stove and started slicing it with a knife. She dished out four slices and placed the first two pieces in front of Luke and Drew.

"Apple," they both said at the same time.

Instinctively, I grabbed at my bag that was slung over the back of the chair. My hand went to the bottom and I fished around until I pulled out the pristine, whole apple. I sighed heavily.

Maddy froze with the other two pieces in her hands. "I'm so sorry. I forgot," she said. "It's not *that* apple, I promise. . . . Should we not eat it?"

"No," Drew said. "It's fine. Sit down."

"Does it make your craving worse?" I asked as I slowly tucked the apple deeper into my bag.

Luke inhaled slowly. "Not really. It's not that these apples are appealing. It's only the one we can't have."

I nodded, feeling a load of guilt for their temptation. What was my mother thinking? Why would she want to lure someone to their death? Did she worry that a dark lord, like Luke, would be following me, and this apple would get rid of him? Had she never considered that Drew could be tempted by the apple, too? But she did know. She knew I wouldn't be alone. She knew someone would eventually take the bite and would become the sacrifice, and that their death would cause me pain. She had said so in her letter.

I looked from Drew to Luke and fought the urge to cry. How could I let this happen? I couldn't. But if not them, then who else would do it? Could I somehow tempt Ella with it? How long would Drew and Luke be able to resist the apple?

"So," Luke said, somewhat cheerfully, and I knew at once that he was trying to change the direction of my thoughts. He knew I was worried. Frustrated. And he feared this could send me into a tailspin of negativity. "Sarah said she's been feeling really good since visiting Nevaeh and Lorendale."

"I'd believe it," Maddy picked up. "I've been feeling pretty awesome, too. Those worlds are amazing."

"Yeah, and I was thinking," I said, "I'd like to go down to the waterfront to take Lucia for a walk tomorrow."

"What about the clue?" Drew asked.

"Assuming it's not opened by then," Luke added.

"But even if it is, I'd really like to do this. I don't spend much time with her anymore and I know that she misses me."

"Sarah," Drew said, "we don't have time to waste here. You only have enough elixir to last nine days. We have no idea how long it will take us to find the next three clues, and then to take back Yelram. I don't think it's a good idea."

"How about," Luke said, "we play it by ear. If the apple isn't open, we'll go. If it is open, we'll see how she's feeling."

Drew nodded his approval, although I didn't get the sense that he felt like the matter was up for debate. But did he have a say anymore?

"While we're on the topic," Maddy said, somewhat uncomfortably. "If the apple isn't open by tomorrow and Sarah's still feeling great, I was thinking that maybe we could all go to that party I was telling you guys about?"

Puzzled, I looked at Luke for an explanation. "What party?"

"Maddy said there's a party going on at the St. Mary's Boat Club," Luke answered.

"Sounds fun," I said.

Drew stuffed a forkful of pie into his mouth and ignored the continuing conversation.

Luke started, "How about we see how you're feeling tomorr—"

"No!" I shouted, more forcefully than I had intended. Then I lowered my voice to continue, "I mean, you always say that, and what you're really saying is that you don't think I should go and you're just hoping something else comes up in the meantime so you don't have to tell me that you disagree."

He looked at me, a smile playing at the corner of his mouth that he was trying to conceal.

"Don't laugh at me," I said. "You know I'm right."

"You are right," he admitted. "I don't want to argue with you and I'm secretly hoping that this stupid apple will open tonight and we won't have to deal with any of this tomorrow."

"Well, at least you can admit it."

Drew had a smirk on his face as he stuffed another forkful of pie into his mouth, which only irritated me. He thought the discussion was over. He thought my silence meant I accepted defeat. He thought that if Luke told me he didn't want me to go the party, or take Lucia for a walk, then I wouldn't. Well, the discussion might be over, but I was far from surrendering.

CHAPTER 8

Forbidden Fruit

~ SARAH ~

MADDY HAD GONE home to sleep, despite her back and forth on the decision. Drew was the one to help the decision process along, reminding her that her house had just as much protection on it as his, so she would be fine to go home.

Maddy took the apple home with her, promising to keep it hidden from her family. As long as they didn't see it, we figured they wouldn't be tempted by it. Mr. Spencer hadn't been tempted until he saw it.

Luke and I slept on the couch again, his arms around me like a warm blanket. Drew wasn't happy about it, and he made no effort to hide his thoughts on the matter.

I woke fairly early—7:38am. Luke was still asleep, so

I slowly reached for my phone on the coffee table and texted Maddy.

MADDY

Today at 7:40am
You awake?

Today at 7:41am
No

Today at 7:41am
How's the apple?

Today at 7:42am
Still there. No bites. Not open.
Good night.

Disappointed, I quietly laid my phone back on the coffee table and tried to go back to sleep too, but it was no use. Lucia, who had been sleeping on the floor by our feet, heard me stirring and was already planting her morning kisses all over my face. I didn't have the heart to push her away, so I let her soak my face while I combed her hair with my fingers.

"Mornin'," Luke mumbled, his voice even deeper with the residue of sleep.

I rolled over and buried my face into his chest, inhaling deeply the scent of his skin—coconuts and sea water, if that was possible.

"Did you sleep well?" I asked softly.

"Always, when I'm with you."

I smiled. "Me too."

His hand was slowly tracing my back and I mimicked the movement with my own hand on his chest and abs. How was it possible that they were still so hard when he was sleeping?

"The apple didn't open," I heard myself say, realizing that this had been bothering me since Maddy told me.

"No?" And I sensed his disappointment, too.

"Do you think someone really has to eat it? And die?"

"I don't know," he replied. "But there's no sense in worrying about it. We can't do anything until it opens, so we'll just have to patiently wait."

"But what if it never opens? What if it wasn't meant to be guarded? What if my mother just expected me to leave it lying around and knew that somebody would come along and bite into it?"

"I don't think your mother would've done that."

But how could he be so sure? He didn't know her. I didn't even know her, and the more I learned about her, the more I realized that she didn't quite fit the image of the mother I had painted for myself.

Luke kissed my neck. "Listen, why don't you get ready and I'll take you out for breakfast."

My heart fluttered, as it always did at the thought of spending alone time with Luke. I had hardly given him my "yes," and I was on my feet and heading for the shower, thankful that my legs were working and I still felt great.

CHAPTER 9

The Enchantment

~ LUKE ~

"HEY," DREW YAWNED as he came out of his bedroom and stretched. "Where's Sarah?"

"Shower," I answered as I folded the blankets on the couch and tidied up the living room.

"D'you sleep well?" he asked, but I knew there was some resentment behind this question.

I just grunted, nodded, and continued folding as if this question meant nothing to me. To Drew it meant more. To Drew it bothered the hell out of him that I was sleeping on his couch with his ex-girlfriend, and I understood that. If it weren't for Sarah insisting, I would've slept on the floor. But Drew knew, as well as I did, that her sleeping in my arms was the best thing for her. She was comfortable and safe there and her night terrors were non-existent.

"Maddy said the apple is still intact," Drew said, slumping down into the chair across from me.

"Yeah, Sarah told me. Were you just talking to Maddy?"

He nodded. "Texted to make sure she's okay."

I grinned.

"What?" he demanded.

"Maddy's cute," I said.

"You want her?"

"What? No. I meant that for you."

He shook his head. "I could never be with Maddy."

"Why not?"

"I don't know. She's too . . . Maddy."

"What? Spunky? Fun? Outgoing? Nice? What's wrong with that?"

"She's Sarah's best friend."

"Sorry, I'm not following."

He threw his hands into his hair. "She'd never go for me anyway. She knows how much Sarah means to me and it wouldn't be fair to her."

I lowered my eyes to the table.

"I didn't mean it like that," Drew continued. "I'm not still in love with Sarah. I mean, I still love her. I always will, but she's more like a sister now. You know? But still someone I need to protect at all costs, even if it means leaving Maddy behind, which I did, if you don't remember, when we went to Nitsua."

"Drew, it's not like you *chose* Sarah over Maddy," I

started, realizing now what his internal struggle was all about. "You chose to *protect* Sarah over Maddy."

"How is that different?"

"Because as Earth's keeper, I would put money on the fact that you've been enchanted to protect Sarah."

"What?"

I stood up and strode to the window. "It makes sense," I continued. "It was your father's mission to protect her. He made the ring of protection for her, and the dream catcher, and introduced you two. When you became the keeper, you would've inherited the purpose to protect her, which would've been so engrained in you that it felt natural."

Drew stood up too. "Yeah," he said, recognition hitting him all at once. "Yeah, I remember the first time I met her. I had just become keeper and we found her in the meadow by the portal. It makes sense now that my father brought me to her so I would meet my purpose. I remember . . . I was so connected to her. I was scared for her because she was in the tree. I wanted her to get down right away. I didn't want her to run, I didn't want her to fall." Drew was rambling faster now, pacing the room. "Every part of me screamed the need to protect her." He stopped suddenly and looked up at me. "You think . . . it's just an enchantment?"

I nodded. "I think so."

"Well, when will it stop? When will it break?"

"I guess it depends what the terms of the enchantment were. But I would think that once she fulfils her purpose, yours will be done too."

Drew's chest was steadily rising and falling and I could see the wheels turning inside his head.

"So maybe," I began, "it is possible to love someone else as much or more than you've loved Sarah. Because your love for Sarah was more from your *need* to protect her."

Drew looked genuinely intrigued by all of this and I wished I had the ability to read his mind to know what he was thinking.

"This could change everything," he said, but it was as though it was meant for only himself. "If her purpose is to take back Yelram, the faster we find her key, the sooner I will be free."

Wow. Drew felt trapped. It was painful for him to see Sarah with me because it was an element of her life that he wasn't able to control, therefore protect. This was agonizing for him, not because he hated not having control, but because the enchantment would only allow him to feel good when he had Sarah under control.

The water in the bathroom turned off and the curtain pulled back. Sarah was done her shower. Her melodic humming was suddenly magnified without the low droning of the shower. A few minutes later, the door opened and Sarah came out, fully dressed, wringing her hair into a towel.

"Mornin', Drew," she chirped.

"You're up early," he said, turning in his seat to greet her.

"Luke's taking me for breakfast." She gave me her beautiful smile, but instead of enjoying it as I always do,

I felt a pang of guilt for Drew. If his purpose was to protect her, every time I did his job for him, he suffered for it.

"Yeah," I added, "I was thinking the four of us could go. We could pick up Maddy on our way." I tried to relay my apologies mindfully to Sarah, but her hurt expression wasn't allowing it.

"I thought it was just going to be the two of us," she said, and a sharp pain drove into my head.

"Ouch!" I said, throwing my hand to my forehead.

Sarah looked taken aback. "I'm so sorry!" she gasped. "Did I do that?"

"I don't know. I think so," I admitted. I wasn't sure how I knew this, but it felt like her doing. Her intention to inflict the same pain.

"Listen," Drew said, raising his hands, "if you planned on a breakfast for two, that's fine with me. I've got things to do this morning anyway."

"No, Drew wait," I tried.

What are you doing? she shouted into my head. *Let him go! I need this time with you.*

But I ignored her because I knew she would understand once I explained it to her, and it was more important for us to consider how we could make Drew's life better seeing as how we had been largely responsible for his discontentment over this last little while.

"Luke," Drew called from his new position in the kitchen, "I know what you're doing. I appreciate it, man, but I'm good. Really."

"Are you sure?" I asked.

"What the hell is going on?" Sarah whispered, angrily.

I shook my head at her. *I'll explain later,* I thought, hoping her mind was open enough to receive it.

"I should really head on over to Etak anyway," Drew added. "Check in and stuff."

I hung my head, guilt washing over me. Etak was my responsibility, and I was shirting it so I could be with Sarah. It was like Drew and I were switching responsibilities—he was taking care of Etak and I was looking after Sarah.

"Thank you," I managed to say.

"Least I could do," he said, returning to the living room, "given all that you've taken on here." He briefly looked at Sarah, and I knew she noticed. "And uh . . . thanks for that revelation earlier. Makes sense and I'm kind of . . . excited to see where this goes."

I smiled and nodded.

"Okay," Sarah interrupted, "whatever is going on here is just weird. Can you please go get ready so we can go eat?"

Drew laughed. "Oh yes, feed the girl already, would ya?"

I laughed too, although it hadn't occurred to me until that moment that Sarah's hunger cranks, combined with a diminishing light soul, could be a recipe for disaster, or breakdown, if we didn't hurry.

CHAPTER 10

The Tormenting Truth

~ SARAH ~

BREAKFAST AT CORA'S was nothing short of perfect, and not for the fact that the bacon and eggs were cooked just right and still piping hot when they were served to us, but because of the fact that Luke and I were finally alone. We requested the smallest table because the closer I was to him, the better I felt. How was it possible that this so-called dark lord could bring me so much happiness?

"Nevaeh's pretty amazing, right?" I snapped off the end of a bacon strip and popped it into my mouth.

"It is," he agreed. "You know, Yelram will be like that one day."

I smiled at the thought of it. "Do you think so?"

He nodded. "It'll be filled with rainbows and

butterflies." He winked. "And beautiful sunrises and gorgeous sunsets. It'll be autumn all year long, just the way you like it."

"With vibrant colours and warm autumn breezes?"

"Just like that."

In actual fact, he had no idea what Yelram would look like, but I let these images fuel me for the rest of what was sure to be a long and arduous journey ahead. I ignored the thoughts of dragons and monsters that lurked in the edges of my mind, knowing that if I focused on the current desolation and destruction of Yelram, it might be too overwhelming to continue the fight. Instead, I allowed myself to imagine the perfect world that Luke was painting for me now.

"I really want to thank you for staying with me," I said as my fork played with my scrambled eggs. "I know you have more important things to do at home."

"After nearly losing you, there's nothing more important than being with you now."

I blushed. "But you're keeper of another world. You can't stay with me forever."

"I told you—Drew's helping me out."

But how long could Drew help him out? Eventually Luke would have to go home, and I didn't want to have to think about that time coming.

"So, earlier, what was going on between you and Drew?" I asked hesitantly. He hadn't brought it up, and although I wanted to respect their friendship, I was too curious to ignore it any longer. "Why'd you invite him along?"

Luke set his fork down carefully and then took my free hand. "Drew's been having a tough time since I came back."

"That's no secret."

"I know, but have you ever wondered why he is still hung up on you?"

My eyebrows furrowed. "I don't know, maybe because I'm pretty amazing." I grinned and he nodded his agreement.

"Yes, well, that part was obvious." He squeezed my hand. "What I mean is he knows you love me, and that it's not likely the two of you will be getting back together anytime soon—"

"Ever," I amended.

He smiled. "I think he's always known that you two weren't compatible, but he was always drawn to you. Always drawn to *protect* you. . . . No matter what."

I was watching his lips as he spoke, and when they stopped, he didn't need to explain further. "You think he's bound to me somehow?"

Luke didn't answer, he just studied my face.

"Well, I mean, I guess it would make sense. I always took his interest in me to mean that he might actually *like* me. But if he was enchanted to protect me, then that would explain why he was always so close to me." I set my fork down, as I suddenly felt full.

"Are you okay?" he asked, lifting my hand to his lips.

I brought my eyes to him. "I'll . . . I'm fine."

"I may be way off on this, but it seems to make a lot of sense. Especially after we discovered that Drew carried the keeper's enchantment for the purpose of helping you find the clue."

I nodded quickly. "Yeah, for sure."

"You're upset," he noticed.

"No, I just . . . I mean, it's like everything I thought I *knew* is kind of . . . not real anymore."

"Sarah, it's not like that. Drew does love you. And I know, even after the enchantment lifts, he will still love you. But maybe not the way that you both thought. And that's good, you know. He can acknowledge it and move on now, and hopefully one day he can focus on someone else."

"Is that what he wants? Am I holding him back?"

"No. No, of course not." He was peddling hard, and I knew he regretted the direction his disclosure had taken us. "Drew just seems a little melancholy, don't you think?"

I shrugged. "It's Drew."

"It's gotta be rough for someone whose sole purpose is to protect a girl who doesn't need protecting anymore. It's like his purpose is in limbo right now."

"Why don't I need protecting anymore?"

"Well, you still do, it's just I'm here now and I'm not going anywhere anytime soon."

This was what I wanted. I didn't want Drew protecting me. I wanted Luke. But if this was really Drew's purpose, then I supposed it could be . . . depressing to have someone else do it for you.

"That's why I invited him to breakfast. So he won't always feel left out."

I nodded.

"But maybe checking in on the beast in Etak will make him feel like he's protecting you from a distance."

I nodded again.

"I shouldn't have told you," he finally said.

"I'm fine," I lied, adding a small laugh to the end so he would relax. "Really. I'm glad you told me. I'll try to be more sensitive to him about it."

I closed my mind off so there was no chance I would send Luke my next range of thoughts. Because yes, this did bother me, but not because I felt sorry for Drew for not being able to fulfil his purpose in protecting me, or for being unwillingly bound to me by some magical enchantment . . . but because I felt sorry for myself. Had Drew's affection and attention only been because of duty? Because of an enchantment? Had his feelings not been organic? If he hadn't been enchanted, would he still have loved me?

CHAPTER 11

Waterfront Walk

~ SARAH ~

MADDY WAS AT Drew's house by the time we got back from breakfast. Lucia was eager to see me, and especially excited when I reached for her leash off the coat rack.

"No luck with the apple?" Luke asked Maddy, and I knew he didn't need to ask. He felt the pull to the apple. His eyes were fixated on her purse that hugged her side.

"Not yet," she replied uneasily, pulling the purse even tighter to her. "But I think I'll go out for a little while and take the apple with me. It's probably best if I steer clear of you guys today."

"Where you going?" I asked.

Maddy shrugged. "Caleb wants to see me."

"Caleb?" I wasn't thrilled about this. I didn't like the

way he had treated her the last time I saw him on Drew's front lawn, demanding to see Luke and calling me a bitch.

"Yeah," Maddy waved it off, "I want to see if I can get my necklace back from him."

I scoffed. "Good luck with that." When she didn't reply, I asked, "Where's Drew?"

"I don't know. He was gone when I got here. I assumed he was with you guys."

"Probably in Etak," Luke muttered.

"Anyway," Maddy said as she went to the door, "I'll see you guys later on?"

"Yeah, sure," I said. "Be careful with Caleb, Maddy."

She rolled her eyes. "Whatever, Sarah. Not everyone can be as perfect as Luke." She pulled open the door and walked through it. "Or Drew," she said under her breath, and I wondered if it was said, or if it was just a thought.

"What was that all about?" I complained the moment she was definitely out of earshot.

Luke let out a heavy sigh of relief and leaned against the fridge. "I don't know, but I'm so glad she's gone."

"Why? Was it really that bad?"

"I won't lie," he said. "There is a strong charm on that apple."

"Maybe you just need a healthy distraction." I went to him and hooked my thumbs into the belt loops of his jeans. "Something else to seduce you." I bit my lower lip and narrowed my eyes onto his lips.

"That could work," he agreed and lifted me up onto the counter. I wrapped my legs around his waist and our lips mated with a desire and need that had been pent up for far too long. He moaned as my hands found their way up his shirt, my nails tracing lines of need down his back. I arched my body into him as one of his hands firmly gripped the back of my neck and the other pulled me closer into him.

Then Lucia whined and pawed restlessly at the door. And we stopped, our foreheads against each other, breaths still heavy.

"We should go," Luke said quietly, as if he thought the interruption was a good thing.

And he was right, really. The sun was shining and the water's edge was waiting for a young couple and their excited dog to come strolling along its paths.

THE WATERFRONT WASN'T as busy as I would've thought for a Saturday. Young families dominated the park with their wild children and crazy dogs. The occasional young couple could be found flying kites and playing Frisbee. Lucia was eager to get our walk started, but patiently waited for us to get car keys, picnic basket, and phones situated.

We walked the path that meandered closest to the water's edge until we came to the end where a lighthouse stood on a bed of rocks that reached out into the ocean, then we turned around and retraced our steps, Lucia walking happily next to us.

"You haven't said much," Luke said after a long silence where our footsteps crunching the crushed gravel beneath us were the only sounds.

I slid my hand into his, and wondered why we hadn't been holding hands up to this point. "Sorry," I said.

"For what?"

"Being quiet, I guess."

"Distracted," he corrected.

I glanced at him for a second and then brought my eyes back to the gravel path.

"I guess so." He was right. I was distracted. As much as I tried to focus on the sunshine beating down on us, or Lucia having the best walk of her summer, or Luke being right next to me and not off in another world, I just couldn't pull myself from the thought of Drew never really loving me.

"Sarah, what is it?" Luke stopped and took my free hand in his. Lucia pulled on the leash to hurry us along, but Luke was only watching me now.

I shook my head and looked away, but realized it made me look guilty, so I brought my eyes back to his. "I'm fine."

"It's Drew," he said, and a part of me loved that he knew. I loved that he could read me so well.

"No," I said quickly. "I mean, yes, but no."

He smiled, but it was forced and I saw the question behind it.

"I just . . . Drew was the only one who ever showed any interest in me before you came along." I looked down at Lucia who was now sitting and waiting patiently. "And I guess . . . it just hurts a little to think that he probably wouldn't have been interested in me . . . had it not been for . . . magic."

He folded me in his arms and I lied my head on his chest, listening for his heartbeat. "Magic or no magic, Drew would've still loved you. How could he not?"

"Thanks," I said, forcing gratitude, "but it's hard to believe when, previous to this, I've never really been loved before."

"Your mother loved you."

I pitched my eyebrows. "Are you sure about that?"

"What do you mean? Of course she did."

"My mother was a murderer, and apparently quite psycho if she planted a clue inside a poison apple where someone I care about has to die in order to open it."

Luke shook his head. "I'm sure she had good reasons for all of that. Reasons surrounding how much she loved you and wanted to protect you."

I took a deep breath and looked away. "Anyway, it doesn't matter. I'm fine, really."

He took my face in his hands and turned it so our eyes met again. "Sarah, I love you more than—"

"You've ever loved anything before," I finished. His puzzled delay gave me time to add, "Because that's not saying much considering you come from a loveless world." I pulled from him and continued walking, but then his grip was on my arm.

"No," he said firmly. "You don't get to make those kind of accusations and just walk away. Sarah, I know what love is. I know it because I've never felt it before. I've felt lust, jealousy, hate, anger, frustration, greed, need . . . but I've never felt love, so when I say that I love you, I know what it is. It's not part of my genetic makeup, so not only does it feel amazing, it also hurts like hell. So please don't tell me you don't believe that I love you. Because there is nothing in the seven worlds that would destroy me more than to lose you again."

My chest trembled with the threat of a sob breaking loose.

"Come here," he said, and he pulled me in again. "Regardless of who loved you and who didn't in the past, I do and I always will."

Being against his chest meant that I could cry and he wouldn't see my tears, so I let them seep down my cheeks and onto his shirt. He kissed my head and although I knew I was the luckiest girl alive, I also wondered what Drew was doing right now in Etak and if he would still care about me when the enchantment was broken.

WE WANDERED THROUGH the park for nearly three hours, enjoying the fresh air and sunshine, and the unmatched excitement of Lucia as she met new people and explored new plants. Eventually she began to settle, and we claimed a quiet patch of grass on a hill near the water where we sprawled out on a blanket and picnicked on grapes, strawberries, crackers, and cheese, while Lucia explored nearby.

"This has been a great day," I admitted.

"Good," Luke said as he kissed my forehead.

"I suppose any day with you is a good day."

"You say that now," he teased, but I knew he worried about my darkening soul and what that would do to my love for him.

I plucked another grape from the stem and pressed it to Luke's lips.

"I'd rather have you," he said as he sucked the grape in and leaned forward to kiss me. I let his lips soften with mine as his hand came up and ran along my face and into my hair. I moaned my approval, and before I knew it, I was on my back and he was hovering over me, his lips still connected with mine.

"Luke," I laughed, "we're in public."

"Let 'em watch." He ran his hand down my side, and I would've let them watch. I wanted to, but a distant, familiar voice had us both sitting up and looking around.

"Sounds like Maddy," Luke said.

"It does," I agreed. I squinted into the sun and saw a couple walking down the path toward our private piece of grass. He was tall, brown-haired, and walked just like Caleb, and she was a petite, blonde that looked just like Maddy.

"Oh crap," I said. "I think that's them."

Luke followed my gaze and confirmed my suspicions by waving a friendly hello.

I sighed heavily. "I don't want to see him."

"Maybe they've worked things out," Luke said as he stood up. "Play nice." He waved them over and it was obvious both were reluctant to come, but decided to play nice, too.

Caleb nodded at Luke. "Hey, man."

Luke held out his hand. "Hey, Caleb. No hard feelings?"

Caleb shook Luke's hand quickly and clumsily,

having come from the wrong dimension for that gesture to be familiar. "Sure, man. No, we're cool."

Maddy and I glanced uncomfortably at each other for a moment during this awkward exchange of pleasantries.

"Nice day, huh?" I said.

"It is." Caleb smiled and pulled Maddy closer to him. "It's always a nice day when you get to spend it with someone as beautiful as Maddy."

Maddy blushed and I tasted bile in my mouth.

"Do you guys want some food?" Luke offered. "We brought lots."

"No, we're good," Maddy said, but Caleb had already accepted the offer and was bent down taking a handful of grapes. "Or we will," Maddy laughed. "Thanks."

Although I wished it were with someone else, I did enjoy seeing Maddy happy. She was wary of us, given that the last time we all saw Caleb was in Drew's front yard when he was freaking out at all of us.

Caleb took a seat on the grass and Luke followed his lead.

"Where's Drew?" Caleb asked, looking up at me as he figured I was the one most likely to know the answer.

I shrugged. "We're not together anymore."

"Yeah, I heard that." He glanced at Luke then looked down.

"So naturally I don't follow his every move," I added.

"I didn't mean that you would, I just—"

"It's okay," Luke interrupted. "We all still hang out together, he's just not with us today, that's all."

"What do you mean you *all* still hang out together?"

110

Caleb asked. He turned to Maddy. "Do you still hang out with them too?"

Maddy, conveniently, had a mouthful of grapes when the question was asked. She mumbled a response while shrugging her shoulders.

Luke gave me a puzzled look.

"Yes, she still hangs out with us, Caleb," I confirmed. "We're her friends. Friends hang out."

"Yeah, no, that's cool," Caleb said, but it was clear he wasn't cool with it at all.

"Come to the washroom with me?" Maddy asked, shooting me a look that suggested I was in trouble.

"Sure." I turned to Luke who was watching me curiously. "Watch Lucia, okay?"

Lucia was rolling around in a patch of flowers nearby, seemingly unbothered by our new company.

"What's up?" Maddy asked when we were out of earshot.

"What do you mean?"

"I mean why are you giving Caleb such a hard time?"

"Oh come on, Maddy, you can't be serious."

"Sarah, he didn't do anything wrong to you, cut him a break."

"Are you for real? He kind of verbally attacked me and accused you of cheating on him."

"Yes, but he was jealous. Which is . . . you know, kind of cute."

"*Cute*," I said disgustedly. "And is it *cute* that he has a problem with you hanging out with your friends?"

"It's just because you and Luke are together, and he's

just a little uncomfortable with me hanging out with Drew at the same time."

"It's almost like you're justifying his jealousy."

"I'm not, Sarah." Maddy sighed heavily. "Can you just please be nice to him? I still care about him. I still . . . love him."

I stopped walking, the washrooms only ten feet ahead. "What did you just say?"

"You heard me."

"Okay, so *why* did you just say that?"

"Because it's not easy to forget the last three months. He was my first, Sarah. My first real boyfriend. He's a good guy."

Maybe I was overreacting. Maybe the darkness made me dislike and distrust people more than I should. Maybe Caleb did deserve a second chance. "Fine," I conceded. "Okay."

"Okay what?"

"Okay, I'll cut him a break." I tossed my hands into the air, signalling my defeat.

"Thank you. And just a reminder, I cut Luke a break after I caught him with Ella."

"That was different. He didn't have a choice."

"Don't kid yourself, Sarah. We all have a choice." She continued to the washroom, leaving me standing there, mouth agape, wondering why this hurt me. Why my chest was on fire with a burning desire to hurt Ella and scream at Luke.

HAVING LOST MY appetite, Luke and I packed up our

picnic and headed back to Drew's. I felt sick and could hardly stand putting on a kind face toward Caleb when all I could think about was Luke being with Ella.

"How was the park?" Drew asked as we came through the kitchen door. He was at the stove, donning an apron, and cooking some sort of stir-fry. I was so happy to see him. So happy that he was okay after his recent trip to Etak, and so appreciative for letting us stay here. A sensation in my chest pulled me toward him and I was hugging him before I knew what I was doing.

He chuckled and patted me on the back. "What's this for?"

"I just wanted to say thank you. For everything you've done for me. . . . For us." I let go of him and watched his eyes dart from mine to Luke's. Was he not sure what he should say? Did he wish we were alone so he could pour out his heart to me? Or was I just in his way and he wanted to get through this mission so he could finally be rid of the enchantment that connected us?

"It's no problem." He turned back to the stove and continued stirring. "So? How was the park?"

My heart sank. I didn't know what I was hoping he would say or do, but I realized that I now had a Drew-sized hole in my heart and I wasn't sure how to fill it.

"It was great," Luke answered. "How was Etak?"

Drew looked sideways at Luke, then said, "It's okay."

I should've tried to tap into his thoughts to discern what he meant by this, but I was too busy rearranging my own. How could I test Drew to see if he really cared about me, or if it was just his duty of protection?

"It would've been nice to have you there," I said as Luke filled a bowl of water for Lucia. "Do you remember when we used to go to the park together?"

Drew's mind was closing quickly, but before it did, I caught a glimpse of confusion and interest. "Uh, sure. Yeah, I remember," he muttered over the steam of dinner.

Luke set the bowl of water on the floor and Lucia lapped it up immediately. "We ran into Maddy and Caleb at the park," Luke added.

"Maddy and *Caleb*?" Drew set the wooden spoon on the counter next to him.

"Tell me about it." I shuddered with disgust.

"Is she coming back for supper?"

"She said she's going out with Caleb for supper," I said. "Apparently she's giving him another chance."

"Why?" Drew sounded as disgusted as I felt.

"Because she believes in second chances, I guess." And this reminded me of the second chance I gave Luke after he cheated on our love with Ella. My stomach turned.

"Are you okay?" Luke asked, putting his hand on my back.

"I'm fine," I said, and I shrugged his hand off. I imagined him touching Ella like this, and speaking to her in that same way. How thick would he have laid on this charm to convince her that he was on her side? How far would he have gone with her for the *mission*?

Drew nodded at Luke. "She should go lay down. Supper will be ready in about ten minutes."

"I'm not hungry," I snapped, again avoiding Luke's hand.

Luke narrowed his eyes on mine, studying my face, wishing he could read my mind. "You've barely eaten," he began. "You need to keep your strength up."

"Why?" I snapped. "So I can die fighting? What's the freaking point anyway?"

"What do you mean *what's the point*?" Drew countered. "We're making progress with the clues, aren't we? We'll find the key, Sarah."

"Yeah? When? Before or after the enchantment breaks and you stop caring? And before or after Luke has to make out with Ella again? The next clues are going to be a hell of a lot harder to find since I'm sure the dark world keepers aren't going to just hand them over. But even if we manage to get them all, we still have to go to Yelram and fight all the monsters before we can find this stupid ingredient needed to heal me. So, chances are I'll be dead by then."

Drew and Luke traded a look of distress over the impending breakdown they assumed I was having. My chest did burn. With a jealousy for Luke and Ella, and a hatred for this stupid enchantment that prohibited Drew from loving me on his own terms.

"Come on," Luke said, this time forcing me with him to the living room.

"Let go of me!" I shouted, ripping my arm from his grasp. "You don't love me! You never did!"

"Sarah, you know that's not true." He moved in front of me. "Look at me, baby."

"No!" I shouted again. "If you loved me, you would never have been able to be with Ella!"

"Sarah, I—"

"I hate that you did that, Luke. I *hate* it," I hissed. "It *burns* my heart. I can't get over it. It kills me to know you were with her!" Tears flowed like lava down my cheeks and I was aware that Drew was behind me now. He placed a hand on my shoulder.

"I know how you feel," Drew said softly.

"You can't possibly know how I feel!" I barked, rounding on him now. "You don't even know *how* to feel unless the enchantment tells you! You've always said you loved me, but guess what? We all know now that it wasn't real. We all know it wasn't your true feelings and if you weren't bewitched, you wouldn't even know my name!"

"Is that what you think?" He looked wounded by this.

"It's what I know, Drew. I've always felt it. It's no surprise. It just . . . it just *hurts!*" I ran from the room and out the front door. I wasn't sure where I wanted to go, or if I even *wanted* to go, but I couldn't continue to stand there, Drew's green eyes burning into mine, and Luke's feelings of hurt seeping through the barrier he fought so hard at putting up for my sake. They just made me angrier. Angry that they felt pain when it was *me* who should be feeling all the pain.

I stopped when I reached the bottom step. My chest rose and fell with the heavy breaths that concealed my screams. Then the door opened and Drew came out alone.

"Can we talk?" he asked as he slowly descended the steps.

"I have nothing else to say, Drew." My jaw throbbed with every tight clench of my teeth. I was working through the anger, through the torturous feeling squeezing my heart.

He stood next to me for a long few minutes, neither of us saying anything, but he left his mind open for me to explore. Despite my curiosity, I resisted. Besides, if I entered his thoughts, would he be able to tell? I couldn't give him the satisfaction of knowing I cared. Nothing was more humiliating than being desperate for the love of someone who only wanted to be rid of you.

"Sarah, who knows what would've happened between you and me if your mother hadn't enchanted Earth's keeper. But I do know that with or without an enchantment, if I had met you, I would've liked you." He paused for a long few seconds, then continued, "Sarah, you're a likeable person. You're funny, smart, kind . . . beautiful."

My racing heart gradually slowed as the burning in my chest began to subside. My throat constricted with the need to cry and Drew folded me into his arms.

"I'm glad I was enchanted, though," he said quietly. "I'm glad I had the chance to love you."

I sobbed in his arms while he rubbed my back and kissed the top of my head, lifting me from my collapse, and mending my heart from the dark side's unforgiving grip.

CHAPTER 12

Unlucky Love

~ LUKE ~

IT TOOK MORE effort than I was used to. It took focused breathing, a closed mind so she couldn't read me, and constant reminders to myself that she was just having an episode—she didn't love him, she was only searching for love. And he was giving it to her. I had given him my consent—he was sensitive enough to ask for it after Sarah ran out of the room crying—and he knew how to calm her down, to reassure her that loving her was not a regret on his part. And seeing her now, folded in his arms, coming out of her dark moment, all at the hand of Drew, made me realize that she still needed him. He still had a purpose.

But it hurt to watch it unfold. Why had my touch been

so toxic for her? Why had my voice been like venom? She recoiled from me—why? Had she been insecure about Ella this whole time? Or was it just the darkness unearthing all this jealousy, hate, anger, and every other dark emotion buried deep inside her?

After a few minutes, and when it was clear that Sarah was in a better place, Drew motioned for me to come take his place. I hesitated, concerned that my touch might set her off again. My heart squeezed with this feeling. I had always been the one to bring her back down, but today it was Drew. Would tomorrow be the same?

The door creaked when I opened it, but she didn't look up or cling to Drew any tighter. Then my fingers touched her arm and she didn't flinch. Instead, she immediately let go of Drew and replaced his embrace with mine. I let out a long sigh of relief as her body, warm with the heat of Drew's, curled into mine.

SARAH STAYED ON the couch for the rest of the evening and night. She only ate what I force-fed her and she hardly spoke a word. Her struggle was ongoing. The darkness was still at the edges of her mind, fighting relentlessly to get in and take over again. I knew this because every so often my vision would flood with an image of Ella and me together. I hated these images. They reminded me of the dark place I had once been. How I missed Sarah so much that I was desperate enough to let Ella change into her so that I could hold Sarah just one more time.

Whenever one of these images floated into my

thoughts, Sarah had an anguished, focused expression. I just bent down and kissed her, whispered how much I loved her, and counteracted the negative images with positive memories of our time together—us at the park, us at Peggy's Cove, our first kiss, the first time I told her I loved her. Her face would soften when I opened my mind to her, and her body would relax more and more. I still wished she would talk to me, but darkness was something I understood all too well, and I knew it was hard for her to fight the urges that were becoming too frequent for my comfort.

THE NEXT MORNING, I woke to a stiff back and sore neck. The floor next to the couch was hard and cold, but I wouldn't take Drew's offer for a bed, not when Sarah refused to move from the couch. As much as I wanted to hold her all night, I respected her need for space, even if she hadn't explicitly asked for it. Halfway through the night, her hand slipped off the couch and I held her fingers in mine until morning. This, I noticed, had stopped the night terrors, too. Drew had come out of his room four times, whining about her incessant screaming: "Please, Luke, just lay down with her. If *I'm* begging you to, you know it's bad." But I wouldn't. Not unless she asked me to. But holding her fingers seemed to make it stop.

The sky was dark with thick, grey clouds, and the rain was beating wildly against the window, causing a dull lullaby for Sarah to sleep to.

"Hey," Drew grumbled as he came out of his room

the next morning, the red, puffy bags under his eyes confirming his sleepless night. "She still asleep?" he asked as he continued his sluggish walk toward the kitchen.

"Yeah," I whispered. I was sitting up now, her hand still in mine. Lucia was curled up next to her, taking my place, and she was as happy and content as ever snuggling with her human.

"So she finally stopped screaming around two in the morning," Drew said quietly.

I nodded and ran my thumb across her hand. "Seems to help if I'm touching her."

Drew flinched and looked away.

"About yesterday, man," I said, lowering my voice further so he had to come closer. "Thanks for calming her down."

Drew shrugged as if it were nothing.

"No, really," I said. "She needed some love, and I wasn't able to give it to her."

He wrinkled his brow. "What do you mean 'she needed some love'?"

"Well, just that the more love she feels, the less room there is for hate. For some reason, she's having a hard time accepting my love right now." Pain pushed at my heart.

"It was just a phase. You know that, right?" Drew said.

I nodded, but I wasn't so sure. "Anyway, I just want you to know that, even though it sucks to see it, I'm glad you're able to . . . make her feel loved."

Drew smiled awkwardly. "No problem."

Sarah stirred and our conversation ceased until her breathing slowed and deepened again.

"Have you heard from Maddy yet?" I asked.

"Yes." Drew visibly relaxed as he sat in the chair across from us, thankful for the change of subject. "The apple's still closed."

"Seriously?" This frustrated me. Was it ever going to open? Were we ever going to be able to move on to the next clue? We needed to find the key for Sarah and find that last ingredient for the cure. If the apple didn't open on its own, maybe I'd have to take matters into my own hands.

"What are you thinking?" Drew leaned forward, resting his elbows on his knees.

"What if we're the only ones who are drawn to it because we're the ones who have to open it? I think if it doesn't open today, we should have Maddy stay here tonight. With the apple."

"And what?"

I took a deep breath, looked over my shoulder at Sarah sleeping soundly, and said, "I'll open it."

"Ah, geez, Luke, I don't know, man."

"If it's the only way to move forward, Drew, I gotta do it for Sarah. I know she's in good hands with you; you're able to bring her out of her episodes. I don't want to leave her, but if I don't, then she doesn't have a chance of survival."

Drew nodded, a look of uncomfortable understanding on his face. "Let's hope it opens today, then."

I nodded, but I had a sickening feeling that it wouldn't. And with Sarah's progressing deterioration, I didn't see another option. She would be safe in Drew's care, and he would be able to continue fulfilling his purpose of protecting her. This was the option that made the most sense.

SARAH SLEPT UNTIL noon, and I only left her once to use the washroom when she rolled away from me and draped her arm across Lucia instead. When she started to stir, Drew quickly re-heated her bacon and eggs, made her some new toast, and set the breakfast down next to her.

"Hey there, sleeping beauty," I said as I kissed her forehead.

"Hey," she groaned, rubbing her head and slowly sitting up. "What time is it?" She reached for her phone, then fell back on her pillow. "Noon. Seriously?"

"You needed the sleep."

"I'm hungry," she said, and then noticed the plate of breakfast on the table next to her phone. "Thank you."

Appreciation was a good sign that she was in better spirits this morning, and I was happy to try my best to keep her there.

"Is Maddy here?" she asked as she stuffed a piece of bacon into her mouth, then chased it down with half a glass of orange juice.

"She's coming over a bit later," I said.

"Did the apple open?" She looked hopeful, and I tried

to think of the most positive way to tell her that it hadn't.

"Almost."

"Almost?" She scrunched up her brow. "How do you know? Is it cracking or something?"

I shook my head and looked away. "No, it's just gotta be close. I can feel it."

A piece of bacon hovered near her mouth as she studied me. "Is the pull even stronger now?"

"No. I mean, I don't know."

She grinned. "You're weird, then."

I reached over and stole her bacon. "*You're* weird."

"Hey!" She tried to snatch her bacon back, but I popped it into my mouth before she got her greasy fingers on it. She jumped onto my lap and straddled me, holding my arms to my side. Then she planted her lips on mine and forced a kiss so needy, desperate, and wanting that I couldn't resist matching the intensity. She let go of my arms so that I could run my hands along her sides and up her back while her own hands went to my hair. I trailed my lips down her neck, savouring the salt on her skin.

"I want you," she whispered into my ear, which made every cell in my body awaken with need.

I sighed heavily, pulling her so close that she coughed. "I love you so much," I said.

"So take me," she said between kisses.

"No," I said definitively. And she stopped.

"Maybe you didn't hear me." She reached behind her neck and unfastened her necklace. "I want you to have this." She dangled her school necklace in front of my face, and I flinched as if it might burn if I touched it.

The blacks of her eyes grew. "What's wrong?" she asked, and it broke my heart to hold her at arm's length like this.

"I don't want it," I confessed. "Yet." I closed my eyes and kissed her again, but her lips didn't move. She was hurt, and I had hurt her. I wanted to make her happy. I didn't want to make her feel anything but love, for fear of another episode, but I also couldn't take her necklace. Not now. Not here. Not like this.

"Why not?" Her eyes were stony now and had lost their needy glaze.

I took her hands and she let me, which was relieving, but they were still. "Babe, I love you, and I know how important that necklace is to you. I know you value it above anything else, even my school ring"—I fingered my ring which circled her thumb—"which is why I don't want it."

"But I *want* you to have it. Why isn't this clear?"

"Because it's not want you really want, Sarah. I know you. This is the darkness talking."

She rolled her eyes and slid off my lap. "I bet you would've taken Ella's."

I inhaled deeply and decided that keeping the peace wasn't going to be an option until this issue was dealt with. "Sarah," I began, "Ella meant nothing to me. She was a chess piece that I had to play in order to find Eli."

"You played her before Eli went missing," she pointedly reminded.

"Yes, I did," I admitted, "and I'm not proud of it. I

missed you so much, Sarah, and I didn't think there was ever a chance of us getting back together. When Ella came to me in your form, I wasn't strong enough to fight it. I couldn't resist."

She sent me a graphic image of her vomiting in the toilet. "Why didn't you think we would ever get back together?"

"Because I thought you were safer with Drew, and I knew about the beast and how it was growing in strength. Drew didn't want me on Earth, and for your safety, I wasn't able to let you come to Etak anymore. I didn't have a choice. I didn't see us ever working a way around this."

She stood and walked to the picture window. The rain was coming down harder now. I knew how much she detested the rain, and I wondered how much this was playing on her mood.

I went to her and pulled her hair back to expose her neck, then kissed it softly. Then I planted another, a little higher, and another. Soon I was nibbling on her earlobe, and I could see her smile in the reflection of the glass. She turned and draped her arms over my shoulders, then jumped up, and I caught her in my arms.

"Hello," Maddy announced cheerfully. "Sorry to interrupt."

I spun around with Sarah still in my arms, but quickly let her down as the lure to the apple in Maddy's hands was too strong to ignore.

"Did it open?" Sarah asked excitedly.

"No," I answered, because I knew it was true. Surely

the temptation would subside once it was opened.

"Not yet," Maddy confirmed. "How are you feeling, Sarah?"

Sarah's eyes flashed to mine for a second before she answered, "I'm okay."

"Listen, I was thinking," Maddy began. "Do you think we should, you know, find someone to open this clue for us?"

"What, like kill someone?" Sarah clarified.

"No!" Maddy quickly covered. "I mean, maybe we should just leave it on a table somewhere public and wait and see what happens."

"What if a kid eats it?" Sarah pointed out. "Or someone who just doesn't deserve to die?"

"But what if someone like Holly eats it?" Maddy pointed out. "There's that party tonight at the Boat Club. Maybe I could drop it off there and see what happens."

"Maddy!" Sarah exclaimed. "Are you actually serious right now?"

Maddy slumped down into the chair. "It's taking too long," she whined. "You might be doing fine now, but tomorrow you're due for another dose of elixir and then you only have six days left. We still have three more worlds to go to, and we have no idea how long that could take, and not to mention—"

"Maddy," I interrupted, "this isn't helping."

Sarah was sitting now, staring at the coffee table in front of her. "You're right," she said. "We have to move this along. We can't just protect the apple and hope that it opens on its own. The last clue was clear—someone has to take a bite."

I gave Maddy a warning look not to discuss it further, then I sat down next to Sarah and rested my hand on her knee. "We don't have to do this right now. Let's just give it another night and see what happens."

"Maddy," Sarah said suddenly as she looked up from her deep thoughts, "if I bite the apple and die, will you finish my mission? Take back Yelram and be keeper for me?"

"Sarah," both Maddy and I scolded.

"Think about it," Sarah said. "What good am I to anyone? Chances are I won't make it to the end anyway, and I'm just holding everyone back. What if I open the clue for you and you all continue on without me?"

"No," I said firmly, while Maddy said, "That won't work anyway. You're the only one who can decipher your mother's messed up nursery rhymes."

Sarah groaned and fell back onto the couch, her eyes finding a resting place on the ceiling above. "Then we search for a victim," she said.

WITH THE APPLE so close, Drew and I were both finding it hard to fight the darkness. It was just after lunch and I was outside on the back deck watching Sarah and Lucia run around when I heard a whisper in my ear: "Take a bite. Just one bite." I spun around, expecting to find someone playing a prank, but no one was there. Maddy had gone to the washroom, leaving her satchel with the apple lying on a patio chair near me, and Drew was inside getting a drink.

"You look pale," Drew said when he came out a minute later balancing four glasses of water. "What happened?"

I shook my head. "Nothing. Just thought I heard someone."

Drew kept his eyes on me while he carefully set the glasses down on the patio table. "About the apple?" he asked quietly.

"Yes," I said.

"I've heard it too."

I slumped down into the chair and pushed my hands through my hair while Lucia came bounding up the back steps, finishing her play with Sarah. She lied down on the step next to Maddy's bag and rested her head on the satchel.

"Leave it, Lucia," I said, and she turned to me for a second before deciding that there must be something interesting inside if she wasn't allowed near it. She pushed her nose into the top and Drew and I both lunged at her. "No!" I shouted.

Sarah jogged up the steps, but Drew grabbed the bag before she saw what the fuss was about.

"I'm so sorry!" Maddy gasped as she came back outside. She took the bag from Drew. "I should've brought this with me. Why did you have it? You weren't going for it, were you?"

"No," Drew chuckled lightly. "Just making sure the dog didn't."

"Are you kidding me?" Sarah laughed. "Have you ever tried to get Lucia to eat a fruit or vegetable? She's a meatatarian." She ruffled Lucia's fur before she picked up a glass and drank half of it. "You two on the other hand—if I catch either of you near that bag again . . ."

"I should go anyway," Maddy said, eyeing Luke and Drew suspiciously and holding the bag close to her side.

"Where are you going?" Sarah asked.

"I don't know. Maybe shopping for a dress. Caleb keeps asking if I'm going to the party later."

"What'd you tell him?" Drew asked as he took a drink of water himself.

"I keep telling him no because I'm spending the evening with you guys, but I don't know. I think he really wants me to go."

Drew rolled his eyes.

"You should go," Sarah said.

Drew opened his mouth to argue, but quickly shut it and took a deep breath—a technique I noticed he did when he was trying to close his mind to Sarah.

"You think?" Maddy asked.

"Sure." Sarah shrugged. "And take the apple with you; these two shouldn't be anywhere near it. You'll have more fun at the party than sitting around with us."

Maddy looked at Drew. "Probably right."

Drew's eyebrows shot up and he laughed. "If you think you'll have more fun hanging out with Caleb, by all means, have at 'er."

"Drew," Sarah scorned.

"No, he's right." Maddy straightened herself up tall and proud. "It's been nice hanging out with Caleb and having someone to talk to who actually cares about me."

Drew's eyes narrowed on hers. "He doesn't actually care about you. You know that, right?"

Maddy's jaw dropped and Sarah jumped right in. "Hey now," she said, putting her hand on Drew's chest. "Regardless whether we have higher aspirations for Maddy or not, we, as her friends, have to support her decisions."

"I don't have to do anything," Drew said, and he pushed Sarah's hand away.

"You're being an asshole," Maddy said, a fire in her eyes like I hadn't seen before.

"Yeah, well you're being stupid," Drew retorted.

"Okay, guys," Sarah shouted. "That's enough!"

"Agreed," Drew said, still glaring at Maddy. "I have better places to be." He took out his necklace and said, "Take me to Etak."

Maddy gasped as the wind caused by Drew's departure whipped at her face and tossed her hair around. "Did that really just happen?"

"Maddy," Sarah tried, "he didn't mean any of that. He's just—"

"The apple is drawing the darkness out of him," I finished. They both looked at me. "It's been really hard staying positive. I'm sure that's his problem."

"Whatever it is," Maddy said, a small quake to her voice, "he's still responsible for the words that come out of his mouth. Until he apologizes, I don't need him in my life."

"Maddy," Sarah tried, but she was heading for the door. "Come on, Maddy. It's Drew. You know what he can be like."

"Exactly," she said over her shoulder, "and I don't plan on letting him get away with it like he does with you." She slammed the patio door closed and disappeared into the house. The front door slammed a moment later, signalling her departure.

"You okay?" I asked after a minute, when it was clear she was still expecting Maddy to return.

"What the hell was that all about?"

"There's some tension there for sure," I said.

"But why?" Then she gasped. "Do you think . . . do you think he likes her?"

He like *her*? I thought it was more obvious that Maddy liked Drew. I shrugged.

"Wow. Okay." She sat down in the chair next to me. "How are you doing? You didn't say much?"

"Not much to say." I sat down in a chair, relieved that Maddy, and the apple, were gone.

"Did you find it harder to be around the apple?"

I nodded. No sense in denying it.

"Well, it's gone now." She grinned seductively, and her hand went to her breast where she began unbuttoning her yellow plaid shirt. "And guess what?"

"What?" I said, trying to keep the grin from unmasking my pleasure.

"We're all alone." She moved her body so that she was now in front of me.

"I see that." My hands reached for her hips, and she let me pull her into me so I could taste her stomach, which was peeking through the gap in her shirt.

She moaned as my kisses trailed up her middle, past her breasts, savouring a few extra kisses around her neck, and then her head was cradled in my hands, and her lips were with mine, mating with a soft, sensual kiss, charged with a need that was growing stronger every time our lips met. This concerned me, of course, but right now I just wanted to enjoy how it satisfied my own burning desire for her.

Our slow and steady kisses quickly turned to passionate, needy ones. Her hands were like warm silk on my chest and back, and I had a vague sense that we were moving toward the house. I continued kissing her, pulling her closer to me. Closer. Closer. The closer she was, the better I felt. We were in Drew's room now, and we fell onto his bed. Sarah was on top and she whipped her shirt off, her hair tumbling down around me as she continued pressing her lips with mine. Her hands went to my belt, and as much as I didn't want to stop, I had to. I couldn't let her do this. She would never have done this otherwise. Not like this anyway.

"Wait," I said, squeezing my eyes closed. I was already regretting my decision.

"What?" she said breathlessly, continuing to trail kisses down my neck.

"We can't do this, Sarah."

A current of her anger, mixed with lust, hit me hard, and I winced.

"Stop trying to be all heroic." She brought her lips to my neck, and my head filled with a foggy ecstasy as I put my arms around her waist and traded places with her, this time pressing my body into hers.

I cupped her head with my left hand as my right ran smoothly over her warm and needy body. She tilted her head back and pushed her hips into me. Every cell and ounce of blood in my body was at its peak, begging to be let free, but as much as my physical wanted her physical, my mind couldn't connect with hers. She wasn't fully there.

"No," I said, pushing off the bed and away from her. I turned away, not able to trust myself while she was lying there, breathless, waiting for me to return. "We're not doing this, Sarah. Not like this."

"Luke." Her voice was soft, and it brought a whimper to my chest. "Do you not love me or something?"

"It's *because* I love you that I won't let you do this, Sarah. Don't you see that?"

"Well, if it's what I want then how are you doing me a favour?"

"Because it's not what you want. It's what the darkness wants. It's trying to destroy your soul, Sarah, and I won't let you go down that easily. Not while I have a say in it."

Her eyes narrowed on me and her lips curled in a sneer.

"What?" I pressed.

She didn't answer, but I found myself thinking of Ella and kissing her, then moving to my bed and lying down with her . . . but I had never been with Ella in my bed. It was my unspoken rule. At her place, yes, but never mine. Even when she appeared as Sarah. My bed was Sarah's.

If I couldn't have her there, I wouldn't have anyone.

Wait—why was I thinking about being with Ella? I hated thinking about Ella. It wrenched my gut with guilt, and left a dry, bitter taste in the back of my throat. Had Sarah put those thoughts there? Did she think this was why I didn't want to be with her? Because she wasn't Ella?

These thoughts consumed me, and Sarah knew it. My head started to throb with the pain of her entering it.

"Stop that!" I warned as I grabbed my shirt and pulled it on. "You're not supposed to be doing this, Sarah."

She looked away and the pain stopped. "Fine," she said. "If you have something to hide, then go ahead."

"I'm not hiding anything. I promise you that I love you. And it's real." A harsh craving for the apple rolled around on my tongue. If that clue was open, we could move on and stop hovering in limbo. This was driving Sarah to have crazy thoughts and unfair accusations.

"I need to get out of here," she said as she clutched her chest. She pushed past me and into the living room.

"Where do you want to go?" I asked, following her.

Her face was distorted with pain, and it physically hurt to see her like this. Then she growled, "Anywhere but here!"

"Let's go for a walk," I offered.

"No!" she shouted. "I can't be around you right now. I have to do this alone."

"No." Drew appeared near the kitchen. "Sarah, you're not going anywhere without Luke."

She shot him a warning look and I worried that she would turn her fury on him. He wasn't as great at managing it as I was, although he did seem to have the ability to calm her once she got it all out. Her eyes bounced to mine, but I didn't say anything. I wasn't backing down on this one, either. She couldn't leave, and there was no way around it.

"Fine," she said, frustrated and defeated. "I'm going to lie down." She walked past me, then turned around. "*Don't* follow me."

She closed and locked Drew's bedroom door, and my heart sank. I had done this to her. My moments of weakness with Ella caused her this deep, unsettling pain.

"She'll be fine," Drew said, patting me on the back.

"It's killing me," I admitted.

"I know, but you're doing the right thing."

"Drew," I said as a lump formed in my throat, constricting my voice. "I need to get out of here for a little while. I don't want to leave her, but I can't be here right now."

"Everything okay?"

"I think my darkness might be affecting her. I just have to go release some of my aggression before I see her again."

Drew nodded. "Probably best."

"I won't be long," I promised. "Don't tell her I've left."

"I don't think she'll be coming out any time soon, anyway."

CHAPTER 13

Parties & Punches

~ SARAH ~

I WAITED UNTIL I heard the sounds of crashing pots and pans and running water, and I knew they were busying themselves with dinner. One of them would come to the door soon to ask if I was hungry, so I waited for that.

"Sarah?" Drew finally called as he knocked lightly on the door. "Dinner will be ready in twenty minutes. You hungry?"

"Geez, Drew!" I snapped, trying to sound shaken from sleep. "I was almost asleep. Leave me alone. I'll come out when I wake up." I was impressed with my mock crankiness. I knew this would be enough to keep them away from my door for at least a couple of hours.

"Sorry," he said, and then the creaks in the floor

confirmed that he was retreating to the kitchen. Why hadn't Luke come? Was he mad at me? Was he considering the possibility that I was right—he never wanted me like he wanted Ella?

Regardless, it didn't matter. Right now all that mattered was my freedom, and the only way I was going to get that was to sneak out through Drew's bedroom window and meet Maddy at her house in thirty minutes as planned. My ruse of taking a nap would buy me an hour or two at least before Luke would come knocking on the door to wake me. Having the door locked might buy me another hour if they believed I was actually sleeping. But I wouldn't be sound asleep. I would be enjoying my youthful freedom at a party with my best friend.

THE PARTY AT the Boat Club was a bigger deal than I had expected. I wasn't even sure what the celebration was for, but knew that every high school graduate in the city was planning on being there.

Maddy wore a sleek black dress that showed off her generous cleavage. She had curled her hair and left it down around her shoulders, and at her side was a small black clutch, which bulged at the seams from where the apple sat comfortably inside.

We had discussed leaving the apple on the hood of her car, but we both had concerns over who might find it, and whether we could ever live with ourselves if someone actually died. So we agreed that she would carry it in her clutch, and I would carry her make-up in mine. Tonight wasn't about finding a victim, anyway. It was about finding some freedom and having some fun. But I wasn't yet ruling out the possibility that there could be a deserving candidate at the party that we could offer the apple to.

Maddy was nervous, which looked cute on her. I wore my favourite yellow, spring dress. Sure it was nearly fall, but the weather was still warm, and yellow made me feel fresh and alive. Maddy had fussed for more than an hour over my hair, calling it unruly and wicked. Finally, we agreed to straighten all the curls out of it, which took far too long, but gave me a completely different look. And I liked it. I felt new and . . . not me.

We made our way through the crowded dance floor, each taking finger foods from the silver trays passing us by. I hadn't realized how hungry I was until I started eating the bacon wrapped scallops and battered shrimp. We saw lots of friends from Xavier High, and we stopped to say hi whenever we could, but there was still no sign of Caleb.

"Where did you tell him to meet you?" I asked over the music and noise of the crowd.

"I didn't," Maddy admitted. "I wanted to surprise him."

I rolled my eyes. "Lovely. What if he didn't bother coming? Why don't you text him?"

She shook her head. "We'll find him."

We headed out the side doors to the wraparound deck and peered down at the pool deck below. It took several minutes to sort through the crowd, but eventually we agreed that Caleb wasn't there, either.

"Okay," Maddy said. "I'll text him." I dug her phone out of my purse and she was about to start typing when her eyes caught something farther down the deck, and her face turned white. I followed her gaze, and tried not to gasp when I saw it, too—Caleb . . . kissing Holly Haverstock.

Caleb's eyes opened, long enough to realize that he had an audience—Maddy—and he pulled back from Holly.

Maddy turned to go, but Caleb yelled, "Maddy, wait! This isn't what it looks like."

Maddy froze, refusing to turn around. "It isn't what it looks like?" She closed her eyes, fighting back tears. "Tell me what it looks like, Caleb."

"It, uh . . . it looks like I was kissing Holly."

Maddy slowly turned around. "Now tell me what it was."

"Well, I . . . I mean, I just—"

She put her hand up. "Save it, Caleb. Drew was right—I never should've trusted you." She lifted her head as if unhurt, but I saw the betrayal and disappointment. "You and Holly deserve each other." Then she turned to leave.

"Let her go, Caleb," Holly said. She was standing behind him now, and slid her hand into his. "She isn't worth it."

Maddy stopped and slowly turned around as Caleb pulled his hand from Holly's. "Enjoy my leftovers, Holly." She was remarkably composed, but all I could see was red. My heart hammered against my chest, begging me to unleash the beast that resided inside. From the moment I saw him kissing Holly, to the moment she said Maddy wasn't worth it, an uprising was happening inside me that I couldn't quite explain or control. I struggled with containing the anger, but Maddy was my best friend and this was a situation that called for anger.

"Sit down," I said to Maddy. "I got this." Then I slowly turned to Holly. "You have six seconds to disappear before I flatten your nose. One . . . two—"

"If you think I'm scared of you, Sarah, you've got another thing coming."

"Three . . ."

"It's about time you two losers got what you deserved."

"Six." There was a crack as my fist connected with her smug face, and an eruption of euphoric pleasure as I realized I had inflicted pain. On another human. Pain. Caused by me. Initiated by me. I struggled with this thought for a moment as a conflict of emotions ensued inside—pleasure versus guilt. What had I done? No! She deserved it. I shook my head, trying to make sense of the arguments wrestling inside of it.

She deserved it. I shook my head again. *You can't heal hurt with hate.* I blinked harder. *You're right, she didn't deserve it. Caleb did! Hit him next.*

Caleb was just as dumbfounded as the rest of the spectators. The gathering crowd whispered their disbelief—had Sarah Marley really just done that?

"What the hell did you do that for?" Caleb shouted.

"I warned her," I heard myself say calmly, eerily calmly.

"You've got some nerve—"

"*I've* got nerve?" I pushed my hands into his chest. "You've been playing my best friend, and you think *I've* got nerve?" I shoved him again, and this time he pushed my arms away, but the reaction was enough to arouse my defensive instinct to crush my knuckles into his nose. He stumbled backwards and immediately brought his hands to his face.

"You should not have done that!" he growled, but when he looked up from his bloody hands, he seemed to change his mind about wanting to hit me back. He just surrendered his hands into the air and said, "You win."

"You're damn right I win." I ripped Maddy's necklace from his chest. It was a proud moment, but as I followed his eyes, and those of the rest of the crowd, I realized that they were resting just behind me. I glanced over my shoulder and found the real reason for Caleb's surrender—Drew and Luke approaching.

"Is there a problem here?" Luke said, a fire in his eyes.

"No, man," Caleb said, backing away. Holly hurried to his side and they disappeared into the crowd together.

"Nice," I said, scowling at the guys. "I totally had this."

Drew nodded while Luke said, "I have no doubt. We were just here to watch."

I scowled and then turned to Maddy, but she wasn't there. "Where'd she go?" I asked, searching the crowd for her small, blonde head. "Maddy. Where is she?"

Luke shrugged, while Drew searched too. "We haven't seen her."

I sighed. "She must have left before I hit Caleb. Damnit. I wanted her to see that. That was for her."

Luke reached for my arm, but I pulled it away. "No," I said. "I'm still mad at you."

"Sarah, come on," he tried, but I ignored him and followed Drew around the deck, in search for Maddy.

We were next to the pool when Luke caught up with me. He grabbed my arm and stopped me from chasing after Drew.

"What?" I shouted, rounding on him.

"Please talk to me, babe."

"Don't call me that," I shouted, feeling rage at the onset of that familiar *love* feeling.

"Okay." He raised his hands to show his compliance. "Can we go someplace private, please?"

I looked around at the dozens of people in party clothes and bathing suits surrounding the pool deck, some lounging in chairs with drinks, others clustered together for gossip. We were not alone, but no one was paying any attention to us. What more could he ask for?

"I need to find Maddy," I said as I backed away from him.

"Drew will find her." He came toward me and tried to take my hand again.

"What is wrong with you?!" I shouted. "Why are you so insistent on fighting with me? Can't you see that we need time apart right now?"

Now people were watching. Luke smiled half-heartedly at a few groups and then came closer, lowering his voice. "I love you," he said, and I knew he was trying to distract me. Distract me from leaving him again and finding Maddy.

He doesn't even care about Maddy. He only cares about himself!

The build-up of pressure in my chest was unbearable now. Every mean word, every sarcastic edge, every nasty facial expression—they all made the pressure lift little by little, but it wasn't enough. I wanted it to be enough, but it wasn't. And the more I tried to protect Luke from my wrath, the more the pressure built. I hated that he was with Ella, and I could no longer hide it.

"I HATE HER! I HATE WHAT YOU DID TO ME! I HATE YOU!" I screamed as my chest exploded. I turned away from him so he couldn't see the tears welling in my eyes, and I wouldn't see the hurt on his face, but when his soft, forgiving hand touched my arm, I couldn't stand what I had done. Before I could spit more fire at him, I turned and ran as fast as I could. I rounded the corner to the stairs and briefly looked back. This time, he wasn't following me. He just watched me go.

DREW AND MADDY were sitting on the stone wall overlooking the harbour. They weren't the only couple enjoying the privacy and quiet of the waterfront, but they were the only two not kissing or sitting on top of each other.

"Hi, I'm here," I announced when I got close.

They both turned. "Why are you out of breath?"

Maddy asked suspiciously.

"Been looking for you," I snapped. "Why'd you take off?"

"Don't worry—I saw you hit him."

I laughed. "Cool, right?"

Maddy forced a smile and then turned away. "I guess so."

"Why'd you leave then?"

"Listen, Sarah?" Drew said, reaching for my hand. He gave it a squeeze and winked. "Why don't you give us a few minutes? We'll meet you up by the pool."

"Are you serious?"

He jerked his head toward Maddy. "Yeah. We won't be long."

Is she mad at me? I thought, channelling a passage from his mind to mine.

Drew shook his head. "No. I got this, though. Trust me."

"Where's Luke?" Maddy asked as I walked away.

"I don't know," I mumbled and kept walking.

"Should we be leaving her alone when she's like this?" I heard Maddy ask Drew.

"She'll be fine," Drew answered.

"Yeah, but will everyone else be?"

Ouch. There was disrespectful sarcasm in her tone, and doubt in her words. She didn't trust me. She didn't appreciate what I had done for her.

I made my way back across the lawn, up the spiral staircase to the pool deck and slowly approached Luke who was leaning forward in a chair near the pool. I hesitated, stopping about ten feet from him, admiring the way he looked with the light of the pool reflecting off his face as he sat lost in thought. I wasn't the only one admiring him, either. The two waitresses, dressed in short, black skirts and too-small, white tops, over by the poolside bar, had noticed him too, and were clearly discussing him. Then one approached with confidence, her head and chest held high.

"Can I get you a drink?" the pretty waitress asked as she flipped her long, silky hair over her shoulder.

"No, I'm good," he replied without looking up. And my heart smiled.

"Aw, come on," she coaxed. "A good looking guy like you sitting here all by himself, you should at least have a drink in your hand."

He tilted his head up at her. "Two bottles of water, please."

"Water? Come on. It's on me. What'll it be?"

"Since you're buying," I said as I advanced, "I'll have a strawberry daiquiri."

Luke reached back and pulled me to his side, a big smile on his face. "You feeling better?"

"I will be once I get that drink." I winked at the waitress who smiled begrudgingly and turned on her heel to fetch our drinks.

"I got you a bottle of water."

"I know," I said. "I don't want the daiquiri, but she seemed so desperate to buy a drink for someone, so why not?"

I sat down on Luke's lap, and he wrapped his arms

around me. "I'm sorry," he said, and I knew he was apologizing for his history with Ella.

"No." I shook my head. *"I'm* sorry. I know I could never apologize enough to make up for what I said to you."

"You didn't mean it."

"I didn't," I assured him. "At all. I have no idea why I said it."

"Because it's the worst thing you could say to someone, and you couldn't help it. You did what you thought you had to do to relieve the pressure."

I was ashamed at my inability to control the darkness, but relieved that Luke understood.

"So how many girls hit on you while I was gone?"

"What? Me? Nah . . ."

"Whatever," I laughed.

"Just a few." He jerked his head to the side, and I followed his gesture to a group of girls sitting near the bar who were clearly making us the object of their conversation.

"Which ones?" I asked.

"Like I'm telling you, slugger."

I stood up and he kept a firm hold on my hands. "Don't worry, I'm not going to make a scene . . . with them."

"Then how?"

"Well, we're not really giving them much to talk about sitting here like this."

Luke stood up too. "What are you proposing?"

I wrapped my arms around his neck. "Shall we

dance?"

He slid his hands around my waist and brought his mouth to my ear. "I have a better idea."

He picked me up and I suppressed a squeal. "What are you doing?" I laughed.

"Taking you swimming." And he took two quick steps toward the pool with me in his arms.

I was only able to let out a small shriek before the water devoured us with its cold bite.

I came up for air, and Luke was treading water nearby, watching me with a huge grin on his face.

"I can't believe you did that!" I laughed as I splashed water at him. "Maddy spent forever on my hair. She's going to kill you!"

He pulled me into him, and I wrapped my legs around his waist and laid back, the water lapping at my chest.

"Have I told you lately how much I love you?" he said as he pulled me up to face him.

I cringed, knowing I didn't deserve his love, especially after what I had just done to him. I laid back in the water again, my arms moving slowly at my sides to keep me afloat, while my eyes searched the sky for stars.

But then he pulled me out of the water again, a desperate set to his face. "I don't care how crazy you get, Sarah. When I said I've always loved you and always will, I wasn't lying. That will never change."

A lump formed in my throat, and I tried to swallow without making it obvious that his words made me want to cry. I wanted to be loved. I wanted it to be just him and me, but I just didn't have enough faith that it was real. How could he love someone like me? Hardly pretty and extremely moody, especially lately.

"You deserve better than me," I said, and the lump grew, threatening to choke me.

"Not at all, Miss Marley. Quite the opposite."

My heart expanded with the rush of love that I felt for him in that moment. What had I ever done to deserve him?

"Look out!" I heard Drew call, and we turned in time to see him and Maddy running toward the pool. Drew grabbed her hand, and they plunged into the water next to us.

Maddy came up gasping for breath. "Fa-fa-fareeeeezing cold!" she stammered.

"Toughen up," I teased as she swam for the pool's edge.

"You feeling better?" Luke asked once she was clinging to the side.

She smiled and splashed Drew in the face who was trying to pull her back out to the deeper waters. "Yeah, I'm good. Sarah, thanks for, you know, giving Caleb what he deserved."

"It was my pleasure," I said. "Really, it was."

Luke chuckled. "I wish I had seen it."

"She's got quite the right hook," Maddy laughed.

Drew was quiet, but I could tell he wished he had been there too, but only so that he could've been the one to hit Caleb.

"What do you guys say we get out of here?" Drew

suggested. "Maddy's coming back to stay the night with us. I thought we could watch a movie."

Why did this hurt to hear? Why was I bothered that Drew and Maddy made plans for her to stay the night? What had they talked about down by the water when Drew had asked me to leave them alone?

"We're ready," Luke said as he swam to the edge of the pool. I ducked under the water and followed him, trying to clear my head with the cool water.

The staff brought us towels, and we used them to dry off. Before we left, another group of people had taken the plunge in their evening attire and were laughing and shouting to their friends to join.

"Looks like we got the party started," I said.

Luke put his arm around me, and we walked to the parking lot. I started toward Maddy's car, which was in a different direction from Drew's, but then Drew tossed his keys to Luke and said, "I'll go with Maddy; you take Sarah home."

Luke took my hand and we parted ways. I watched over my shoulder as Drew chased Maddy to her car. I couldn't explain why this bothered me. I had everything I wanted right here, attached to my hand, so why was my heart still aching for Drew's affection?

"That was more fun than I thought it was going to be," I admitted as we pulled out of the parking lot.

"Yeah, about that," Luke started. "What were you expecting by coming here tonight?"

"Just to let loose a little," I confessed. "I'm sorry if I worried you, but I needed this."

"I wasn't worried about you. I knew you'd be fine." He watched me with a mischievous grin on his lips. "I *was* worried about that apple."

"What—you thought I came here to look for a victim?"

He kept his gaze on the road and nodded.

"I mean, I'm not gonna lie—after we found Caleb kissing Holly, I did consider making him some apple cider."

Luke was quiet.

"But obviously I wouldn't do that." When he didn't respond, I continued, "I just want the damn thing opened, you know? I want to move on to the next clue. And if someone has to die in order to open it, then what the hell are we supposed to do?"

Luke took in a long, deep breath, then let it out slowly. "Well, regardless how it happens, I want you to know that continuing this mission, taking back Yelram, and finding that cure, is the most important thing. If someone has to die for that, then it's a worthy sacrifice." It felt scripted, and I noticed the whiteness to his knuckles as he gripped the steering wheel, but his mind was blocked, and the only thoughts that seeped out were of how much he loved me.

"My mother's a twisted person," I finally said, returning my attention to the road ahead. "I mean, who does that?"

Luke grinned. "She may be twisted, but she wasn't stupid. If that clue fell into the wrong hands, she was guaranteeing they would never live to find the next clue."

"I guess you're right," I acceded.

After a few minutes of silence, Luke changed the subject. "I think you broke Caleb's nose." He chuckled.

I laughed too, happy for the change of subject, and even happier to replay the look of shock on Caleb's face. "I kind of wish you guys didn't show up."

"Why?"

"I think he wanted to hit me back."

"I would've killed him."

"Which is why he didn't, I'm sure. But I would've loved to have kicked his ass in front of everyone, especially Holly."

"And I have no doubt that you could've easily done that."

"I can't believe how good it felt to hit him."

"Like an eruption of all your pent of frustration from the last few days?"

"Exactly!"

"I know what it's like."

My excitement dwindled as I realized the magnitude of this. Luke knew what I was talking about because he dealt with it on a daily basis. He fought the urges, and he knew how hard it was for me. Except with me, there was an element of fear there. I wasn't born to be dark. I couldn't go around hitting people or lashing out at the people I loved. The darkness was turning me into someone I wasn't born to be.

"How do I go back to normal? I don't want to be a monster," I admitted.

There was a pause before he answered, "We have to

open that clue so you can find the cure."

"So *we* can find the cure."

He just nodded, and for the first time since we started this mission, I felt his uncertainty.

CHAPTER 14

The Sacrifice

~ SARAH ~

AFTER A LATE night watching movies, morning came early. I had slept well with Luke's warm arms around me all night, but now there was a chill to the air that I didn't like. He wasn't with me anymore. Washroom, I imagined. Maybe he was showering. Maybe the apple had opened and they were getting ready to go, waiting for me to get my rest before that time.

I stretched, but a pain shot through my legs, and I realized that my whole body was aching as if I had run a marathon the day before.

I slowly sat up and reached for my phone, confirming that it was just before noon. Drew and Maddy would be up by now. They never slept in this late. My legs screamed with pain, but I forced myself to stand, holding onto the side of the couch, then the end table, and then the chair, for stability.

"Hello?" I called, but no one answered.

Then I saw it. The apple was sitting on the kitchen table, unattended. I hurried to it, ignoring the stabs of discomfort from my body. I picked up the apple and rotated it, but stopped when I saw the white fleshy inside. It slipped from my hand and fell to the floor.

"Luke? Drew?!" I yelled as I turned toward the kitchen. "Maddy?"

No one was in the kitchen. I ran down the hall. "LUKE?!" I screamed, tears stinging my eyes as they hovered on the edge of desperation and devastation.

"Sarah!" Maddy called as the patio door pulled open.

I spun around and headed back toward the patio. She me in the dining room and folded me in her arms as she burst into tears.

"Who is it?" I cried. "Who did it?" I tried to pull away, but she held onto me.

"I'm so sorry," she sobbed. "I didn't know. I didn't know."

I pushed her away and stumbled to the patio door, Maddy hot on my heels. I fell through the doorway, my eyes scanning the backyard for Luke or Drew.

And then I saw them.

Drew was standing over Luke who was on his knees, hunched over. Drew came to me and tried to stop me from going farther, but I didn't hear a word he or Maddy were saying to me.

"LUKE!" I screamed, fumbling my way to him, my legs working against me.

Luke slowly stood and turned to me, his eyes swollen and red, his expression a portrayal of defeat. I threw my arms around him and he caught me, burying his face into my neck as he quietly cried with me.

A flood of emotions spilled over me—relief that he was still alive, guilt that this was because of me, anger that he had taken this risk for me. But he hadn't died. Why hadn't he died? Was there time to save him like there was me?

And then I saw his mind. It was wide open, and he was filling it with images that confused me.

Images of sorrow and regret.

Images of love and happiness.

A memory of us at the park walking Lucia.

A memory of him sitting on the floor next to me, watching me sleep while I was snuggled up on the sofa next to Lucia.

A memory of us sitting on the front step while Lucia covered me with her love.

An image of Lucia. Just Lucia.

And that image stayed, lingering in his mind like a broken spirit.

"Lucia?" I gasped, my breath escaping the moment I said her name. Luke stepped aside, holding me firmly, and there on the ground at his feet laid my beautiful girl.

"NOOOOO!" I cried as I collapsed next to her. I buried my face into her soft fur, her unmoving body giving no warmth. "Lucia," I cried. "No-o-o-o. Lucia-a-a-a-a!"

Why? Why had she done this? She didn't eat fruit. She hated apples. Why would she do this? Why??

"Lucia, wake up, girl," I cried. "Please, wake up, Lucia. Don't leave me! Don't leave me-e-e-e!" I lifted her limp body and cradled her in my arms, rocking her back and forth as my body shook with heavy sobs. "Please, Lucia," I cried. "Please come back. Please, Lucia."

I cried over her for a long time, and they let me. When my body was too tired to hold her any longer, I curled up next to her on the ground and placed her head on my arm, exactly how she liked to snuggle, except that her fur was matted with my tears. Her nose was now dry. Her body was now stiff. Her soul was now gone.

"Sarah," Luke said softly, waking me from my dreamless sleep, "it's time to go."

Drew knelt down on the other side of Lucia and put his arms under her lifeless body as Luke did the same to me. I watched as Drew gently lifted her and held her close to his body, then brought her away so I didn't have to say good-bye. I buried my face in Luke's chest as he carried me into the house. Maddy was sitting on the couch, her face solemn and regretful with her own grief.

"Sarah, I'm so sorry," she said gently. "I didn't think she could get it."

"Where was it?" I asked, not because I blamed her, but because I needed to know. I needed to know what Lucia's last moments were like.

"It was in my bag, and I was sleeping with it," she said. "Drew was on the floor and you and Luke were out here, so I thought it was safe to keep it in bed with me." She reached for another tissue, blew her nose, and then added it to the pile of others on the coffee table.

"So she went into Drew's room and somehow got it out of your bag?" I asked.

Maddy shrugged. "Must have."

Luke left the room and returned a minute later with a familiar-looking bottle containing the elixir. "Here," he said, handing it to me with a glass of water. "It's time to take this."

I was curled up on the couch where he had set me only a moment ago, unable to move due to the screaming in my body, so I happily drank the elixir and waited for the pain to subside.

Luke sat down between Maddy and me. He handed me a tissue and I caught the silent tears sliding down my cheeks, but he didn't say anything. He knew there wasn't anything he could say that would take the hurt away.

The patio door opened, and Drew appeared in the living room a minute later. He was holding the apple in his hand. "Why haven't you opened this yet?"

Luke shook his head. "Not now, man. She's grieving."

"I know that, but we're kind of pressed for time here."

"Drew," Luke started, but I silenced him.

"He's right," I said. "Bring it to me."

The second I put both hands on the apple, the top twisted from the bottom, and it came apart. I reached in, pulled out more pages, and read them aloud:

I am so sorry, my sweet Sarah. I wish I could be there to hold you in this time of loss. Lucia's purpose was to be your companion through these years without a mother. This was her mission, given to her by your father, and she promised that she would always protect you, and do whatever it took to help you take back our world. Being the sacrifice for this clue was her purpose, and she was honoured to do this for you. For us. And most importantly, for Yelram.

1

I set the pages down and covered my face with my hands while I cried. Lucia was given this purpose. My parents raised her to protect me, and then to die for me.

Luke pulled my head into him and I muffled my cries with his chest. Maddy took the pages from me and continued to read:

The next lag of your journey won't be so easy, I'm afraid. I hope you're not upset with me for making you go on this quest. Yelram was once a beautiful world, my princess, and if this key falls into the wrong hands, it would be too easy for them to turn it into a dark world. I have to ensure that you are the one to find the key. That you are the one to take back Yelram. And I have to be sure that you are ready. This quest will prepare you for the obstacles you will encounter in Yelram.

2

Maddy stopped reading and set the paper on the table.

"Is that it?" Drew asked. "That tells us nothing."

"There's another page here," Luke said as he took the last page from my hand. "Did you want to read it?" he asked me. I shook my head, so he continued.

When any hidden thing appears lost, the quest to find it can seem unbearable at times. The next world is full of darkness, and you will have to use your mind. Nothing is as it seems here. Be careful who you trust as they may not be who you think they are. Take this blue ribbon and tie it into the hair of the young girl who helps you. She is a good friend of mine. She will be waiting for you, and you will know her by her ability to communicate with you through your thoughts.

I lifted my head. "The young girl from Nitsua," I said. "The one I met in my dream, and the same one who helped us find Eli."

"Are you sure?" Luke asked.

"Not entirely, but she has helped us before. The clue says she'll find us." I looked inside the apple and found a blue ribbon at the bottom. My tired, trembling fingers pulled out the long piece of silk. "I have to tie this into her hair for my next clue." I considered the ribbon and my mother's words about the girl being a good friend. "How do you think she became friends with a young girl from Nitsua?"

"She may not really be a young girl," Luke said. "She'd be a shapebender, so this could just be the form she uses to stay small and inconspicuous."

Drew added, "And she could've known her from Earth—a friend who died and crossed over to Nitsua."

"But that would mean she wasn't a good person," I deduced.

Drew shrugged. "Not necessarily. Just didn't have time to rectify some bad choices, maybe."

"You don't think my mother belongs to Nitsua now, do you?"

Luke and Drew both shook their heads.

"She killed a keeper," I reminded them. "She wasn't a saint."

No one said anything.

"And isn't murder one of the strongest laws?"

Again, silence.

"Well?" I pressed.

Drew cleared his throat. "Yes."

"If she broke the strongest commandment, she could be in Leviathan right now." My stomach squeezed.

Luke shook his head, but didn't comfort me.

"But we could rescue her, couldn't we?"

Again, I was treated with silence.

"Guys?"

Luke finally spoke, "When souls come to rest in Etak, they are forever tethered to that world. Unless there's a trade." He squeezed my hand. "I'm sorry, Sarah."

"A trade?"

Drew glared at Luke before answering, "It'd have to be an equal trade of a soul for a soul, and the keeper would have to agree to it, which Victor would never do." Drew's voice softened. "Even if your mother was there, Sarah, you may not even recognize her. She could've been changed into any creature. She could be a fire-breathing dragon, or even a demon."

"But her soul wouldn't change. She would still be the same. She would know me. . . . Right?"

Drew was quiet while Luke answered, "Hard to say."

This new discovery that my mother could still be "alive" in Leviathan or another world was mind-numbing. I already had a million and one questions for her, and I was finding it difficult not making her my final mission.

"What if we go to Leviathan next, find her, then she could tell us where the key is? And we could try to rescue her at the same time."

"Sarah," Drew said, appearing next to me. He took my free hand (the one not being held by Luke). "Your mother created this mission for you because this was what she wanted you to focus on. Not her. We need to stay focused."

Luke refolded the pages and handed them to Maddy. "Sarah just took the elixir," he said. "We should go while she's in good health."

Maddy was on her feet now. "Come on, Sarah. Let's go get ready. The faster we do this, the faster we find your key and take back your world. Your mother's not going anywhere. There's time to find her later."

I nodded, realizing there wasn't anything I could do at that moment, anyway. I followed Maddy into Drew's room where we got changed and ready for our next destination. Nitsua. Ella's world.

CHAPTER 15

I is for Ingram

~ SARAH ~

ELLA'S CASTLE WAS the last place we saw the little girl who helped us rescue Eli, so that was our next destination. We ported into the woods nearby and once we had our bearings and knew which direction the castle was in, we set out together.

"We need to be quick," Luke said. "She's expecting us, so she'll probably have guards waiting for us."

"Why is she expecting us?" Maddy pressed a little nervously.

"She tried to have Sarah killed," Luke said, as if that were enough.

"Then we get what we need, and we get out of here as quick as possible."

"Yes, and cover our tracks," Luke said.

Luke had his hand on the butt of his sword, his head constantly in motion, looking for a threat. Maddy and Drew both had arrows ready in their bows, walking with a bend in their knees, also anticipating the enemy's arrival. I, however, wasn't afraid. Maybe I had convinced myself that I wasn't going to die in this world—that if Ella hadn't killed me already, then maybe she didn't have it in her. Or maybe I just didn't care if I died. Lucia's death was hard on me, I realized. I hated knowing she was gone, because of me. I hated knowing that my mother planned for it to happen this way. Did Lucia even know what was happening to her? Did she have any control over it? Or was it a subconscious decision that took her life from her? Had she cried for me? Had she tried to wake me?

"Sarah," Maddy whispered, "I'm feeling a lot of negative energy coming from you. Mind toning it down a little?"

I scowled, then turned to the guys who made no attempt to soften her request. "Am I bothering you?"

"No," Luke said quickly, shaking his head, while Drew said, "It's annoying, yes."

Luke's hand rested on my shoulder as we walked, but I made no effort to move closer to him. I was lost in my own misery and I didn't want to share it with anyone. It was bad enough that my suffering was transferring to them. I needed to be better at building my own wall for my mind. They were all working hard at blocking me from entering their minds, but obviously it was too difficult. Why hadn't I been working at blocking my thoughts and emotions from escaping my own head? This was what I would have to do. This was my new mission—protect my friends from my own slow, agonizing demise.

We trudged through the thick forest for hours, stopping only to eat nuts and dried berries to keep up our energy. The sun was starting to fall in the sky, and I worried that we weren't going to be able to make it to the castle until nightfall. We had done well to avoid any confrontations at this point, but we had been quiet and keeping to the deepest, darkest part of the untouched forest.

"How much longer?" Maddy quietly asked when we stopped for a drink of water.

Luke and Drew were crouched over an old map that was laid out on the ground at our feet. Drew traced his finger along the map, which moved us away from the castle, and then traced another line back to the castle. Luke nodded his approval.

"A few hours," Drew finally responded.

"Why is this taking so long?" Maddy whined. "It didn't take us this long last time we came here."

"We weren't expected last time," Drew reminded her. "If we go this way"—he traced the line again on the map—"then we'll reach the Forest of Fear by nightfall. You can't port in or out of this forest so she won't expect us to go there."

"And we can get into the castle from the Forest of Fear, so that's the plan," Luke added.

"Okay," Maddy said, crouching down so she could jab her finger into the large dark mass on the map. "So we land *here*, in the Forest of *Fear*, at *nightfall*. Does anyone else think that's a stupid idea?"

Drew looked up at Luke before responding. "Again, they'd never expect us to do that."

Maddy's eyebrows shot up. "Probably because no one in their right mind would ever do that. Perhaps we should take lead on that and, you know, save our death wish for the morning?"

Luke wasn't engaging in the argument. He was watching me, but I pretended not to notice. His mind was closed—he had gotten really good at that—and all I could tell was that he wished he knew what I was thinking or feeling.

"I think we should camp out," I finally said, "when we get to the Forest of Fear."

"Are you nuts?" Maddy nearly shouted.

"I agree with Drew," I said, my eyes flickering to his for a brief moment. "They won't expect us to be there, so we'll be safe from Ella's army."

"What about all the other things that *live* in there?" Maddy challenged. "I assume it's called the Forest of Fear for a reason. I'm sure it's not filled with butterflies and bambis."

Drew grinned, admiring her wit. "I won't let anything happen to you, Maddy."

This caught her off guard for only a few seconds. When she had recovered, her face a light pink hue, she said, "You can't go making promises like that, Drew. If you can't port in or out of there, will you even be able to use your craft?"

They were quiet. They wouldn't have their powers, but they didn't think they'd need them.

"We'll have ours," I reminded her, which was also a painful reminder to me that the last time I was in a dream world, my power had been firebending—the craft associated with Leviathan, the darkest world. Although it hadn't made sense at the time, it sure made sense now. Of course I was destined for the darkest world. My soul was full of darkness and my body was crippling from the weight of it. It didn't matter that I was a princess of a light world, without my key, I was just a regular girl, destined for whatever world my soul took me to.

Maddy inhaled deeply, exaggerating her frustration. "Fine," she said. "I don't like the idea, but if the rest of you think it's our best chance of staying alive, I'll trust you."

Luke began folding up the map. "We'll take shifts sleeping," he said. "Two at a time."

"We'll figure it out when we get there," I said. "Let's go."

I hadn't wanted to get into the discussion about who was sleeping with whom. I would be paired with either Luke or Drew, and I didn't want to think about who I would rather spend the quiet hours of the night with. It should be Luke. It was always Luke. I would normally do anything to spend time with him. To feel his skin brush against mine. To hear his words whispered in my ear. But lately my heart cried for the reassurance that Drew loved me. That what he felt for me was real, and not just an enchantment.

I wrestled with this as we trudged through the sharp brush, waded through rivers so our tracks would be lost, and stopped periodically for water and food. Hardly a word was spoken. Their minds were closed tight, and although I tried to break into Drew's, he wasn't budging. Not until the woods became thicker and the sky was nearly black. It was the first time any of the three brought their defences down long enough for me to feel what they were feeling.

For Maddy, every sound frightened her. Her palms were sweating and she kept drying them on her pants. She wondered if the rest of us could hear the distant howling too. She migrated closer to Drew, and he noticed. He put his hand on the small of her back and brought his other hand to his belt where his sword waited.

Drew hadn't felt like this since he was young. He had just found out that his mother was dead, and he was having a hard time coping with the news. He began sleeping with his bedroom light on, believing that as long as there was light, he would be safe. He grew out of it, but now those feelings were coming back. His heart was racing, and he worried. He worried about death, and memories of his own mother's death were lingering near the forefront of his mind.

Luke wasn't scared. The energy that was coming from him was powerful and confident. The fear he sensed from the forest ahead was exhilarating, although he didn't want to admit it. But he didn't have to. I knew how he felt, and I could relate. I felt it too. I wasn't afraid. The fear was awakening the darkness inside me. It made me stronger. Tougher. Invincible.

"I think we should go back." Maddy stopped, causing me to nearly run into the back of her.

"The forest starts just up there," Luke said, pointing to a row of tall trees lining the edge of darkness.

"And I'm already scared to death," she admitted, her body shaking. "Can we please do this tomorrow?"

"She's right," Drew added. "The fear is strong in there. I can feel it from here." He looked at Luke. "I suppose you can't?"

Luke shook his head. "It's not a problem for me. I think we should keep going. We'll be safer in there. I can protect you guys."

Maddy was clinging to Drew and they were all watching me now.

"It's your vote," Drew said. "What do you want to do?"

What were they so scared of? Sure it was dark, but that meant we would be well hidden. The only fear I sensed was theirs. Like Luke, I felt empowered and suddenly very awake. But I knew telling them this would unsettle them. It would mean I was more like Luke than them. But wasn't this the truth anyway? My soul was more dark than light. I feared less, loved less, angered easily, and even felt hate.

"We should go in," I heard myself say. "We'll be fine."

"Are you serious?" Maddy said. "Can't you feel

that?"

I paused, looking at Drew, then Luke, before I answered, "I only feel your fears. For me it's . . . kind of exciting."

Drew narrowed his eyes, studying my face. "Let's go in then," he said. "We need to hurry this quest up."

There was an obvious coldness the second we crossed the border from the regular forest to the Forest of Fear. Maddy was shivering uncontrollably, even with Drew's sweater wrapped tightly around her shoulders, and was unable to hold a weapon of her own. Luke had his sword drawn, and Drew's bow was readied with an arrow and aimed straight ahead as we walked. I chose my bow as my weapon of choice, taking up the rear of our pack and scouring the trees for any movement or threat. The farther we ventured into the forest, the colder it became.

"C-c-c-can we st-st-stop here, pl-pl-please?" Maddy shivered.

"Yes," Luke answered. "Here's good. We'll stay here for the night and start out in the morning."

Maddy collapsed on the ground, ensuring the three of us were close. She wrapped Drew's sweater around her tighter and held her knees to her chest.

"Maddy should rest first," Drew decided.

"She's freezing," Luke said, "and we didn't bring sleeping bags. Someone should lay with her."

My stomach clenched, threatening to throw up, as I knew Luke meant this for Drew, but Drew was busy gathering sticks and brush for a fire.

"I got this," I said before Drew responded. I sat down

next to Maddy and pulled her into me.

"Y-y-you're just as c-c-cold as me," she stammered.

"Am not," I argued. "Drew will have the fire blazing in a minute. You'll be warm soon."

Luke released a thought of hurt before he answered, "I'll keep Maddy warm. You and Drew keep watch."

No! I thought desperately. *Why would you do that?*

You want to spend time with Drew. I get it, he thought back. *It's either me or Drew lying down with her. I can guarantee it will mean nothing to me, but I can't make that promise for Drew.*

Drew wasn't paying attention to our silent exchange. His eyes, and aim, were on the forest around us.

I'm not going to pretend I'm okay with it, Luke added. *But if it keeps you happy, it's a sacrifice I'll make.*

How was I supposed to respond to that? I didn't want Drew with Maddy. I didn't want Luke with Maddy. I wanted them both to myself. But I knew Luke was mine. He was devoted. I couldn't say the same for Drew. What if he *was* enchanted and didn't love me after this? I wasn't ready to let his love go. He was my longest friend. My first crush. The one person who always loved me. I couldn't let him go. Not yet.

Luke was on the ground next to Maddy now, his back against a tree. He pulled her into his lap and wrapped his arms around her as she buried herself into his embrace.

"Thank you, Sarah," she mumbled into his chest, the blaze of the fire revealing the mask of pleasure on her face.

I turned away from them, unwilling to commit the

visual to long term memory.

"Guess it's just you and me," I said as I joined Drew on watch duty, the fire crackling behind us.

"Yeah," he grumbled, and I wondered if he was as uncomfortable as I was with Luke and Maddy lying together.

"I'm sorry," I whispered.

"Me too," he said.

"Why are you sorry?"

"Because I didn't volunteer myself up." His reply was so low that I almost didn't hear it.

"Yeah, why didn't you?"

"I . . . wanted to be with you," he said, and my breath got caught on the inhale.

"Why?" I managed to say.

"It's been awhile since it was just the two of us."

"It has."

"And it's nice."

"It is."

Our backs were together now, Drew facing Luke and Maddy on the other side of the fire, and me watching the rest of the dark forest. We stayed like this for a long time. Every now and then he pressed his back into me, and I focused on the way the warmth from his body felt against mine. But soon I found myself worrying that Luke would notice. Could he feel my connection to Drew right now? Did he know that my heart was racing? And if he did, what would it do to him? He didn't deserve my unfaithfulness. I loved him, but the darkness made me needy and greedy, and as much as I tried to stop it, I couldn't.

A low, guttural growl spliced through my gyrating thoughts. Was it Luke? Did he see what was happening between Drew and me? I turned quickly to face him, but he wasn't angry. He was slowly transferring Maddy to the ground, being careful not to wake her. He had heard the growl too, and the glint in his eye suggested he was more excited by it than anything.

CHAPTER 16

The Forest of Fear

~ SARAH ~

DREW'S ARROW WAS pulled tight, his eyes bouncing from left to right, anxiously searching the perimeter.

Sticks cracked behind me, and Drew spun around, his arrow leaving his bow and whizzing through the air next to me. It missed its target, and he launched another before I could react.

"What's out there?" I said as Luke flanked my left side, holding his sword out steady in front of him.

"Panthers," Luke answered. "Ella's favourite animal. The forest will be stocked with them."

"Probably would've been nice to know that before," I muttered.

"We're surrounded," Drew said as he released

another arrow.

"Don't waste your arrows," Luke said. "You'll need your sword for these animals."

Drew tossed his bow to the ground and pulled his sword at the same time I did.

"Make sure they don't get near Maddy," Drew ordered.

From the corner of my eye, I caught a yellow light flicker in the blackness ahead.

"Found one," I said as I stepped forward, but Drew held me back.

"I got this one," he said.

The panther met him in mid-air as they leaped toward each other. Drew didn't have time to slice his sword, and the animal wrestled him to the ground.

"Drew, catch!" I pulled my dagger from my boot and tossed it to him. In one swift movement, Drew caught the handle and drove the blade into the panther's side, then pushed the animal off and finished it with his sword, driving the metal deep into its chest.

"Thanks," he panted.

"We're not done yet," I said as he tossed my dagger back to me.

Drew traded his sword for his own knives, and I tucked my dagger into my belt, keeping it nearby for when the panthers got too close for my sword's advantage.

Three panthers stepped into the light of our campsite. Their heads were low, their yellow eyes flickered with the threat of revenge, and their growls were felt deep inside my chest. I knew their greed, their vengeance, their anger. I tasted it, and it made me hungry for my own.

With a loud growl, I sprinted toward the panthers. I leaped into the air at the same time the middle panther lunged toward me. Using every muscle in my body, I swung my sword, beheading the animal before his body crashed with mine. I landed on the ground, a black, lifeless body confining me to the earth.

Drew and Luke were battling with the other two panthers, and then there was an ear-splitting scream of terror. I felt it before I heard it. Every fibre inside of me had been alerted to her accelerated emotion. It was Maddy, and she was now awake.

Maddy was standing when I reached her, hugging the tree as if she could disappear inside if she squeezed hard enough.

"Maddy," I urged, "calm down. Shhh. It's okay."

But she wasn't listening. She couldn't listen. All she could see was the bloodbath that was happening in front of her—Drew and Luke battling now four panthers.

"Maddy, just stay here," I instructed. "Take your knives, but just stay here."

She was sobbing and shaking uncontrollably at this point, and I doubted whether she understood me.

"Knock her out!" Luke shouted over his shoulder as another panther lunged toward his sword.

"What?"

"Her fear is drawing the panthers!" he shouted. "KNOCK HER OUT!"

I suddenly noticed we were surrounded. There were

at least two dozen beady, yellow eyes glaring at us. My fist was in Maddy's face before I had time to think it through.

"I'm so sorry, Maddy," I gasped as I watched her body fall to the ground.

"Now come help us!" Drew shouted.

I killed three panthers by the time I reached Luke's side and finished one of the four that he was still fending off. Together, the three of us slowly eliminated the crowd of panthers, which were no longer multiplying now that Maddy was sleeping again. When the last panther fell at Drew's sword, we all collapsed by the fire.

"Are you okay?" Luke asked as he touched my arm.

"I'm fine," I answered between breaths.

"You're bleeding." Drew nodded toward my ripped shirt soaked with blood.

"It's not my blood. I'm fine."

Luke moved my hair aside and ran his fingers along my cheek, which stung, but I managed to keep a straight face. "You've got a pretty deep cut."

"Yeah, I felt that," I admitted.

"I have something in my bag for that." Drew dug through his bag and pulled out a topical ointment. "Until we get back," he said as he applied the cream while Luke handed me a canteen of water and handful of nuts.

"How's Maddy?" I asked, my eyes still avoiding her, although I could feel the buzz of thoughts from her dreamless sleep.

"She'll be fine," Luke said.

"I feel so bad," I said.

"Had to be done."

Drew didn't say anything. He, too, hated seeing her knocked out.

"You should rest," Luke said. "Why don't you lie down next to Maddy?"

"I'm not tired," I said. "Why don't *you* lie down with her?" There was jealous venom in my words, which he heard.

"I'll rest," Drew interrupted. He stretched out on the ground next to Maddy, keeping a knife clutched close to his chest.

"Looks like it's just you and me," Luke said, his words too familiar for my liking. He had heard me talking to Drew earlier. He knew I had wanted to be alone with Drew. And he wanted me to know that he knew. This hurt. I was hurting him. Part of me was enlivened by his jealousy. This was the dark side, I knew. But a smaller part of me still hurt. This was the only good left in me. So I clung to this hurt because it made me feel human.

A half hour passed without a word. We both paced around the perimeter of the campsite, passing each other every minute or so. At first there was cold distance between us, but with each pass, we got closer and closer until our arms brushed each other. I liked it. It was electrifying to feel his skin against mine. I loved him. I would always love him.

As my bow became heavier and heavier, it soon only rested near my side. Luke's sword trusted the silence too, and we were both comforted by the low crackle of the fire. Drew was asleep, propped up against the tree with one arm over Maddy who was still curled up on the ground near him.

The next time Luke and I passed, he reached for my arm and held it. Our eyes met, and I felt drawn to kiss him. But did he want the same? Or did he want to tell me he was done with my games? I couldn't blame him if he found it too hard to love me given all the conflicting feelings I continuously showed.

His lips came closer to mine, and I knew he still loved me. I felt it. He needed me as much as I needed him. But before we finished our apologies, our faces were bitten with a cold frost that swept through the campsite. Our fire crackled viciously, resisting the cold, but it didn't win the fight and was extinguished almost as quickly as it started.

"Drew!" Luke called, squeezing my arm and pulling me toward Drew and Maddy.

"I'm up," Drew said. "What's wrong? Why's it so cold? Where's the fire?"

"It just went out. Something's not right," Luke said, but I knew what he meant—something was *very* right. Suddenly the Forest of Fear was awake, aware of our presence, and taking back its territory.

CHAPTER 17

Fear's First Victim

~ SARAH ~

DREW WAS ON his feet, and he searched for my hand until he found it. "Are you okay?" he asked.

"I'm fine. What do you think it is?"

"I don't know, but we need to get that fire started."

Suddenly I remembered that, as a dream warrior, I might still have powers here, even though Luke and Drew didn't. And if I still had powers, then I was able to create fire with my hands. I quickly rubbed my hands together, then threw them toward the ground. A small fire ignited, much to my surprise and excitement, but the coldness snapped it in two, extinguishing the flame before our eyes.

"Do it again," Drew ordered.

The second time was more successful. The flame was larger, more intense, and lasted a bit longer. Long enough to survey the area and confirm that we weren't surrounded. This provided some comfort and Luke let go of my arm, allowing me to continue working the fire with my hands.

And that's when I felt it. Or didn't feel it. Maddy. I couldn't sense her presence. I couldn't hear her muted dreams. I couldn't feel her. I spun around, letting the fire die a little. "She's gone!" I gasped.

Drew grabbed his sword. "Where is she?" he demanded loudly. "Maddy!"

Luke was at my side again, one hand on my arm and the other holding his sword out as his eyes searched the area.

"Make light for us, Sarah!" Drew demanded. "We have to find her!"

With Drew beside me, and Luke taking up the rear, his hand on my waist, I led the way through the woods with a ball of hot light in each hand.

"Maddy!" We all took turns calling into the night.

"Can you sense her, Sarah? Can you read her thoughts?" Drew pressed.

I hesitated because I didn't want to admit it. "No."

"Damnit!" Drew slammed his fist into a tree.

"What do you think happened to her?" I asked, unsure of whether I wanted to know the answer. Terrified for my friend whose fate was uncertain. I felt the guilt of knowing she didn't want to go into the forest at night, and that she relied on my vote to keep us out. This made my legs move faster, and the fire in my hands shine brighter.

"What was her biggest fear?" Luke asked.

"Coming in here," Drew said between gritted teeth, and I felt the stab of his accusation.

"Exactly," Luke said. "But why? She was scared of something. The forest is pitching our biggest fears against us."

I stopped walking. My feet stayed planted as I thought this through. "It's Maddy," I said, turning to Drew as I knew he would understand my next words. "She's a fighter. Her fear would be that she couldn't help us. She'd be immobilized."

Drew nodded. "So what does that mean, though?"

"They'll take her to the castle," Luke said. "They won't kill her."

"How do you know Ella won't kill her?" I said, the taste of bitterness on my tongue.

"She's not a murderer," he said, which made me want to be sick.

Drew hissed, "She's a dark lord, Luke. Murder isn't beneath any of you."

Luke sniggered. "We do what we have to do, Drew. You're not so innocent, either, if you haven't forgotten."

"Stop it," I said, and the light from my hands diminished to a flicker. "Why don't you think your precious Ella won't kill Maddy?"

Luke inhaled slowly, trying to ignore my reference to Ella. "She'll use her as bait, and then as collateral. If Maddy's dead, she won't have anything to bargain with."

"What do you mean?" Drew snapped.

"She knows Sarah will come for her, and she'll expect Sarah to take Maddy's place."

"No," Drew said quickly and assuredly. "That's not happening."

"I didn't say we would have to," Luke said. "I'm just saying that's why I don't think she'd be stupid enough to have Maddy killed before we get there."

My stomach was turning over and over and I was thankful for the darkness that concealed my jealousy. Luke was defending Ella. And he basically just said she was smart. Smart and kind. Kind because she wouldn't murder Maddy, and smart because she knew the trade was more valuable than the kill.

His hand touched my back and I recoiled. "No," I said, trying to keep the shake from my voice.

He knew what I meant. I couldn't handle his touch. Not when I felt like it was Ella he would rather be touching.

"Come on," Drew said, grabbing my hand and pulling me forward. "We need to get to the castle. It's our best chance of finding Maddy."

"Then what?" Luke said. "She'll want Sarah in exchange for Maddy."

Was this what *he* wanted? Maybe he planned for this.

"Well, they're not having Sarah, either," Drew said definitively.

There was no closure on the matter as we all just kept our focus on running through the Forest of Fear toward Ella's castle. Toward Maddy.

WE RAN FOR what seemed like half the night, with no one saying a word. The forest was slowly lightening as the sun showed its tired face. Suddenly Drew stopped and I ran into the back of him, bounced off, and landed in Luke's arms.

"What is it?" Luke pressed.

"Maddy!" Drew gasped as he stared off toward a body of water in the distance. He ran through the brush, jumping high to avoid the brambles. "Maddy!" he shouted again. Soon he was at the water's edge. A large pond, or small lake, that was covered in a thick fog.

"Where is she?" I shouted as I pushed past Drew and took a few steps into the bitter cold water.

"Sarah, get back!" Luke said, reaching for my arm. I pulled away, but he managed to get a grip on his second try. He yanked me out of the water as Drew caught sight of Maddy again, then pushed past us and dove into the freezing cold water after her.

"Drew, wait!" Luke yelled, but Drew was already under the water.

"I don't see her!" I panicked as Luke kept a firm grip on me.

"Me, neither," Luke said, but there was no surprise in his tone.

Drew came up for breath almost a minute later and searched the water. "Maddy!" he shouted again and desperately swam farther out.

"Drew!" Luke yelled. "It's not real!"

"What are you talking about?" I pressed as we both

watched Drew take another deep breath and plunge under the water again.

"You can't see her, right?" Luke asked.

"No."

"Can you hear her?"

"No."

"I think only Drew can. I think it's another fear."

"You think his fear is Maddy drowning?"

"Or losing her."

Why did my heart constrict at those words? There was a time when Drew wouldn't have left my side for anything. And now he was leaving me in the Forest of Fear while he risked hypothermia in a lake that was more than likely just luring him to his death. But on the other hand, I thought to myself desperately, this meant Maddy wasn't drowning.

Drew came up for breath again, and Luke and I both yelled for him. When he turned his attention to us, I waved him in while Luke called, "It's not real, Drew!"

Drew took another look around the lake and decided that maybe we were right. He began to swim back into shore, but as he did, the water in the middle of the lake formed a peak, and something began to move quickly toward him.

"Hurry, Drew!" I screamed as I conjured a ball of fire and threw it over top of Drew toward the thing closing in on him.

Luke drew his sword and ran through the water until he was waist deep.

"Luke, no!" I screamed. "I can't lose you!"

Luke retreated back to shore, but paid no mind to my words. I pulled out my bow and began firing arrows toward the creature, and when the thing was almost on top of Drew, Luke took a few steps back and then sprinted forward and leaped off a boulder, flew through the air over the water, and drove his sword into whatever it was that was about to devour Drew.

Drew scrambled to shore, catching his breath. He reached into his boots and pulled out his daggers, then dove back into the water to help Luke who was now beneath the surface. I stood, frozen in fear, as I watched the two of them wrestle with a creature that had the advantage of being able to breathe underwater.

My bow was at the ready, my eye lined with the arrow, waiting for a clear shot. But was it the creature? Or Luke? Or Drew? Suddenly the beast reared out of the water, its slimy grey body more enormous than I imagined. I released the arrow into its chest. Then another into its head before it fell back down into the water . . . right on top of Luke's sword.

The creature was dead. Luke was alive.

But where was Drew?

Luke disappeared under the water again and appeared a few seconds later with Drew, whose arm was mangled and bleeding, hanging loosely next to him. I helped Luke set Drew down away from the water's edge, and tore off the bottom part of my shirt and wrapped it around his arm to help stop the bleeding.

"I'm sorry," he panted. "I . . . I thought I saw her. I swear I did."

"It's okay," Luke said. "I'm sure it felt real."

"It did."

A thought was haunting me and I couldn't ignore it. "Do you think Maddy disappeared in the first place not because of her fear, but because of yours?"

Neither answered.

"If your biggest fear was losing her, maybe that's why she was taken," I said.

"No," Drew said, shaking his head. "My biggest fear is losing *you*."

Luke looked away, but I could tell he wanted to hit Drew for saying it. And because I didn't want to admit that there was a part of him that feared losing Maddy too, I didn't press the matter.

I picked up my bow from the ground, slung it over my shoulder and said, "Which way to the castle from here?"

Luke didn't answer, he just led the way.

AN HOUR LATER, Luke was still a few strides ahead of Drew and me. I sensed his agitation with Drew and his frustration with me, and it was exhausting. I detested having to try to read his feelings and thoughts when they were all over the place and completely void of any merit. Well, maybe not completely.

"Can we stop for a few minutes?" I finally asked, my legs burning with the need to sit.

Drew immediately stopped, retrieved some dried nuts and berries from his backpack, and a canteen of water, then handed them to me as I sat down on a rock.

Luke stopped too, but kept his back to us. "Her castle's just up ahead," he said.

"I just need a couple minutes." I ignored that it was *her* castle and not *the* castle.

"She needs a break," Drew started. "Just let her rest, man."

Luke turned on Drew, but before he could say his next words, his eye caught sight of something on Drew and he stopped.

"Why are you wearing that?" Luke demanded, pointing to Drew's key hanging around his chest.

Drew looked down and touched his key. "It's mine. Why?"

"Like the hell it is," Luke hissed, and he lunged for Drew. Drew fell out of his way, and I jumped between them.

"Luke, what the hell!"

"It's not yours, man," Drew said confused as he read the fire in Luke's eyes.

This didn't seem to be the right thing to say. Luke pushed me aside and went for Drew again, and this time his fist connected with Drew's face.

"LUKE!" I gasped, running to Drew's aid. "Drew, are you okay?" I pushed Luke three times until I was sure he wouldn't attack again. "What the hell is wrong with you?!"

"Of course you'd side with him!" Luke shouted.

I shook my head. "What has gotten into you?"

"How, Sarah? Just tell me *how*?"

"Okay. How what?" I asked, trying desperately to

determine the root of his problem.

"How could you do that? Just because I wouldn't take it from you? You give it to Drew?"

"Luke, I don't know what you're talking about. That's Drew's necklace. It's always been Drew's."

"Dude, it's not Sarah's," Drew said. "Look"—Drew held up his key, confirming that it was indeed his—"and it's definitely not yours."

Luke let out a growl and dove for Drew again, but this time I was faster and got in the way. It lessened his fury, but he still managed to make contact with Drew.

"Wait!" I shouted, realizing that this was far too strange to be normal. "I know what's going on!" Both turned to me, Drew confused as hell and nursing a bleeding lip, and Luke angry . . . but fueled by jealousy.

I went to him and touched his face. There was so much hurt there.

He pushed my hand away. "I thought you loved me," he said, his voice a soft whimper.

"I do. I love you."

"Then why would you give him your necklace?"

"What?" I heard Drew say, more to himself.

"Luke, this isn't real. That's not my necklace. Look." I pulled my school necklace from my shirt and brought his fingers to it. "Do you see this? It's still mine. I'm keeping hold of it for you. For us." I nodded toward Drew who was standing behind Luke. "And *that* is Drew's key."

Luke softened slightly, took a quick and awkward look back at Drew, then sat down on the ground and threw his hands into his hair.

"What just happened?" Drew said after a minute.

I squatted down in front of Luke and kissed his forehead. "It was just a fear."

"That what? I took your necklace?" Drew was still confused.

"That you took *me*."

Drew licked the blood from his lip. "I need to take a piss. I'll be back in a minute." I appreciated this for his attempt to leave us alone.

"Are you okay?" I asked Luke once Drew was gone.

He nodded and looked up at me. "I'm sorry."

"Don't be. It's this awful forest. I know you would never get that jealous otherwise."

Luke shook his head and looked away. "But I have been."

"What do you mean?"

"I've been so jealous over how you've been looking at him. And how he looks at you. And how I know you want his touch over mine."

"I don't."

"Sarah, do yourself a favour and don't get into the habit of lying."

"Okay." I looked down and took a deep breath. "So maybe I've missed him a little, but I—"

"You don't have to make excuses. I get it. The darkness plays tricks on you all the freaking time. I know what it's like."

"But in my moments of clarity, I know I love you, and I want nothing to do with him."

He nodded. "I know."

I wanted to ask how he knew, but I wasn't sure I wanted the answer. I didn't want him to tell me that he felt the same toward Ella. A false love that kept him drawn to her.

"First Maddy, then Drew, and now you," I said. "I wonder what my episode of fear will be like."

"Do you want to know what I think?" he said. "I think you've already had it."

"What do you mean?"

"I think when Maddy went missing, that was Drew's fear coming alive. And when Drew nearly drowned to try to save her, that was your fear."

"What? No." I shook it out of my head, pretending that he couldn't at all be right about this. I wasn't afraid of Drew choosing Maddy over me. Well, I was a *little*, but not more than I was afraid of losing Luke.

He shrugged. "It was just a thought. Would make sense. Especially since we're at the edge of the forest and you haven't had an episode."

This made me angry. Angry that he was accusing me of fearing losing Drew to Maddy! Maybe I was unsettled by the thought, yes, but it wasn't my biggest fear! I feared losing Luke to Ella far more!

"That wasn't my fear," I said firmly.

"Sarah, I'm not mad," he said. "When you have darkness in you, you have a harder time controlling your thoughts and feelings and urges. I get it. I was born into darkness and I've been fighting these things my whole life. Sometimes your body wants something that your mind doesn't. That's what the darkness does. It tempts you."

"Stop talking," I said.

"Why?"

"Because my fear is losing you to Ella. I can't go through that again, Luke. And the more you talk about being tempted and having feelings for someone else, the more I think you're going to tell me you still want her." I paused because I wanted to give him an opportunity to jump right in and squash that thought, but it took longer than I expected. "I think I'm gonna be sick." I stood up and stumbled away, my head spinning with the realization that I was right. He did still have feelings for Ella.

"Sarah," Luke said, taking my arm and steadying me. "You're wrong. That might be your fear, and that might be what Ella tries to convince you when we get in there, but the forest can't make me feel something for her that's not there. I only love you. That's all. Forever. I promise."

He pulled me into him, and I let myself trust him. I let myself believe that he loved me and only me.

Because he promised.

CHAPTER 18

The Dragons' Den

~ SARAH ~

THE CASTLE'S EAST side was protected by the Forest of
Fear. It was the safest entrance as no one ever willingly
went into this particular forest. No one but us. And with
one less person than we went in with, I now knew why.

From our vantage point in the woods where we now
crouched, assessing our options, we counted seven
dragons tethered to the entire east side of the castle, each
having just enough chain to reach the next. There were
three arched entrances, spread about a hundred feet
apart.

"What should we do?" I asked as Drew and Luke
studied the map.

"It looks like two of those entrances are traps." Drew

pointed to the map where the two entrances on either end led to dead ends. "I'm willing to bet that they aren't just there for looks. They'll lead to a pit, or something else is sleeping inside those rooms."

"So this is the real one?" I asked, pointing to the entrance in the middle.

"According to the map," Luke said.

"Where did this map come from anyway?" Drew's question was for Luke.

"Ella," Luke answered quieter. "She gave it to me when she trusted me because she wanted me to know how to get around the castle."

"Has it always been accurate?" Drew asked.

"Yes," he said.

My stomach turned, knowing he had been here numerous times to see Ella. "Did she tell you about the Forest of Fear?" I asked, fighting hard to keep the jealousy from my voice.

"She did. That's how I knew about its threats."

"So then she would know that if you were ever to come through the castle on this side, then you would be doing so without her approval," I gathered.

"I guess so. What does that have to do with this?"

"She wouldn't have bothered to tell you if the map was misleading then."

"You think it is?" He was curious. He trusted my instincts, and I liked that.

"I do."

"And that would explain why there are three archways," Drew began. "Because if there were just two, we would assume it was the other one. But with three, we now have options."

"So which one is it?" I said, turning back to the dragon-guarded archways.

I studied the ground near the entrances. All were scuffed up and void of grass. The first one also had black scorch marks around the door, as if someone had gone through and was closely followed by the breath of a dragon. The second one had three of the seven dragons guarding it, the middle dragon being uncomfortably irritated. And the third entrance was guarded by two rough-looking dragons, with sores and battle scars.

"The first one has scorch marks," I began. "The middle archway is guarded heavily, but I think that's just to make it look like it's the right one. The dragon in the middle has a long enough chain to reach the two end archways, so really, each entrance has three dragons guarding them. The farthest one is guarded by two gangly looking dragons, which could mean they're being picked on by the other dragons. If they had an important job of protecting the right entrance, then they would be respected more, I'd think."

"The first one looks interesting," Luke said, following along on my same line of thinking. This was the entrance with the highest probability with the scorched stone.

"Okay, well then I think the first door is the best bet," Drew agreed. "We try that one."

Luke drew in a deep breath. "I'll go first."

"No," I said, instinctively trying to protect him from another possible bad decision made by me.

"It makes the most sense, Sarah. Drew and I both agree."

"I'll go too, and try to fend them off with my fireballs."

We took out our swords and descended the hill together. Luke led the way, I kept to his right, and Drew to his left. It was clear the moment the dragons detected us. One of them let out an ear-piercing screech and began flapping his wings, preparing for his attack. Another stretched his neck long and blew a stream of fire toward us, which spread and billowed into smoke before it reached us. Two more ran toward us, stopping only when they reached the end of their leads.

"We need to go quickly," I shouted over the noise of the dragons. "They'll attract the guards"—I looked over my shoulder—"and whatever else is in that forest that we've been lucky to avoid."

"Sarah," Drew began, "do you think you can make that wall of fire that you made to stall the beast?"

"Uh, yeah. Yeah, I think I can."

Maybe it was the heat from the fire being thrown at us, or maybe it was the clanging of the chains threatening to break and unleash the dragons, or the glass-shattering shrieking coming from every direction, but it wasn't as easy creating a flaming barrier to protect us than it was when I made the wall of fire for the beast. It should've been easier. We had a lot more to lose this time.

Streams of fire were being hurled at us from all seven dragons, and the heat, combined with the smell of scorched grass, made it difficult to concentrate on making even more fire.

When I threw my hands toward the dragons, I felt an eruption from my palms, but where I expected to see a wall of fire, something else was there instead.

"Water!" Drew exclaimed. "How did you do that?"

We didn't have time to sit around and discuss what this meant—waterbending was Nevaeh's craft. How was that possible? Wasn't my soul getting darker by the day?

Luke and Drew pressed on, using the wall of water as a shield from the dragons' wrath. We were near the first entrance now. The dragons were vicious, but when they got too close, Luke was able to fend them off with his sword, and Drew was aiming well with his arrows.

I sensed the danger before I saw it. There was something lurking in the shadows just beyond the archway of the first entrance. Something big, something hungry, and something ready for its prey.

"Not there!" I yelled to Luke who was pressing forward. Instinctively, I turned away from the entrance, realizing that we were wrong; the first entrance was a trap. But my change of plan left Luke exposed, and he was hit by a blast of fire. He flew back through the air, chased by another stream of fire.

I threw my hands toward him, sending a torrent of water in his direction to extinguish the flames before they turned him into charcoal.

Drew dove behind a boulder, avoiding another wave of fire. I threw my hand behind me, toward the dragon, and to my surprise, a ball of fire left my fingertips, striking the dragon in its side.

I ran to Luke's aid, fending off more breaths of fire, while we both hurried back up the hill to a safe distance from the dragons.

"There was something in there," I panted, explaining why I had abandoned our course, leaving Luke exposed. "Are you okay?" I helped him sit up as he regained his strength. "I'm so sorry."

He squeezed my hand and smiled. "Don't apologize. You were awesome." His clothes were scorched, and I tried to ignore the melted skin on his chest.

"So you think it's the last one then?" Drew asked, eyeing the third archway.

"I don't know if I can do that again," I admitted. "It was so hard to focus over all their screeching!"

"They weren't screeching," Drew said, confused.

"Are you kidding me? I couldn't hear anything else," I said.

"You're hearing them communicate with each other," Luke realized. "Sarah, do you think you can communicate with them and find out which entrance is the real one?"

I was on it before he finished, unsure why I hadn't thought of it sooner. I connected with the dragon in the middle. It was the one paying closest attention to us. The one with the longest chain, allowing her to reach the two side entrances. While the others were erratic, throwing their tails, spitting fire, and shrieking randomly, this one was pacing and pulling against its chain, and never took its eyes from us.

I slowly descended the hill, keeping my eyes locked

with hers. I knew it was a her. I felt it. She was angry at my presence. She was nervous at my descent.

What are you afraid of? I thought.

Her eyes burned with a deep red, one that refused to let me into her mind.

If not your mind, then I'll take another's.

Her chin lifted, and the sharp ears on her head twitched, telling me she didn't like my threat. She shrieked with an anger that was meant for me.

Fine, I thought, and I broke eye contact with her and peered onto the dragon on her left. I pointed at him, narrowing my eyes to his and capturing his mind, which was much softer than hers. *You will bow down*, I commanded, and he did. Immediately. *You will tell me which entrance leads into the castle.*

NO! the first dragon shrieked. She opened her jaws and scorched him with her fiery breath, adding yet another wound to his already pathetic appearance. He fell to the ground in a defeated heap while the other dragons looked to her for answers. *Don't tell her anything!* she shrieked to her companions.

You will harm one of your own to protect what? A castle? We don't want to hurt you! I told her. *We only want to pass through and get what is ours.*

For a brief second her eyes flickered to the entrance, not in which she was directly in front of, but the one to her left. The one she truly guarded.

That's the entrance, isn't it? I asked.

An image flickered in front of my mind. An image of a young dragon, hardly old enough to breathe fire. A crippling pain flooded my heart as this dragon finally let her guard down. She wasn't protecting an entrance. She was protecting her baby.

"There's a dragonling in there," I relayed to Drew and Luke. "The dragon in the middle—the one with the longest lead—is the mother."

"Do you think it's the entrance we need?"

"Yes. I think that's why her baby was put there. To guard the entrance, but also so that mama dragon would be more protective."

"And that's why the two dragons in front of that entrance have wounds. From her," Drew realized.

"That's so cruel," I said, my eyes stinging with this affliction.

"She's just protecting her young," Drew added.

"No, I mean it's cruel to keep them apart. It's cruel to keep the baby dragon prisoner just to protect the castle."

If you help us get into the castle, I will free you. And your baby, I thought to her.

The massive dragon considered this as she paced restlessly. I knew, with enough effort, I could *make* her do this, but it didn't seem right. She wanted it, but years of mistrust for humans fueled her hesitance.

"What are you doing?" Luke questioned as I stood up tall and began walking toward the row of dragons, the other remaining four pulling hard against their tethers.

"I need to get close enough to break her chain," I told them.

"Are you crazy?" Drew shouted. "Why would you do that?"

"Because then she'll trust me to free her baby, and we'll be able to get into the castle."

Just you, the dragon screamed into my head.

"She doesn't trust you yet," I said. "You two stay here."

"That's not happening," Luke said, at the same time Drew said, "Nope."

One of the dragons let out a ferocious shriek and blew a stream of fire at us, which we rolled onto the ground to avoid. In response, our mother dragon scorched him with a breath of her own.

"What is she doing?" Drew pressed.

"She's going to help us," I realized as I kept my eyes on hers. I had a connection with her and could feel her every emotion. She desperately wanted to be freed. She desperately wanted to see her baby.

"Drew, you take the two on the left. Luke, you take the two on the right. I'll free mama dragon."

"Sarah," Luke tried, but I couldn't lose this opportunity. She trusted me. She believed in me and our best chance for survival and for finding Maddy was to make this happen.

Drew was already gone, releasing arrows as he ran down the hill. I conjured two strong, bright balls of fire and threw one at each of the two dragons. Stunning them would allow Drew and Luke to get in there and finish them off.

I slowly approached Mama. Her tail swished slowly behind her. Her breath was heavy through her nostrils, but her mouth remained closed, a good sign that she wasn't planning on frying me. But I was still nervous. Scared that this could be a trap.

Bend down, I directed. *I will break your chain.*

I slowly pulled my sword from my belt as she lowered her head. The chain was heavy and thick, and I doubted my sword could even make a dent in it. Her head was next to mine now, and the collar around her neck was solid and even thicker than my body. Blood stained her leathery skin where the collar dug deep.

Searching for a way to break the chain, I slowly ran my hand along it, under her chin, and around the other side.

"Use the heat from your hands!" Drew shouted, out of breath, and I pictured him struggling with the dragons. But I didn't want to break the connection with Mama so I couldn't react. Couldn't look. Couldn't respond. I could, however, take his suggestion.

I laid my hands on the collar and let the heat flow through my body, out of my hands, and onto the thick metal. My hands burned, but the skin never sizzled. The metal, however, glowed a yellow, then orange, then bright red before shattering into a million little pieces.

The moment the chain fell and she knew she was freed, Mama reared onto her hind legs and shrieked ferociously. I jumped onto her wing and clambered up her side onto her back.

"Easy, girl," I said into her ear as she ran toward the two dragons Luke was fighting—the dragons guarding her baby. She grabbed one of them with her teeth and ripped its head clean off. The other fell from Luke's blade ripping into his chest.

Mama stuck her head into the entrance, but that was all that would fit; her body was too large.

My baby! she cried.

There was a small whimper in response, but nothing more.

"We'll go get him," I told her. "Trust us."

She backed away from the entrance, slowly deciding whether to believe us. I had kept my promise this far, and she had no other options.

Luke and Drew joined me a minute later, keeping their distance from the dragon, and their swords at the ready.

The dungeon was dark and dank, but I could make out a silhouette of something large in the far corner. Its breathing was heavy and erratic, and I couldn't get a strong mental reading. As we got closer, it was clear that the little dragon was nearly dead.

"Oh no," I sighed.

"There's the door into the castle," Drew said, pointing past the dragon. "Let's go."

"No!" I shouted, appalled that he even suggested it. "I made a promise. We need to free this dragon."

"It's too late, Sarah," Drew began. "It's dead."

"No!" I said. "I can hear him breathing. He's not dead . . . yet."

"Come on." Luke hit Drew in the arm and then approached the small dragon. "The sooner we get this guy out there, the sooner we can find Maddy."

With Drew and Luke standing close by, I broke the

chains tethering the young dragon to the wall. He didn't move. He made no attempt to get up.

"Carry him," Luke said. "On three."

Working together, the three of us half-carried, half-dragged the creature out of the dungeon.

Mama was waiting outside, pacing back and forth. When she saw her baby, she shrieked. *What's wrong with him?!*

I think he's sick, I told her as we laid him down on the ground.

She wasn't listening. She swiped her strong tail, catching Luke and Drew, and flung them into the forest, then she came at me and pinned me down to the ground, her nostrils spitting smoke and sparks at me as I tried to breathe.

You killed my baby, she cried. *You lied to me!*

"No!" I shouted back. "He was already like this—"

Liar! she shrieked.

My fingers hunted the ground, searching for the baby dragon. *Come on, little guy,* I said, directing my thoughts to him. *You're free now. You're safe. Feel the sun. Feel your mother's love.*

I didn't think it would work, but at this point, we had no other options. Drew and Luke were attacking the mother dragon, trying to draw her wrath to them, but they were no match for her grief. Her tail was powerful, and she was only interested in me. But she didn't want to kill me. I saw it in her eyes. She did, however, want to inflict pain on someone. She needed someone to blame for her baby's condition.

My fingers finally connected with the dragonling's tail, and I stroked my trembling fingers along its dry, scaly skin as Mama's foot crushed a little deeper into my chest.

Give your baby love, I cried to the mama dragon.

Yes, lack of food and water and mistreatment from the guards and other dragons was likely the root cause of this young dragon's condition, but a lack of sunshine and love was also to blame. And I felt it. He craved his mother's touch. He craved any loving touch, which was why, no matter how much it hurt, I continued stroking his long tail.

Finally, the dragon let out a small cry, and his legs trembled as he tried to stand. He inhaled slowly and deeply then blew a spark of fire at his mother, telling her to let me go. She backed away immediately, giving Luke and Drew a chance to come to my aid.

"Sarah, are you okay?" Drew said desperately as he collapsed next to me and began assessing my body.

"It hurts a little," I downplayed. "But look"—I gestured to where Mama was now nuzzling her baby—"he's going to be okay."

"Fabulous," Luke shouted. Then he turned to the mother dragon and raged, "LOOK WHAT YOU'VE DONE?! SHE WAS TRYING TO HELP YOU!"

"Luke," I said, my chest burning with the words, cautioning me to the fact that my ribs were likely broken. "I would've done the same, and so would you."

Drew was helping me sit up, and I tried to keep the agony of my broken ribs from reaching my face. But then something amazing happened that made me forget about the pain crippling my body—Mama bowed to me. She rested her eyes on the ground at my feet, then lowered her head. She exposed her neck completely, a gesture I took as a display of her new-found trust in us.

I smiled, tears escaping as I did. It was a beautiful moment, and I felt the enormity of this gesture.

"Great," Drew grumbled. "So we have the respect of a dragon. Still doesn't change the fact that we're even further behind now."

I took a deep breath and, clutching my side, slowly got up with Luke's help. I leaned on him heavily as my leg was hardly any good to me. Was it broken too? I cupped my hands and formed a small bowl of water, then I brought it to the dragonling, and he lapped the bottomless bowl of water for nearly a minute, his thick, rough tongue scraping desperately against my palms.

"Get out of here," I said to the mother. "Go as far away as you can. Take your baby and go!"

The small dragon knocked his head into me, which hurt like hell, but I managed to keep from flinching because he hadn't meant to hurt me; he only meant to thank me.

The two turned, flapped their wings until they were high above the castle, then they fled, not daring to look back for even a second. They were finally free.

IT TOOK AN hour, but Luke insisted that we not move forward until I could walk without wincing and breathe without clutching my ribs. Drew was agitated as he was sure Maddy would be dead by the time we found her. This made it harder for me to focus on working through the pain and accepting it for what it was, as all I wanted to think about was Maddy and how to rescue her. Eventually though, I learned how to mask the discomfort and we continued on.

"I think we should find the clue first," Luke said, and there was hesitance behind it. He watched Drew carefully.

"That's ridiculous," Drew countered. "Why on earth would we do that?"

"Maddy is sure to be with Ella by now. She's waiting for us. We won't have much hope of finding the clue after Ella knows we're here."

I nodded. This made sense. If we already had the clue when we found Maddy, then we could just grab her and escape.

"You're not seriously considering this, are you, Sarah?" Drew said, a look of grievance on his face.

"Sarah, you decide," Luke said.

This brought a painful reminder of when Drew and Maddy had trusted me to make the call about whether or not we would camp inside the Forest of Fear, or outside. I chose the inside. I thought it would be safer. I let my thirst for the adventures of darkness supersede my common sense and respect for my friends.

"We find Maddy first," I decided.

"What?" they said in unison, both surprised by my decision.

"I let her down once. I won't do it again." I pulled

both daggers from my boots and led the way into the dark dungeon, Luke and Drew hurrying to catch up. My leg throbbed with every step, but I did not let it take me. I did not let the sharpness in my lungs hold me back. It was time to find Maddy.

CHAPTER 19

The Exchange

~ SARAH ~

FOLLOWING THE MAP, we made our way through the dungeons without incident. There was only one giant blocking our way to the staircase, but Drew was able to take him down with an arrow between the eyes. I had wanted to try to bend his mind to let us pass, saving us from taking yet another life, but Luke argued that it was a waste of my energy and before I could object, Drew agreed with Luke and took out the giant. Only mildly phased by this, I pressed on, Luke soon taking the lead again, and Drew bringing up the rear.

We decided that Ella wouldn't be holding Maddy in the dungeons. She would be too much at a disadvantage down there—too many dark places and blind corners.

Plus, we had already succeeded in rescuing Eli from the dungeons. She wouldn't take the same risk with Maddy.

"We don't need to find her," Luke said after I became frustrated with the realization that Ella could keep her well-hidden for as long as she wanted. "We only have to wait for Ella to find us."

A few minutes later we were entering a breezeway that would lead us to the large open courtyard in the middle of Ella's castle. The courtyard was deserted, no sign of life or activity of any kind.

"She knows we're here," Luke said. "So we wait."

"Hold up," Drew said, grabbing his arm. "We don't have a plan yet. What's our plan?"

"Sarah stays between us. I'll take care of the rest."

Just as he had predicted, Ella appeared almost immediately. She announced her presence by clapping slow and loud.

"I must admit," she said, "I did not expect you to get *inside* the castle."

I opened my mouth to speak, but Luke squeezed my hand, reminding me that he knew her best.

She smiled, bothered by our silence. "How did you get in, can I ask? I should know where my weaknesses are." She circled, from a distance, and watched us curiously. When we didn't answer, she said, "What brings you here today?"

Finally, Luke spoke. "You know why we're here, Ella. Name your terms."

"Why, whatever do you mean, Luke?" Her eyebrows were propped in a mock display of curiosity.

"We need your help," I said, and Luke squeezed harder.

Ella let out a burst of laughter. "*My* help." She narrowed her eyes at me. "The *princess* wants *my* help."

"Yes," I said.

Luke glared at me. "Would you let me do the talking, please?" he growled.

"I thought you came for revenge, no?" Ella asked.

"I don't want revenge," I said, and this seemed to confuse her. "Ella, I've forgiven you."

"I didn't ask for forgiveness," she spat.

"I didn't do it for you. I did it for me. There's no sense in harbouring hate over the past."

"Let me guess," she said, "you can't heal hurt with hate." She glared at Luke. "Now where have I heard that before? . . . Oh, right. Your *boyfriend* tried to convince me of that once upon a time."

"Ella," Luke interrupted, "you know why we're here. Can we just get on with this, please?"

"Fine," she said, a look of disappointment on her face. "Bring me the girl!" she shouted over her shoulder.

Two men dressed all in black and holding tall, shiny battle axes came through the door pulling a bound and muzzled Maddy behind them.

"Maddy!" Drew shouted, and he almost broke away from us, but his hand stayed on mine and seemed to root him to the spot.

"Okay, so this is good," Ella said. "I see you want what I have, and I want what you have."

"You're not getting Sarah!" Drew shouted.

"Then you're not getting Maddy," Ella retorted. "And if you don't want her, and I don't need her, I see no reason to keep her alive." She raised her hand and one of her guards raised his axe.

"Wait!" Luke said, stepping forward. "You can have me. I'll take Maddy's place."

My stomach turned. Was this always his plan? Did he *want* to be alone with her? Did he *want* to have an excuse to be with her again?

Ella looked intrigued by this. "Oh, that's tempting, Luke, I won't lie. But as pleasurable as that promises to be, I have my eye on a bigger prize now."

The word "pleasurable" rotated in my mind, making me dizzy and sick.

"Ella, please," Luke said. "I'll give you anything."

"I thought you already had." She smirked, and I dropped Luke's hand.

"I promise if you let Maddy go, I'll come with you," I said, stepping away from Luke and Drew. Both tried to follow, but I held my hands up, signalling for them to stay where they were.

"Sarah, I can't let you do this," Drew said, and he took my hand, squeezing it firmly.

"Drew, you have to."

"No, I mean I physically can't. My job is to protect you. This defies all logic. This is not protecting you. This is crazy." His grip tightened.

"You'll let me go because you know it's our best chance of survival. Ella will be preoccupied with me, which will give you time to go get the clue." I hugged him.

I can do this, he thought. *This is how I will protect her. It's the only way. She will be safer.*

He wasn't expecting me to bend his mind, which is why it worked so well. I massaged these thoughts further into his mind until he believed entirely that my life depended on him letting me go.

"Take this," I said as I gave him the blue ribbon. "Go get the next clue and I'll meet you at the lake in the Forest of Fear."

"No," Luke said definitively as he snatched the ribbon from Drew and handed it back to me. "This is insane. I'm not letting you do this."

"That's not your choice," I said. "Get the clue, and I'll get out. I promise." My eyes stung with the realization that this might not be the truth, but it was either me or Maddy, and at least I had the advantage of bending Ella's mind.

I took a step closer to him, but was careful not to let our hands touch. "I will use my craft," I whispered.

"You can't let her know," Luke said as his eyes glistened. "You can't let her catch on to what you're doing."

"I won't," I assured him. Then, stuffing the ribbon into his hand, I turned away so that he wouldn't see my uncertainty.

"We have a deal," I announced to Ella. "Release her."

Ella motioned to her guards who pushed Maddy forward. Maddy scrambled to her feet, blindfolded, and Drew ran to meet her.

Drew steadied Maddy while he pulled off her blindfold, untied her hands, and then she ran to meet me as I prepared for the trade with Ella. There was no backing out now. We were surrounded.

"I'm so sorry, Sarah!" Maddy cried. "Please don't go with her. We can fight our way out of here."

"I made a promise," I said loud enough for Ella to hear. "And I will honour it." I lowered my voice for only Maddy. "It's the only way I can guarantee your safety. And I owe you. I'm sorry."

Ella raised her chin, curiosity painted on her pretty face. "You are mine now, princess. Come. Now."

I took out my sword and handed it to Maddy, then gave her my bow and satchel of arrows. I left a knife in my boot, although I hoped I wouldn't need it.

I turned to Ella. "Do you promise to let them walk out of here, giving your guard orders not to touch them until they are out of the castle?" We were walking toward each other—her flanked by guards with spears pointed at me.

"If they promise to leave and not try any heroics, then I do," Ella said. "Besides, I have what I want now." She grabbed a hold of my arm.

Luke yelled, "Ella!"

"Yes, lover?"

I cringed at the way the word rolled effortlessly off her tongue.

"I'll give you whatever you want if you let her live," he answered, and it made the lump in my throat grow.

"You had your chance to give me what I wanted," she said. "Our alliance is over."

Ella snapped her fingers and we disappeared, leaving my three best friends in the middle of a courtyard, completely surrounded by Ella's best guards.

What had I done? I hoped I hadn't just made a colossal mistake.

CHAPTER 20

The Shape of a True Friend

~ LUKE ~

SHE WAS GONE, and all I could do was stare at the place she once stood. She was alone and at the mercy of Ella. She would have a fighting chance if she was able to bend Ella's mind, but what if Ella was expecting it? What if Ella, like the rest of us, had spent years trying to figure out what Yelram's craft was? And what if she had figured it out? My palms sweat, and my heart pounded with these menacing thoughts.

Maddy and Drew both had their bows drawn, watching the wall of guards carefully.

"Ella gave orders to leave us alone," Drew reminded the guards.

There was a murmur of disgust, but then the guards

parted, creating a path for us to exit.

"I'll take it from here," one of the larger guards said to the others as he pushed Drew into the hall. "I'll make sure they don't ever come back." He chuckled darkly, in a way that I didn't like.

When we were alone with the guard in the hallway, he pulled a sword and pushed it into my back. "Keep walking," he ordered.

"We're leaving," I told him, but my hand hovered near the handle of my sword. We were still too close to the swarm of guards to make a move.

When we rounded the corner, and I thought it was safe to behead the guard, I wrapped my fingers tightly around the hilt of my sword. Just as I was about to pull it out, the guard stopped and sheathed his own sword.

We turned around and the guard was smiling.

"You're not going to give us any trouble?" Maddy asked. Her fingers were outstretched, and her hands were trembling. She was ready to send a tremor through the hallway. But then the guard shook his head, and his body began moving, morphing, and shrinking, and the next thing we knew, we were staring at a small, frail child with brown hair.

"The girl," Maddy gasped.

"I'm sorry if I scared you," she said. "I saw them bring you in, and I changed into a guard so I could be there when the rest of you arrived."

"Yeah, no, that was smart," I said, relieved that I hadn't accidentally killed her. "Thank you."

"Get the ribbon," Drew said.

I pulled the ribbon from my pocket and held it out. "Sarah asked us to give this to you. You have something for her in return."

She made no effort to take it from me.

"Tie it in her hair," Maddy suggested.

I crouched in front of the child and tied the ribbon around the end of one of her braids. As soon as I finished, her fingers went to the ribbon and felt it. Then she reached into her dress pocket and pulled out a small envelope.

"My instructions were to give this to Sarah only," she said, hesitating.

"I know." I nodded. "But as you know, she's kind of tied up at the moment. She told us to get the clue and then she'd meet us in the Forest of Fear."

"The Forest of Fear," the girl repeated, a little less comfortable with the arrangement.

"But as soon as you hand over the clue," I added, "we're going back to rescue her."

She studied me for a moment. "Who are you?"

I let Drew start the introductions, knowing that my name and title might not help our cause.

"I'm Drew, Earth's keeper, and this is Maddy, Sarah's best friend."

The girl nodded, then her eyes returned to mine.

"I'm Luke. . . . Etak's keeper."

Her eyebrows raised, and the clue slid back into her pocket.

"He loves Sarah," Drew added, "and she loves him."

A curious grin crept across her lips. "Leah never

would've imagined that this is how her plan would've played out."

"He's on our side," Drew said. "He's one of us."

"Please," Maddy said, "just give us the clue. We're wasting time here."

The girl reached into her pocket and pulled out a long, slender tube. It was not the clue. "I'll come with you and personally deliver the clue as per Leah's wishes."

"It's dangerous," I told her.

She laughed. "I'm used to danger. Besides, I know this castle like the back of my hand. I've been living here and studying the labyrinth of secret tunnels since before your time. I needed to be sure I could help Sarah when the time came." She raised the slender metal tube. "This is a dart gun. It puts people to sleep and erases their memory of the last ten seconds. I know the best way to get into Ella's personal chambers. I'm sure that's where Ella would've brought her."

"It is," Maddy added.

Drew glanced down at her. "Is that where she took you?"

Maddy nodded.

"What did she do to you?"

"Nothing," Maddy lied.

"Did she hurt you?" Drew demanded.

"Come on," I urged Drew. "Ella will get what's coming to her. But first, let's get Sarah out of there."

WE FOLLOWED THE tiny child back through the dark corridor. It felt strange allowing a child to lead the way, but I also knew that she wasn't a child. If Leah entrusted her with the clue, that had to have been at least fifteen years ago.

"How *old* are you?" Maddy asked.

"Age is just a number in the dream worlds," she answered.

"Okay," Maddy said, "then how do you know Leah?"

"We were friends on Earth. We grew up together. And when we were seventeen, I was possessed by a shadow."

"A shadow?" Maddy asked.

"Yes. It's sort of like a virus, or snake, that you can become infected with while you sleep. It corrupts your mind, causing you to say, do, and think things that you normally would never otherwise."

"Sarah had a shadow," Drew told Maddy.

"What? When?" Both Maddy and the girl asked.

"A few months ago."

"How did she get it out?" the girl wondered.

"She managed to convince it to come out and fight her. Then she killed it." I shook my head, still marvelling at how she did it. I had been sick about having to extract the shadow, for fear the extraction would kill her. She never ceased to amaze me.

"Wow." Maddy turned to the girl as we continued down the hall together. "Okay, go on."

"Well, I spiralled into a deep depression and I saw no way out. Suicide was the only thing I could think to do to end the constant battle inside my own head. So I did it." We slowed and rounded a corner. "Leah was devastated. She spent days crying, and she slept a lot, and one night she dreamed into Nitsua and we found each other. I told her all about the dream worlds and assured her that I was okay. I had tried to reach friends and family after crossing over to Nitsua, but human minds aren't geared for this sort of stuff. Leah was different, though. She was . . . a real dreamer. That's how she got introduced to the dream worlds. She kept visiting, and then one day she told me she met a guy, a prince from one of the good dream worlds." The girl smiled. "They fell in love and, well, the rest is history."

"Wow," Maddy said. "So you and Sarah's mom were best friends."

"Yes," she confirmed. "My name's Rayna."

"Why are you only little then?"

"It's one of my shapes," she explained. "I'm less conspicuous in this form."

Suddenly, Rayna stopped. She put her hand up to silence us as she craned her neck and listened to the air.

I slowly pulled out three throwing knives from my boot and balanced one in my right hand. Drew quietly retrieved an arrow from his satchel and readied it in his bow. Maddy had Sarah's sword at the ready.

Rayna motioned for us to follow her quietly, and then she pushed on a stone in the wall and a secret door slid open. We followed her inside and the wall returned into position.

"Cool," Maddy said.

The room was dark but it felt small. I ran my hand along the edges of the stone, hating that my eyes were wide but unseeing.

"There are lots of these safe rooms in the castle. You won't find them on any maps, though. I'm sure even Ella doesn't know about most of them," Rayna whispered.

"You know this place well," Drew said.

"I've been here a long time," she reminded him.

"Are you stuck here?" Maddy asked. "Or can you leave the castle? Seems like an awful place to live out your life."

"I could leave the castle," she explained, "but I made a promise to Leah and I will fulfill that promise first."

"Why here, though? Why keep the clue in the castle?"

"Believe it or not, it's the safest place for it."

"How so?"

"They think this place is so well protected, so impenetrable, that they never look for traitors on the inside. They use up all their resources looking for me in the rest of the world, but they don't know I've been living right here under their noses all this time."

"Why are they looking for you?" I asked.

"I used to be one of the queen's most trusted guards," Rayna began. "I applied for the position after Leah fell in love with the prince of Yelram. I knew one day Leah would need an ally on the inside, and I wanted to be that person. But then the queen created this horrible beast to kill King Jefferson and Leah . . . and their heirs. After it killed King Jefferson, Leah was desperate to save Yelram and Sarah. She had me arrange a meeting between her and the queen. Leah thought she could convince the queen to stop the beast, and in exchange, Leah would let the queen kill her right there on the spot." Rayna's brow creased as she recalled the story. "But the queen was not a stupid woman. She figured out why Leah was so desperate to stop the beast—if it wasn't to spare her own life, then there must be another living heir. She guessed that Leah and King Jefferson had a child, and Leah was never a good liar, so the secret of Sarah's existence was out." Rayna looked up, as if breaking from her revelry and returning to reality. "And that's why the queen had to die. She knew about Sarah, and there was no choice but to kill her. And after that, Leah began making plans to hide the key and protect Sarah until the day came where she was old enough to begin the quest."

"Wow," Drew said, but that's all he said. Maddy was silent too.

I hated hearing the truth about the queen of Nitsua's murder. It was done to protect Sarah. The rumours had always been there—King Jefferson's wife was responsible for the queen of Nitsua's death, but I never wanted to believe it. Mostly because I knew Sarah never wanted to believe it.

"Come on," Rayna said. "I think they're gone." She slowly pulled the door open, and we cautiously slipped back into hallway. We weren't fifteen feet down the corridor, though, when someone shouted.

"Hey, you! Stop there!"

Drew and I spun around. Drew was aiming a cocked arrow, and I had a throwing knife ready above the shoulder. Four guards wielding long spears were coming toward us.

Rayna pushed past us. "I have this," she said. Her

small body morphed into a young woman, her thick, dark blonde hair spilling over her shoulders.

The guards hesitated. Then one shouted, "It's Rayna! Get her!"

"I'll lead them away," Rayna said. "I've bought you some time. Go to the Forest of Fear and when I get free, I'll rescue Sarah."

"We can help you fight!" Luke protested.

"No," she shouted. She pushed the white envelope into his hand. "Take the clue and get the hell out of here. If they catch you, they'll destroy that clue and it's the only hope you have of re-opening Yelram."

Rayna ran full speed toward the guards, changing again into the small child just as one of them swung his sword at her head. She tucked her small, slender body between two guards and sliced both of their Achilles tendons with her knives, then she caught one of their swords as they fell and changed back into her true form, sword fighting the next two guards.

"Come on!" Maddy urged, pulling my arm. "We have to get out of here."

There were more guards coming now from the other direction. Maddy was pulling me down a small corridor.

"Duck, Luke!" Maddy shouted. I dove to the ground and she shot an arrow toward two guards that had just rounded the corner.

I scrambled to my feet and chased after Drew and Maddy who were meandering through the dark passageways ahead. Every stairway was blocked by guards or giants. Our only way out was the way we came in—into the Forest of Fear. They probably thought they were forcing us into a death trap with seven ferocious dragons waiting for dinner on the other side, but we knew otherwise.

"Maddy, shake the ground!" I shouted. The rumble shook them so violently that the guards trampled each other while we escaped, and they were none the wiser about us evading the dragons.

We didn't stop until we were deep into the Forest.

"We need to keep going," I pressed when Maddy tried to stop near a tree.

"Give me a second," she panted.

"Sarah could be waiting for us!" I barked.

"Luke," Drew started, "I want to know Sarah's okay just as bad as you do, but Maddy needs a rest."

I shook my head at him, picked up Maddy, and hoisted her over my shoulder. "We don't stop until we find Sarah."

Finally, the lake where Sarah told us to meet her was just up ahead.

"Sarah!" I shouted. "Sarah, are you here?"

My heart was racing as I searched through trees for her, running in circles around the clearing at the lake, calling her name. But Sarah wasn't there.

"Damnit!" I threw my fist into a tree. "We should've gone back. We should've fought the guards."

"We didn't stand a chance," Drew said.

"I should never have let her go." Why hadn't I fought harder for her? I could've convinced Ella to take me over Sarah. All I had to do was tell her I loved her, but that would've broken Sarah's heart. But this—this stupid idea could kill Sarah.

But it wouldn't. If Ella really wanted Sarah dead, she had plenty of chances. And suddenly it hit me. Ella had other plans for Sarah. She wasn't stupid. She had banked on Sarah surviving the beast's attack. She hadn't wanted the beast to kill her. She only wanted the beast to poison her!

My thoughts were interrupted by Maddy screaming and Drew saying, "What the hell?"

I followed her terrified gaze to the darkest part of the forest where something big and large was lurking.

CHAPTER 21

The Art of Temptation

~ SARAH ~

"**WHAT DO YOU** want from me, Ella?" My voice strained from the silence of the last ten minutes.

She continued pacing, her eyes focused but darting around the room as she walked. She was contemplating. Strategizing. Considering. I left her to her thoughts as she wondered why Luke let me take Maddy's place. She wondered why he didn't fight harder. She wondered if my craft was so incredible that he knew I'd be no match for her. She had also seen the way Drew ran to Maddy, and a part of her softened with a jealous loneliness. But mostly, she wondered why we were there. She assumed we were there to kill her—but why hadn't we even tried? And if my craft was so amazing, why wasn't I fighting her now? This both confused and unnerved her.

"Why did you come here?" she finally asked, turning to give my answer her full attention. She pressed her hand into the back of the chair that I was tethered to. "Revenge?"

"What? No!" I said too quickly.

"Then why?" she pressed. "What do I have that you want?"

How was I to answer her? In all the time I had to sit there and think about a reason for why we were there, I could only think about whether Luke, Drew, and Maddy had escaped the guards and found the clue. My silence angered her, but what reason could I give? I couldn't tell her that I was there to get a clue to help me find my key and take back my world—the one thing she would kill me to prevent from happening.

She lowered herself over me and stared into one eye, then the other. "You're not so good anymore, are you, princess?"

And how was I supposed to answer *that*? I supposed it wasn't a secret that the beast nearly killed me. Surely she could easily guess that I had been poisoned.

"What happened to you?"

"I was poisoned by the beast."

She studied me carefully, her eyes slowly narrowing as the corner of her mouth turned up. "So you're converting to the dark side. How's it feel to be tainted?"

"I'm dying, Ella. It doesn't feel great."

"Good."

"I don't think you mean that."

"Oh, you don't?"

"You had a chance to kill me but you didn't."

"You stole Luke from me."

"I *saved* you from him. He never loved you. I did you a favour."

"Is that what you tell yourself so you can sleep at night?" Her jaw hardened, but then she continued pacing. "Maddy tells me you haven't found your key yet."

Maddy! What had she told her? Ella would've tortured her for information, but would she have given up anything?

"No," I answered, and I looked away.

"Have you been looking?" she asked, interested.

"I'm more concerned about finding a cure right now, to be honest."

"It's Luke, isn't it?"

"Huh?"

"Luke doesn't want you to find the key. He probably wants to keep you all to himself, am I right?"

I shook my head. "I don't know," I said, hoping this was the best way to answer.

"Why are you here?"

"I need a cure or I'll die."

"You'll die," she chuckled under her breath. "And you think the cure is here?"

"I think there's something here that I need, yes."

"What is it?"

"I don't know."

"You're lying." She was getting impatient.

"Ella, I'm running out of options here. I'm dying and the only way to save myself is to find the cure."

"Stop being so dramatic," she scoffed. "You're not *dying*. You're just . . . *converting*."

"What do you mean?"

"It's just taking over your body. It *might* kill you, but I doubt it. You're too . . . stubborn for death." She turned away.

Wait—what? Why hadn't anyone told me this before? Why did they lead me to believe that if I didn't find a cure, then I would slowly die? Was it possible that I wouldn't actually *die* if I couldn't find the cure, but that I would just transition to a dark lord?

"Which is why I'm not sure I want to kill you yet," Ella continued. "If I let you live and you do survive the turning, Yelram will be a dark world and the balance will be set in favour of the dark worlds. But on the other hand, if I let you live and you find a cure, you'll be my nemesis again. You see my dilemma?"

I kept my focus on the gardens below, not giving a reaction. Mostly because I still needed to process what this meant.

"It's pretty, isn't it?" Ella said as she followed my gaze out the tall window.

"It is," I admitted.

"Being a dark world isn't all bad." She waved her hand and the ropes restraining me fell to the ground. "Come see for yourself."

I slowly got up from my chair, watching her movements carefully, but she was only interested in the gardens outside the window. The beautiful gardens. Full of colour and shape and mystery. She could've been right. Maybe the dark worlds weren't all bad. What did I know about them, anyway? Luke was a leader of one, and he wasn't a terrible person. Yes, his world was corrupt, but it probably wasn't much different than Earth. And he seemed happy. For the most part.

"Do you know what the best part of being a dark lord is?" When I didn't answer, she continued, "It's being able to use the gift of temptation."

"*Gift?*"

"Well, the light lords might call it cruel, but that's why they don't get graced with it." She turned me to face her and waited until my eyes found hers. "Watch how it's done." Her eyes were a chocolate brown and seemed to somehow melt right into mine, as her soft pink lips bulged with anticipation.

"What are you doing?" I asked nervously, uncomfortable with the sensation that tickled my skin.

Her moist tongue slowly ran across her bottom lip, then her perfect white teeth came down onto her lip, and she held it there, begging me to bite it too.

"Do you like it?" The words rolled off her tongue fluidly, seductively.

"No," I said, forcing myself to look away.

"You're strong," she said, as if she admired this. "No one has ever been able to resist my temptation." There was a flicker of hesitation, and I saw that she held back the rest of her thought—Luke was able to resist her, but not once she changed into me.

I pinched my eyes closed as my jaw instinctively clenched. I didn't want to think of her changing into me and Luke not being able to resist her. He should've been stronger. He should've known better.

When I opened my eyes, Drew was standing in front of me, instantly changing my already piqued interest into needy arousal.

"I want you," he said, moving his body into mine. He touched a strand of hair near my face and brushed it away softly.

Breath filled my lungs as I worked hard at steadying my heartbeat. This was Ella. It was not Drew. Although Drew did have the same comforting smell, and the voice was exactly like his.

With his fingers now on me, my skin tickled exactly like it always did when he touched me. And just like every other time, it left me wanting more. I wanted to feel his hand in mine, his arms around me, his lips with mine, our bodies connected . . .

"No," I said, my voice weaker than I had intended. But my legs couldn't move. I was drawn to him. Crippled by the curse of this temptation.

His eyes were darker than normal, but I wasn't focused on them. It was his mouth that I watched as it slowly lowered to mine. And as our lips connected, the warmth and softness from his sent electricity coursing through my entire body. My hands were in his hair before I registered what I was doing, and there was no going back now. I couldn't stop. The temptation, the lure, was far too strong.

But soon it wasn't his short, blonde hair in my fingers that I felt. It was Ella's long, silky hair. I pushed her away, immediately repulsed by what I had done.

"How *dare* you!" I shouted, pushing her away again, but this time she caught my arm, twisted me around, and had a knife at my throat before I could react.

"I could kill you." Her breath was heavy in my ear.

"I know," I panted. "But you won't."

"Why won't I?"

"Because you know if I don't find a cure and I survive as a dark lord, you'll have an ally and we could take over Leviathan together. That's what you really want, isn't it, Ella? All the power for yourself."

"You wouldn't align with me," she said, but I heard the question and curiosity that lingered.

"We could be friends, Ella."

She shook her head vigorously. "You and I could *never* be friends."

"Why not?"

"Why would I? So I can invite you into my home and you can stab me in the back like your mother did to mine?"

"Ella, that wasn't me. I would never do that."

She shook her head. "Doesn't matter. I won't help you find a cure, Sarah," she finally said. "I'd like to see you join the ranks of the dark world leaders."

I wasn't going to argue with her. Mainly because the more she talked, the more time I gave Luke, Drew, and Maddy to find the little girl, get our next clue, and get the hell out of there. But also because I wasn't entirely against the idea. If I wasn't able to find the cure, maybe being a dark lord like Luke wasn't such a bad alternative. The thought circulated in my mind, arousing the darkness that was loitering at the edges, begging to come out and play.

"You're strong, Sarah," Ella continued. "You resisted the temptation better than even Luke ever could. *And* you stopped it."

"What do you mean?"

"It was you who changed me back."

My heart beat wildly. If I was in control of it, and I was able to change her back better than Luke could, how far had he gone with her? My stomach clenched, and I swallowed back the unpleasant taste in my mouth.

"How was the kiss?" she asked, her voice careful and calm.

"Drew's a far better kisser than you." I glared at her, causing a look of interest to cover her face.

"Drew?"

My narrowed eyes flickered away from hers, and her eyebrows shot up.

"Seriously?" she laughed. "You just . . .? I was . . .? That was Drew?"

"What game are you playing, Ella? You know you changed into Drew."

She shook her head. "I only change into whoever you desire most."

My heart stopped, along with my breathing. "What?"

Her smile spread. "When with Luke, I always changed into you because that's who he wanted most. It was his desires that changed me, not mine. And you . . . you desire Drew."

"I do not!" I protested.

"Well, this is an interesting plot twist, princess. Does Luke know about this? Better yet, does your little friend Maddy know how bad you want Drew? I saw the way Drew ran to her when our guards released her. Sounds like a little love triangle to me."

Before I could answer, an arrow flew through the window and pierced Ella in the shoulder. She stumbled forward and I hesitated before deciding whether this was my chance to escape. I was halfway bent over to help Ella when I recognized the arrow. It was Drew's! I ran to the window and found Drew riding on the back of mama dragon, hovering below Ella's window!

"JUMP!" he shouted. I didn't think twice about it, and as Ella turned and threw an open hand toward me, I propelled myself through the window, her curses flying out after me.

Drew caught me and pulled me in front of him so I could hold onto the dragon's scaly mane. He covered my body with his as the dragon soared through the gardens then up into the sky, far away from Ella's castle.

Once we were out of danger, I asked, "Where's Luke? Maddy?"

"They're on Duke."

"Duke?"

"Yeah, we named them. Mama wasn't working for Maddy. So this one is now Duchess, and the dragonling is Duke. They're on their way out of the Forest of Fear so they can port out and meet us in Etak."

"Why didn't Luke come?" I asked, feeling extremely guilty over my kiss with Ella . . . or Drew.

"I'm a better shot with an arrow," he said. "He didn't like it, but Maddy had the deciding vote and she knew I'd be better for the job. Plus, Ella has a hate-on for Luke right now and seeing him come to your rescue would likely empower her."

I nodded and tried not to think about his arms around me, his breath on my neck, and his body pressed into my back. He was right, though—Ella probably enjoyed the fact that Drew was the one to rescue me.

We soared over a row of trees and through a canal. Once we cleared the other side, Drew said, "Take us to Etak," and Nitsua's landscape disappeared.

CHAPTER 22

Darkness & Desires

~ SARAH ~

"YOU GOT THE clue?" I asked the moment we landed.

Duchess crouched low and we slid off her wing.

"Luke has it," Drew answered.

"Did you have any trouble?"

"Not at all."

A minute later, we heard the familiar cry of the baby dragon. Duchess cried back to him, and he appeared a few seconds later through the thick clouds above, landing next to us with Luke and Maddy as his passengers.

Luke jumped off Duke before he had touched the ground, and I was in his arms seconds later.

"Are you okay? Did she hurt you? What did she do to you?" He pulled me away to look at my face, then pulled me back into him. "I was so worried about you."

"I'm fine. She didn't hurt me. Turns out she doesn't want me dead after all."

"Why not?" Maddy asked.

"She wants . . . she wants me to switch teams."

"What do you mean?" Maddy laughed. "Like, she has a *thing* for you?"

"No," I said with an awkward laugh, but I felt my face flush and I looked down to hide my chagrin. But Luke noticed. And I knew he would.

"What did she do to you?" he demanded.

I looked up at him only for a second, then turned toward the dragons who were reuniting.

"How did you get the dragons to help you?" I asked, searching for a change of subject.

"Oh," Maddy piped up. "These beautiful beasts were hiding in the Forest of Fear. Nearly scared the pants off me, but they were friendly. It was Luke's idea to see if we could get them to help rescue you."

"Good thinking," I said, but didn't turn my eyes from the dragons.

Drew was next to me now, and he touched my arm gently. I jumped away from him. "Geez, Drew, you scared me."

He looked confused. "Are you okay? Sarah, what happened to you in there?"

"I'm fine. Nothing!"

"Are you sure?" he pressed.

"Well, actually, yes, something *did* happen. When were you guys going to tell me that I'm not actually going to *die* if we don't find a cure?"

"What?" Maddy said, as surprised as I was when I had first heard the news.

Drew and Luke exchanged a look, then Luke said, "You *may* survive the transition, Sarah, but—"

"What transition?" Maddy said.

"The poison is turning her to the dark side," Luke explained. "It isn't exactly killing her, although it's true that there's a chance she won't survive it."

"Don't you think I deserved to know this?" I said.

"I didn't want—" Luke began.

"We didn't want you thinking it was an option," Drew finished for him.

"What do you mean?"

Luke turned away from me while Drew answered, "I know how much you love Luke, Sarah. If you thought becoming a dark lord and being able to rule alongside of him was an option, then maybe you wouldn't have wanted a cure."

He reached for me, but I stepped back. "Are you kidding me right now?" Drew shook his head, but Luke still wasn't looking at me. "Luke?"

He inhaled deeply. "I'm sorry."

I couldn't believe what I was hearing. "Yeah," I said, "I'm sorry, too. I'm sorry that a lifetime of happiness with me as a dark lord could be so appalling to you."

"It's not that, Sarah," he began. "I would love you regardless. I just know you'll be happier without the darkness."

"And if that means we can't be together, then so be it,

right?"

"Sarah, please," Luke begged. "I just want you to be happy."

"Save it," I said, cutting him off. "I spent enough time with Ella today to know that you've got a good back-up option. You won't miss me for long when I take back my world."

"I won't miss you at all because I'm not going anywhere."

I closed my mouth before anything else could be said in anger. "Where's the clue?"

"I have it," Luke said. "But we need to get to my castle. You're not safe out here."

"I want my clue." I held my hand out. "*Please.*"

He clenched his jaw, reached into his pocket, and pulled out an envelope. "You can read it when we get back to my place." He picked me up before I could protest, then nodded to Drew and Maddy who quickly held on too. Then he muttered something and our surroundings disappeared, being replaced seconds later with the grey stone walls of a large bedroom that was Luke's home.

Luke set me down and immediately walked to a counter near the door and poured a drink for both him and Drew. I ignored that he was frustrated with me.

Maddy led me to the fireplace where we sat down on the comfortable sofa next to it. "Go ahead," she urged as I stared at the envelope in my hands. It was our fifth clue. Our next clue would be here in Etak, and our last clue was in Leviathan. We were almost done, and this, for some reason, scared the hell out of me.

Drew and Luke joined us, and all eyes were on me, so I sucked in a deep breath, and opened the envelope.

My Darling Princess,

You have now met my sweetest and best friend, Rayna. Although she is really my age, she prefers her 8-year-old identity best. She always said her happiest memories were when she was eight years old. She is a good ally to have and will help you whenever you are in Nitsua.

1

I quickly, and irritably, continued to the second page.

Remember in this next world that kindness has the power to overturn evil. You will win more wars with love, kindness, and forgiveness, than you will with hate, jealousy, and vengeance. I know these light world attributes come easily to you, so I don't worry that you will ever possess the negative qualities of a dark world, but I should warn you nonetheless that even dark souls crave love.

2

These words stung as I read them over and over in my head. She had so much faith in me. She didn't know me—I did possess the negative qualities of a dark world. But she was right about one thing—dark souls did crave love. I sensed it with Ella. I knew it with Luke. And even I craved the love and acceptance more and more as I slowly transitioned.

I wiped away a tear that slipped down my cheek, and then I flipped to the last page.

Now get inside that memory of yours, and remember when we would play in the grass. Remember the song we would sing?

If you go down in the woods today
You better go in disguise.
For every <u>bear</u> that ever there was
Will gather there for certain because
Today's the day Big Ben will have his picnic.

"A bear?" Maddy said, puzzled. "Is there someplace bears congregate in Etak?" Her question was for Luke.

While Luke thought, I shook my head. "I don't remember the song that way."

If you go down in the woods today, you better go in disguise. For every . . . bear? . . . No, that's not how she sang it. "For every *giant* that ever there was."

"What?" Luke said, a sudden look of angst on his face.

"It wasn't a teddy bear's picnic. It was a giant's picnic."

"The giants' forest," Luke concluded.

"That would make sense," Drew concurred.

"Only problem is that it would've been impossible for her to hide a clue in there," Luke said. "The giants are extremely territorial over their forest. They would never have let an outsider in."

"Well, is there another possibility?" Drew asked.

"That's the only forest with giants," Luke said.

"Then we go there," I decided. "She talked about dark souls craving love. Maybe that's what these giants need."

"Sarah, it's not safe," Luke argued. "These giants aren't afraid of anything, and they certainly don't want to be *loved*."

"If my mother did it, then so can I."

I could feel Luke watching me, trying to decide what he should do with me. Trying to figure out what Ella had said or done to bring this coldness between us. Did he know she changed for me? And if so, was my awkwardness toward Drew giving away who she changed into?

"We'll go in the morning," Luke said. "We *all* need some rest."

Drew nodded his agreement.

"And I could use some real food," Maddy added.

LUKE HAD CARTS of hot food and fresh fruit delivered to his room for us, and we laid out a blanket near the fire and had a picnic of sorts.

"So are you going to tell us now what happened to you back there?" Drew asked before stuffing a forkful of steak and potato into his mouth.

"We just talked," I said.

"She didn't try to hurt you?" Maddy asked, seemingly unconvinced by this.

"No," I admitted.

Drew turned to Maddy. "Why? Did she hurt you?"

Her eyes flickered to his before she looked down and chose her next grape carefully. "It wasn't pleasurable," she said.

My face flushed at the word 'pleasurable.' She hadn't meant anything by it, and by the way she had been shielding the left side of her face with her hair, I knew her encounter with Ella was much different than mine. Ella hadn't tried to seduce her. She only wanted to inflict pain, to show Maddy her power and what she was up against.

Drew was glaring at his plate of food as he chewed his steak with vigour.

"I'm fine, though," Maddy added. "It wasn't anything I couldn't handle." She looked over at me and forced a smile. "What'd she do to you?"

I swallowed before answering. "Her plan wasn't to hurt me," I said quietly. "Now that she knows I've been poisoned, she wants to . . . be friends."

"How does she plan to convince you of that?" Maddy scoffed.

"She tried to tempt me by showing me what dark lords are capable of," I said, mesmerized by the fire.

"And I suppose she showed you how to use the art of temptation?" Luke said, his voice low with a trace of anger.

"She did," I answered, keeping my eyes on the fire, as much as they wanted to see Drew.

Luke took a slow, deep breath. "I'm sorry. That couldn't have been easy."

"I broke it," I said.

"What?"

"I resisted her. I mean, I was pulled in for a minute, but then I stopped it."

"Wow," he said. "That takes strength."

"I know. Apparently *you* weren't even able to resist her."

"I wasn't able to resist *you*, Sarah."

"Oh really? You don't seem to have a problem resisting me now."

He recoiled as if I had slapped him. "Because my head isn't clouded with need and greed. She floods your body with these feelings that you can't get away from. Then she changes and it's . . . impossible."

"*Almost* impossible," I reminded him.

"What do you want me to say, Sarah? That I'm not as strong as you? Because obviously I'm not. Obviously you're able to resist me far better than I could ever resist you."

The argument was on my tongue, but I swallowed it. I couldn't tell him why I had been able to resist him better than he could me—because it wasn't him that I had resisted. It was Drew.

I took a bite of my dinner and resolved to let the discussion die. But for Luke it wasn't that easy. He threw his fork down and mumbled, "I'm going for a walk."

It was quiet after he left, my heart constricting with every breath I took. Where was he going? Was I slowly killing him? What was wrong with me?

"You should go," Drew said softly, and Maddy nodded her agreement.

"All I ever seem to do lately is hurt him," I said, a quiver to my voice that I didn't want to let out.

"It's not the real you, though," Drew said, "and he knows that. We just have to get through this. Together."

"I don't know what I want anymore," I said, and the tears fell before I could stop them.

"What do you mean?" Maddy asked.

"I don't think I'm ready for the responsibility of owning a world. Like a whole *world*." I dropped my face into my hands. "But if I don't, then I either die or become a dark lord. If I turn to the other side, I'll be even more horrible to Luke. There will be no kindness left in me."

"Okay, that's enough," Maddy said, putting her fork down. "It's about time you got off your pity pony and go apologize to the one guy who loves you despite all your faults right now."

Drew looked down at his plate, and I hated that I noticed his uncomfortableness.

I stood up. She was right. All I ever did was take from Luke. He needed me now, and it was my turn to be there for him.

I didn't have to look far to find him. He was at the end of the hallway staring out the window. He looked over his shoulder when he heard me, but returned his watch to his kingdom once he saw it was me.

"I'm sorry," I said, keeping my distance until I knew he wasn't going to send me away again. I deserved it, anyway.

"It's okay," he said, although I could've been mistaken since it was said so quietly.

I took a few steps forward. "I shouldn't have accused you. I know you're not proud of what you did."

He turned slowly and extended his hand for me to take. My body sighed as I let him pull me to him.

"I just wish I could've resisted her," he grumbled. "I hate that she had that control over me."

"I probably wouldn't have been able to resist you, either."

"But you did. That took strength."

"It wasn't you she changed into," I admitted, and I closed my eyes waiting for his response.

"It wasn't?"

I swallowed hard. "It was Drew."

His eyes went to my forehead, then to the ceiling, and finally closed as he inhaled then exhaled sharply.

"Luke, I am so sorry."

"Don't be sorry," he said. "She's a bitch for doing that to you."

"She didn't do it," I said meekly, my voice trembling.

"What do you mean?"

"She told me that she doesn't choose who she changes into. It's us who chooses."

"What are you saying?"

I was crying now. "For you, she always changed into me because that's who you desired most. It was you that changed her."

"Sarah?"

"I'm so sorry, Luke." I fell to my knees, burying my face in my hands, and letting myself cry for the first time in a long time. I wasn't doing it for his sympathy. I wanted him to just leave me to my pathetic, horrible self. I was a terrible person and couldn't live with myself for what I was doing to him.

But then his hands were on me and he was lifting me up. He held me in his arms and I felt his forgiveness.

"I don't know what's happening to me," I cried.

"It's okay," he said, pain in his voice, too.

"I love you," I cried.

At his silence, I felt his uncertainty.

CHAPTER 23

A is for Anderson

~ SARAH ~

THE MORNING CAME too quickly, but the moment I woke and saw the sun filtering through the window and drawing an orange line across the fireplace, I couldn't go back to sleep.

I watched as the light slowly climbed the wall, marvelling at its beauty and the contentment of this one moment. Luke's arms were around me, and he was sleeping soundly, the rhythm of his breathing lulling me back to sleep, but I fought it. Just so I could enjoy this quiet moment alone.

Luke was changing. I could feel it. His soul was darkening and I hated watching it. It was because of me, I knew. When he loved my good soul, he was a better person. And now I offered him nothing but grief and heartache. I stiffened at this thought, and Luke's arm tightened around me.

"Morning," he whispered in my ear in his gruff morning voice. "D'you sleep well?"

"I did," I whispered back. I rolled over and nuzzled my face into his chest. "I always sleep better in your arms."

"I love you, Sarah," he said, but I felt it more than I heard it. His heart was beating harder, his arms were tight around me, his lips were on my head. The energy coming from him was pure love and I drank it up, fuelling myself for another difficult task ahead.

Maddy moaned and stretched, her little arms poking up above the back of the sofa near the fire. Drew was now quickly standing up from his place of rest near the fire, too.

"I guess it's time to get up," Luke said.

I pouted and wrapped my arm around him tighter. I just wanted to stay right there. Forever.

A knock sounded at the door, causing Drew to grab his bow and aim it in that direction.

Luke jumped out of bed. "It's okay," he laughed at Drew. "It's probably just breakfast."

I sat up and noticed my clothes neatly folded at the end of the bed. Luke had taken them away to have cleaned while I was enjoying a steaming hot shower that I needed more than a good sleep. He had replaced them with one of his own white t-shirts and a pair of flannel pajama pants, which I swam in, but slept well in.

Carrying my clean clothes, I followed Maddy to Luke's bathroom where we freshened up and got dressed.

"Sleep well?" I asked as I squirted toothpaste onto a toothbrush and began brushing.

Maddy did the same. "Mm-hmm."

Then we heard the sound of a deep voice getting louder. Both of us stopped brushing and turned our heads to the door.

I spit into the sink and tip-toed to the doorway. Drew was standing behind the bedroom door with his finger raised to his lips, signalling for us to be quiet. Luke was in the doorway arguing with someone. Who would argue with Luke? His brother, the only one I could think of who might dare to, was in prison, was he not?

"I swear, Luke, if you have her in there and we're losing people out there because of it—"

"Devon," Luke interrupted, "you're out of line." His voice was hard and firm. "I'm only going to tell you this one more time—get the hell off my chamber floor."

"Luke, you need to think long and hard about what you're doing to your own world. That's all I'm saying about it."

Luke slammed the door then threw his fist into the wall. I slowly emerged from the washroom, unsure of whether he'd want to see me or not.

"Why are you losing people?" I asked.

His forehead was pressed into the stone wall. "Because they're stupid."

"Luke," I warned, "tell me the truth."

"The beast."

"How?"

"He's learned how to bring down his wall of defence when he's hungry, apparently. He puts it up when they attack, but lets it down when he wants to eat."

My hand clutched my chest as I found a seat nearby to sit down on.

"But he's never eaten before," Maddy said. "Why is he hungry now?"

"Because I'm here," I answered. I looked at Drew, then Luke. "Right?"

Neither of them answered.

"I need to get out of here then." I searched the room for my belt and sword.

"The beast can't get into the castle," Luke said. "You're safe here."

"But your people aren't!" I shouted. "Luke, I'm not more important than your own people! We should've just gotten the clue last night and left! Why would you bring me here?"

"Because I wanted to have one last night with you," he blurted. "I wanted to share my bed with you. I wanted to hold you while you slept in *my* home. Not Drew's."

It took a moment to thaw, but then I touched his sad face. "And I love that you wanted that." I waited for his face to soften before adding, "Let's find my key first, then once I have my full powers, we can kill the beast together and have our sleepovers." I smiled at him, but he didn't smile back.

"What is it?" I pressed.

"Once you find your key, you won't want to come back."

"Of course I will."

"Once you become a light lord, Sarah, being in a dark world will disgust you."

"Luke, what are you talking about? That's not true. As long as you're here, I'll always want to come back."

"It won't be good for you." He took my hand. "But we can still see each other on Earth," he said.

I shook my head. What was he saying? Was it true? Would being in Etak disgust me? And to just see him on Earth—that seemed hopeless. We would both need to be with our worlds. We couldn't keep abandoning them to meet on Earth.

"It's still better than you becoming a dark lord, Sarah," Maddy added, somewhat reluctantly, as I'm sure she knew that becoming a dark lord would occur to me as being an option.

"So let me get this straight," I said. "You want me to find my key. You're *helping* me, even. But once I find it, we won't be able to see much of each other anymore."

He nodded.

"And this is okay with you?"

"No, Sarah!" he shouted, making me realize that I had been shouting, too. "No, it's not *okay* with me. I would much rather this not be the case, but you've been poisoned and we need to find you a cure, which just so happens to be in Yelram. You either find the key and we accept the fact that we won't be a good match for each other anymore, or you become a dark lord and we live happily ever after." He was being sarcastic, which didn't help my hopelessness.

"Neither of those options sound good," I said, my voice trembling.

"Baby," —he crouched in front of me— "we will build a home on Earth together. We can still be happy."

"And who will look after our worlds while we do that?"

"We will," he said. "Just part-time."

I wanted this to work, but I knew it wouldn't. He was already losing control of his world by being with me so much. But for now it would have to be enough to give me hope.

"I'VE BEEN HERE before," Maddy said as we surveyed our new surroundings. We had just ported to the edge of the giants' forest, with a cliff as a backdrop, and a forest of tall trees in front.

"You came here in your dream when you were trying to follow Sarah," Luke reminded her.

Maddy nodded, but then her smile faded. "Those giants were scary," she recalled, "but I was able to keep them away with the light from my hands. They were afraid of the light."

"Yes." Luke snapped his fingers. "That's how we'll do it. Sarah, you can ward off the giants with fireballs. Drew and I will attack if they get too close."

"Are you crazy?" I said. "Luke, these are your *people*. Why would you want to hurt them?"

"Only if they try to hurt you!" he defended.

"No," I said, shaking my head. What had gotten into him? He was willing to sacrifice his own for this mission? "I'll go in on my own," I decided.

"Like the hell you will." Luke pushed his way past me and started into the forest first.

I rolled my eyes to Drew, who shot me a warning look. He sided with Luke on this one.

Before long, the ground began rumbling. Two trees in the distance broke apart, falling slowly in opposite directions, as the heavy steps of a giant came closer and closer.

Then the giant burst through the trees, and the sight of him nearly knocked me over. I hadn't expected him to be the size of a two-story house, or have a face with such massive and angry features that instantly provoked a deep fear inside. The giant roared like a lion but stopped when Luke stepped forward.

"BE STILL!" Luke shouted.

The giant stopped, breathing aggressively as he sniffed the air around us. His gaze fell over Drew, then Maddy, and then me. I stepped out from behind Luke and raised my hands.

"Get back," Luke growled to the giant, and the giant stepped back. "Show us where the clue is," Luke ordered.

The giant scrunched up his face, his anger and abhorrence apparent.

"Maddy," Luke said over his shoulder, "shake the ground."

"No!" I barked, stepping in front of Luke. Maddy's hands were out, ready to be thrown into the ground, as she moved beside me. "Maddy, don't you dare!" I warned.

"Maddy, I'm giving you an order!" Luke shouted.

I shoved both hands into him. "Cut it out!" I yelled. "He's not going to show you where the clue is!"

"I can *make* him show me!" Luke challenged.

"I don't want to *make* him show us! My mother was friends with these giants!" My eyes stung with the threat of tears, but I choked back the cry that was pressing even harder.

Luke held my stare for a long few seconds, then dropped his sword, held his hands up, and stepped back. Maddy lowered her hands too, which confused the giant as he looked from them to me.

I reached into my boots and slowly took out my daggers, then I tossed them to the ground. Next, I threw my bow and sword on the ground. I felt Luke's resistance, but he didn't complain. I raised my hands and slowly reached my right hand out to the giant.

"I'm Sarah Marley, Yelram's heir, daughter of Leah."

He recognized me. I read it on his face and felt it in every fibre inside of him.

"Are you Big Ben?" I asked, hoping this wouldn't offend or upset him somehow.

His brow creased, and then his face brightened with recognition. A smile began to form at his lips, and then he left out a large, deafening sound, resulting in the four of us clutching our ears. Within seconds, the ground began rumbling again and a dozen more giants joined him.

I heard the sound of Maddy's sword being drawn, and saw Drew's bow raise out of the corner of my eye. I held out my left hand to them.

"Put your weapons away," I said. "You can come only if they let you. Otherwise, you'll stay here and wait for me to get back."

Luke made a sound as if he was going to protest, but decided against it. I stepped forward and the giant bowed his head to me and reached out his hand. I took it, my hand barely able to hold onto his index finger. He slowly turned and the crowd of giants parted, giving space for us to walk through together. I was not able to keep up, so he gently scooped me up and put me onto his shoulder where I held on and let out a nervous, but happy, laugh.

I felt Drew's anxiety, Luke's bewilderment, and Maddy's excitement. I hoped they were able to see that showing respect to a misunderstood creature would get them further than force. They followed us, having to run to keep up, and I was pleased that the giants let them come.

Several minutes later, we stopped. This part of the forest looked only slightly different than the forest we had just trudged through. It was thick with trees, but the ground around the trees was well trodden.

One of the smaller giants, in his still enormous blue shoes, waddled over to a bed of brush, then curled up for a rest under the canopy of leaves. This, I realized, must be one of their resting grounds.

"Thank you, Big Ben," I said as he lowered me to the

ground.

I slowly walked through and around the trees, feeling each one as I did, squinting up to the tops of them, which seemed to stretch on to impossible heights.

The giants were all making their way into the resting place, surrounding me, but I didn't feel threatened or scared.

Big Ben was the largest. He must have been their leader. There wasn't another that compared, in height or command. Most had old rags tied around them for clothing, helping to differentiate the men from the women.

And then there were the young. Aside from their smaller size, they were recognizable by their spunky clothing and longer, more unruly hair. And then there was the smallest of the giants, who was resting comfortably in his nest, playing with the strings of his blue shoes. Of course they were untied, as his fingers were too fat to master the technique.

Big Ben spoke, which startled me as I had assumed that he couldn't. His voice was deep, muddled, and void of any hard pronunciations. "Welcome, Leah's daughter!"

The others roared as I took a bow, but then Luke, Drew, and Maddy broke into the circle, and the noise died down immediately.

I took Luke's hand and pulled him to me. "This is your keeper, Luke."

The giants bowed to him, but I didn't sense the same respect and admiration that they had just given to me.

"Underneath all that toughness, there's a real sweet guy in there," I said, a smile playing at the corner of my mouth for Luke's benefit.

He squeezed my hand. "You're making me look weak," he muttered. "You don't know these creatures like I do—they need to be controlled."

I laughed. "Sure. Looks like it."

Luke narrowed his eyes at me, then watched the crowd of giants cautiously.

"My mother left something for me in your care," I explained to Big Ben. "Do you have it?"

Big Ben laughed. "Do we have it? Of course we do! When we're given a task as important as this, nothing will get in our way."

I smiled up at him, and he winked at me, his big features looking almost impossible. Then, Big Ben reached for the massive tree in front of us and pulled. It took two hands, which he hadn't expected, but soon the ground began to shake and tremble until the tree finally uprooted, revealing a large metal box in the ground.

"For you, princess," he said, bowing low as he motioned for me to approach the trunk.

Together, Drew and Luke heaved the chest out of the hole and onto the ground by my feet.

I knelt on the ground and touched the buckles on the trunk, then ran my fingers across the details of leather and metal, but I couldn't bring myself to open it. There were at least two dozen large giant eyes staring down at me. Drew, Luke, and Maddy were behind me, and their anticipation and anxiety was real and overwhelming.

"Are you okay?" It was Luke and he was kneeling beside me now, at the surprise of the giants who seemed to take this gesture of kindness as something they had never seen or expected from their keeper.

I turned to him, my eyes filled with tears. "What do you think is in it?"

"I don't know," he answered. "Should we open it and find out?"

I looked up at Big Ben, smiling down on me as if pride were his utmost feeling at that moment. He knew what was inside. He knew my mother. They were friends. She was kind and loving enough to befriend a giant from a dark world.

Suddenly, the ground began to rumble. The giants' heads popped up and turned eastward. Big Ben shouted to them: "He's come for her! Attack!"

Luke pulled me from the ground, and we stumbled back as the giants grabbed their oversized weapons and hollered, running through the forest away from where we came. The smaller giants were corralled together by a female giant who led them deeper into the forest.

"What's happening?!" I screamed.

"Drew!" Luke shouted over the noise. "Take Sarah and the chest back to Earth. I'll meet you there."

Drew obeyed immediately. He grabbed my arm but I pulled away, joining Luke as he readied himself for an attack.

"Is it the beast?" I asked, trying to ignore the anguished screams of the giants.

"Take us to Earth," Luke said, and we were gone.

"LUKE!" I CRIED the moment we landed in Drew's backyard. "You left your people!"

"I had to," he said. "The beast was too close. I couldn't risk getting thrown from him like last time and not being able to protect you again."

"You have to go back!" I shouted. "Drew and Maddy! They're still there!"

"They'll be here in a minute," Luke said, and he began pacing Drew's backyard.

We waited a long minute but they didn't return. I stopped Luke in his pacing. "We need to go find them."

"I can't," he said, his eyes watering. "I . . . just can't."

"Why can't you?"

"I need . . . to keep you safe."

I felt my eyebrows raise. "You *need* to?"

He clenched his jaw. "Yes."

There was an eeriness to the way the words were said. An unnatural desperation. My heart constricted around the words "I *need* to keep you safe," and the thoughts that lingered around them. The last time I had heard the word "need" was when Drew described his *need* to protect me. The enchantment caused that need. Had Luke been enchan—

The air blew viciously around us, whipping my hair and causing me to grip Luke for stability. Then Maddy and Drew appeared, breathless.

"What happened?!" I demanded. "Are you okay?"

"We couldn't get the chest," Drew gasped. "We were thrown from the beast."

"He chased us over a cliff," Maddy added.

"We have to get that chest!" I shouted. "We have to go back!"

Luke nodded. "I'll go back. You stay with Sarah."

"No," Drew said. "Sarah's scent is all over you. I'll go."

"We'll all go," I said. "We get in, we get the chest, and we get out."

"You're insane if you think we're taking you back there," Luke said.

"No, she has to go back," Maddy said. "We'll use her to draw the beast out of the forest first." Maddy turned to Luke. "Can you port us somewhere nearby, then when the beast gets close enough, we port back into the giant's forest, get the chest and come home?"

Luke closed his eyes tightly, shaking his head.

"Luke, we have to get that chest," I said. "What if the beast destroys it? What if someone else finds it first? We need to do this. And we need to do it *now*."

"I can't believe I'm saying this," Drew said, "but she's right. Maddy's plan will work."

Luke opened his eyes, appearing defeated. He finally nodded, took my hand, and we disappeared.

MOUNTAINS SURROUNDED US, but I could see the massive trees of the giants' forest far below.

"He's down there!" I shouted, noticing the trees parting and moving with pronounced force.

The beast appeared in the clearing at the base of the mountain and sniffed the air viciously. When he caught my scent, he disappeared.

"Where'd he go?!" Drew demanded.

And then a second later, the beast reappeared on the edge of the mountain, only a hundred yards from us, clinging to the rock face and moving purposefully toward us.

"What the hell!" Luke shouted. He grabbed my arm and we disappeared too, reappearing a minute later in the giants' forest, next to the chest. Drew and Maddy appeared a few seconds later.

"How'd he do that?" I gasped.

"I don't know," Luke admitted, his brain searching for an explanation. "He's getting stronger. Smarter."

"Let's just grab the chest and get out of here," Drew said as he took one handle of the chest. Luke grabbed the other handle but before I took his hand, I noticed something that made me stop.

It was a shoe. An extra-large blue shoe with untied laces. I was inexplicably drawn to it, and when I picked it up, I saw the matching one, about fifty feet away. I ran to the next shoe, vaguely aware of their shouts coming from behind me. But when I picked up the second shoe, that's when I saw him. He was lying on his back, a blank stare gazing past the treetops.

"NO!" I shouted as I ran to the young giant. I collapsed next to him, my whole body only covering a small part of his chest. He wasn't breathing. There was no pulse. He was gone!

"NOOOOO!" I screamed again. But then Luke was there, dragging me from his body and pulling me back to the chest. I was no match for him as my fight had diminished. The beast, as a result of me, had killed the most innocent of souls.

CHAPTER 24

H is for Haigh

~ SARAH ~

LUKE WAS STILL holding me when we landed in Drew's backyard. My heart was racing uncontrollably, and I felt nothing but the young giant's cold body and saw nothing but his ashen face. Luke caressed my back, but offered no words of encouragement. I only assumed he was mourning too, in his own way. He must have been. How could he not?

"I will kill that beast," I said once my voice returned to me. My grief was turning into anger. I wanted blood for this.

Luke didn't answer, but I knew he was thinking the same. The darkness filling the air around us was not only my own.

"Forget about the beast," Drew said. "We have to find your key and then find the cure. That's what's important here."

"Yeah, 'cause god forbid I change into a dark lord," I snapped.

"Yes, Sarah," Drew snapped back. "That would be a bad thing."

Luke squeezed tighter. "We'll figure it out," he whispered in my ear, which was comforting if nothing else.

It took several minutes before the images of slain giants subsided in my mind. The bright blue shoe was always there, though, and no matter how hard I focused on the green grass, or the red brick on Drew's house, or the yellow shutters, all I could see was the blue shoe.

I squeezed my eyes closed and felt tears run down my cheeks. My jaw clenched as an intense mixture of angry emotions bubbled up inside my chest, replacing the image of the blue shoe with the beast's heart at the end of my sword.

Luke touched my back, and a shock of energy pierced through the tightness in my chest. Our eyes met and I saw the concern in his, but underneath that was anger, too. He wanted the beast's blood as much as I did.

I knelt down to where the trunk now laid at my feet. Opening it, I smelled the richness of leather and sharpness of metal. An envelope laid on top of various pieces of shiny armour, which I quickly took note of—a helmet, breastplate, and sword, to be sure.

My fingers fumbled with the envelope as the presence

of the heavy armour failed to give a feeling of ease. I pulled the three pages from the envelope and began to read aloud:

My Sweet Sarah,

The giants have always been one of my long-time greatest allies. In a world that is so divided, with a king that mistreats his subjects, the giants have always appreciated a kind and caring companion. I visit with them often. You've even come with me on occasion. I wonder if they will recognize you when they see you again.

1

My heart constricted at the thought of my mother with the giants. All of them happy in a world that forbade their happiness. Luke's hand was on my shoulder, and I brought my attention back to the pages in front of me, hoping the second page offered less torture.

There is nothing I can say that will ever prepare you for your next destination. It was my first destination when hiding these clues as I had to work backwards to ensure I didn't lead you on a dead end mission. It has taken a long time to recover from that visit. But remember, my sweet girl, our struggle is not against flesh and blood, but against the powers and spiritual forces of evil of this dark world. This is the last, and most difficult, lag of your journey. Be safe. Be brave. Be wise.

2

I eagerly brought the third page to the front and began reading:

These are the pieces of armour you will need for protection. Let this belt remind you of the truth, so you will not be strayed by lies. Take the breastplate to protect your pure heart, and to remind you to always choose love. Have faith that the shield will repel the flaming arrows of darkness. Wear the helmet to protect your mind against evil, manipulating thoughts. And finally, the sword, which was handcrafted in Nevaeh, will guide you to where you need to go. I believe in you.

I slowly laid the pages on my lap and carefully peered into the trunk. There was the helmet, the breastplate, the sword, and the belt. Just as my mother had written. She wanted me to wear them. She thought I would need them for protection.

"This is insane," Drew said. "There is no way in *hell* I am letting you do this, Sarah."

I reached in and pulled out the sword. It was heavier than the blade I was used to carrying, not to mention shinier. The studded jewels sparkled against the dying light of the sun.

"It's beautiful," Maddy whispered.

"Put it back, Sarah," Drew snapped. "I'm beginning to think your mom was half crazy."

"Watch it, Drew," Luke warned.

"What? Are you seriously telling me you think this is a good idea?"

"I didn't say that," Luke answered.

"But you don't think it's a *bad* idea," Drew pointed out.

"I don't think it matters what I think, Drew. We are at the end of the race. We don't have a choice but to go through the finish line."

Drew threw his hands into the air. "Did you happen to notice that there's only enough armour for *one*, Luke?"

Luke nodded.

"She's not going on her own, I'll tell you that right now," Drew cursed.

"She won't," Luke added.

"Then what about the rest of us? What about Maddy?"

"Maddy can stay here," Luke said.

"Hold on a second!" Maddy jumped in. "I don't think so. I'm going."

Drew glared at her with a look of frustration mixed with concern. "Maddy, Leviathan isn't like the other dark worlds," he said. "There is absolutely *no* good in there."

"Watch it," I said. "My mother might be in that world."

"Huh?" He looked at me, then realized his mistake. "I'm sorry. I didn't mean that."

"Luke and I will go," Drew decided. "We can do this ourselves. We don't need you two coming along and getting yourselves killed." He picked up the breastplate and tossed it to Luke. "If the sword leads us to the clue, then we'll take the sword and—" but the moment his fingers made contact with the sword, an electric current went through his body and he flew back ten feet.

"What the hell—" Luke began. He reached for the sword too, and when his hand touched the hilt, he, too, was thrown back.

I tried not to laugh. "It looks like I'll be needed after all."

Drew was dusting himself off, frustrated with his lack of control over the situation.

"Guys, we've come this far together," Maddy began, "and I don't want to sit on the bench for the rest of the game."

"It's not a game!" Drew shouted.

"You know what I mean, Drew," Maddy shouted back. Then she looked at me with her big brown, pleading eyes. "Sarah, please. Don't keep me out. This is the most *alive* I've ever felt."

She had me, and she knew it. It was the most alive I had felt too. We were Dream Warriors, navigating the dream worlds. Together.

"She can wear my armour," I said, standing up.

"What?" Luke grabbed my arm. "No."

"We'll share it," Maddy offered. "You wear the helmet because your mother said something about it protecting your head, which I think could have something to do with protecting your thoughts. And you take the sword as it'll lead us where to go. I'll take the breastplate and the belt. Fair?"

"Fair," I agreed.

"Can we at least sleep on it?" Drew asked, sounding more defeated than I felt.

I nodded. I still needed to process the atrocities that had happened to the giants, and I was more exhausted than I could ever remember being.

Luke led me into the house while Drew and Maddy carried the trunk of armour. I curled up on the sofa and imagined Lucia was lying there next to me. My eyes felt as heavy as the armour I would have to wear the next morning, but I tried not to think about it. I pushed every thought out of my head and focused on the inside of my eyelids with little moving, red lines and white stars that my vision chased but couldn't catch.

WE WERE ARMOURED up and ready to go the next morning by eight o'clock. I felt ridiculous wearing a helmet and didn't like the idea of using a different sword. I laid the sword that Luke had made me on the coffee table and ran my fingers down the blade. I wanted to bring it, but Drew had argued that it would just weigh me down and was unnecessary since I had the new sword.

The second we landed in Leviathan, the sword began vibrating in my hand. I held it up, and it thrust to my right, nearly slicing Luke's body.

"What are you doing?!" he shouted as he jumped out of the way, but his question was answered when my sword pointed straight to the east and pulled me with it.

I hardly had time to notice the deep red surroundings. The mountains in the distance were the darkest red, the sky was even a lighter shade of red, and the dirt beneath our feet was reddish-brown.

It was cold here. I had expected it to be hot, so this was a surprise, and I immediately regretted not dressing in more layers. But soon the atmosphere changed. We weren't racing across a plateau in a sea of red, we were running down the side of a mountain toward a river of lava, and the temperature was quickly rising.

The pull from the sword wasn't as intense in the ravine, and now it only pointed straight across the river toward the base of a mountain with deep crevices and dark corners.

I pulled off the helmet and gave my soaked head some relief from the intense heat inside, desperately wishing the river was cold water so I could plunge my body into it.

"Now what?" Maddy asked as she loosened her breastplate.

Drew took a few steps back and then ran and leaped, with ease, over the river. "My powers still work here," he called back to us. "I'll jump us across."

He came back, landing next to me. As soon as he did, though, a loud screech came from above. We all looked up to find a large, black winged creature flying toward us.

"Take her!" Luke said, thrusting me into Drew. "Get into the mountain now!"

"Wait!" I shouted, the black creature eyeing me as she came closer and closer. Her large brown eyes were familiar. I knew them. I knew her.

"It's my mother!" I shouted as I ran to meet the magnificent, beautiful creature.

"Sarah, no!" Luke yelled.

But I had a connection with this creature, and I felt it implicitly. *Mom?* I called to her.

My darling, she answered.

I laughed as tears of joy sprung to my eyes. My arms were open and I expected her to sweep me up onto her back and take me to our final clue.

But I didn't get to greet her with the warm hug I had imagined. Drew flew past, his sword held high and firm, then as if in slow motion, he drove his sword into my mother's chest.

"NOOOOO!" I screamed, falling to the ground. "DREW, THAT'S MY MOTHER!!"

Luke picked me up from the ground and pulled me back. "Sarah, let's go. NOW!"

"Let go of me!" I shouted as my mother quickly recovered from the treachery. She reared up and threw her head toward Drew, pitching him across the river and into the side of the mountain. My heart palpitated at this sight as I imagined, for a split second, that he could've fallen into the river and been gone. Just like that. But no, my mother would never have allowed that.

"Leah, I'm so sorry!" I cried.

It's okay, she said, her voice quivering from the pain of her injury.

Luke was still pulling me, and now Maddy was too, and my struggling was no match for them. Drew flew back over the river and tried, yet again, to kill my mother. Then Luke gave up restraining me and joined Drew in his effort. I tried to stop them. I screamed. I shouted, but neither of them listened. Maddy was flying arrows at my mother, and all I could see were her large, sad eyes as she fought back.

"Put on your helmet!" Maddy screamed at me from her position of weakness under my mother's enormous body. Maddy sliced at her legs, and I wanted to shoot an arrow at all three of them!

Luke threw his hand toward my helmet, and a wind caught it, bringing it to my feet. "Put it ON!" he shouted.

I bent down and picked up the helmet, then slowly put it on, anger boiling over inside me. Why was I listening to them when they were trying to kill my mother?!

But the second the helmet was fitted snugly on my head, everything changed. The creature was no longer beautiful and magnificent; it was ugly and ferocious. Her eyes were no longer large and innocent. They were narrowed and red. She wasn't my mother. I had fallen prey to the darkness and trickery of Leviathan.

I pulled my studded sword from my belt and ran to the creature, but Drew was running toward me and before I could plunge my sword into her chest, he grabbed my arm and took me in another direction, leaping across the river.

"Get inside the mountain!" he ordered, throwing me toward the cave. He turned to go back for Maddy, but they were running from the creature back toward the mountainside we had just come from.

"Maddy!" I screamed.

"GO!" Luke yelled back. "We'll find a way over!" They dove behind a rock, narrowly missing the creature's jowls. And when it couldn't reach them, it turned its sights on us.

"Run," Drew said, grabbing my arm and stumbling backward. "Come on!"

I broke eye contact with Luke, and I let Drew pull me toward the mountain. We escaped just in time.

"We can't just leave them there!" I shouted, trying to free myself from Drew's hold.

"Luke still has his powers," Drew reminded me. "He can fight the creature."

My heart was racing. "What do we do now? Wait for them?"

Drew put his hand over mine, which was clutching the sword with all my strength. "They're not going anywhere any time soon," he said. "Let's go find that clue and then come back."

I hurried back to the entrance of the cave. "We'll come back for you!" I shouted.

Maddy nodded while Luke motioned for me to keep moving. The creature dove at me one last time before I disappeared with Drew into the mountain.

"You okay?" Drew asked after several minutes of hiking through the dark cavern. He knew I had been crying. He heard it, as much as I tried to keep my sniffles to myself.

"Uh-huh," I said.

"Don't beat yourself up," he said. "Could've happened to any one of us."

"Uh-huh."

"Sarah," Drew said as he stopped, causing me to run into the back of him. "We survived. It's fine." He knocked his knuckles onto my helmet. "Just make sure you don't take this off again, okay?"

"I'm sorry," I said and I let myself fall back against the wall. "You could've died. I was so angry with you for trying to kill her. But then she threw you, and I thought you were going to land in the river, and I . . . I could never live with myself."

Drew brushed a wet strand from my face. "I'm okay," he said. "And if I died trying to save you, then that's how I would want to go, Sarah." His eyes were burrowing into mine, and I felt the physical connection. His lips were moist, and parted slightly. I ignored the memories of kissing Ella when she was in his form, because the euphoric thoughts made me eager for his touch. I looked down at the butt of my sword, which was still trying to pull me through the cave.

"We should go," I said.

"Yeah." Drew stepped back. "Uh . . . still straight ahead?"

"Yeah," I added quickly.

Drew led the way again and soon we saw the light from the end of the tunnel ahead. We walked through the exit together, and as Drew held me close to his side, we discovered a pool of lava below, and the most magnificent display of waterfalls surrounding us. Except, if it had been water, it might be inviting, but these were lava, and they were anything but inviting.

"Firefalls," Drew said. "I read about this place. My powers won't work in here."

"Great," I muttered.

The sword stopped vibrating, and I knew this was the place. The place my mother hid the last clue.

Drew shuddered. "I can feel the darkness here. Can you?"

I nodded. There was an eerie familiarity about the place. A feeling that wasn't brought on because of a memory, but because of a connection inside of me. It was stirring the darkness and calling for emotions that I was trying so hard to bury. Why had my mother chosen *this* forsaken place to hide the last clue? It had *death* written all over it! I would have given up if it weren't for the vengeance I swore to get on the beast for killing the giants. I took a step forward and my knee buckled. Drew caught me before I fell.

"What happened?" he said.

"My knee," I said as I rubbed it vigorously. "It hurts."

Drew looked left, then right. "Come on. We need to

find that clue."

He pulled me to the right, a direction that I agreed would be our best bet as the ledge on the left tapered off and led nowhere.

Soon we were edging our way carefully and slowly behind a firefall. The heat was nearly unbearable. Drew ripped off his shirt, wiped his face with it, then threw it to the ground. I debated doing the same, but instead, rolled up my t-shirt, exposing my stomach to the thick air.

When we came out on the other side of the firefall, I instinctively looked up the side of the pit. "It's up there," I said, feeling it more than anything.

"Up there?" Drew's gaze followed mine up the length of the wall. "How?"

"I need to climb," I said. I was sure about this. I felt it. I knew it. I found a place for my hand and a foothold then hoisted myself up, ignoring the screaming pain in both my legs and arms.

"I'll go," Drew said, pulling me back down. But I had come too far to let the darkness take my body now.

"No," I said. "Once I get to that ledge up there, there is a small opening to a cave. The clue is just in there. You won't fit." I wasn't sure how I knew this, but I did. I continued searching for holds and hoisted my body higher and higher.

"Be careful," Drew called up to me.

I was almost to the ledge when an electric current of pain bolted through my body. I screamed in agony before losing my grip and falling thirty feet back down. Drew caught me in his arms, and we both fell to the ground.

"Are you okay?" he pressed as he quickly stood, cradling me.

"No," I admitted, holding back to the screams that tried to escape with the pain.

"We need to find Luke," he said. "He has the last elixir."

I hated the truth of this. I didn't want to need the last elixir. My fate seemed so definitive once I took it. Once I drank it, I would only have three days to find the key and then the cure.

Drew was running now. I pressed my head against his shoulder as the heat of the firefall engulfed us. Then Drew stopped to catch his breath and to wipe the sweat from his brow.

"Drew," I said, my body coursing with pain. The only relief was that I was in his arms, and I wanted to be. This relieved the pain. My desire to be held by him was keeping the pain from reaching my head. My need for him, which was completely wrong, was the only thing giving me comfort.

"Yes?" he said.

"Kiss me," I exhaled.

He looked at me, as if considering this and its implications.

"I want you," I said again. I slowly slipped out of his arms and my feet found the ground.

"You can stand," he noticed.

"Because my body wants you." My hands were in his hair and I pulled his face to mine, which he didn't fight.

The kiss was soft at first, but then my body was fueled with a power that wasn't mine. I forced him against the wall and pressed the skin of my stomach against his. His hands held me there, as needy as mine.

But then we weren't alone.

Luke and Maddy had appeared suddenly behind the firefall with us. I pulled away and my body crumpled.

"What's going on?" Luke demanded.

"She . . . she needs the elixir," Drew said as he crouched down and picked me up. "Here." He handed me to Luke and backed away. "Take her back to Earth. Maddy, you come with me. We know where the clue is but Sarah collapsed before she could reach it."

Maddy looked at me in Luke's arms. "She looked fine a minute ago," she said, a taste of venom in her words.

Drew ignored it and turned back to Luke. "She's losing herself. Bring her back to Earth."

CHAPTER 25

Burned & Betrayed

~ LUKE ~

IT WAS A strange feeling cradling her in my arms and knowing she had just been in Drew's. The more I thought about it, the angrier it made me. I had half a mind to go back and beat the hell out of Drew.

She felt like a rag doll, bouncing around in my arms, as I ran as fast as I could through the firefall. We meandered through the cave's passageways and came out on the other end of the tunnel. I grabbed my key, held tightly to Sarah and said, "Take us to Earth."

The minute my legs touched down in Drew's living room, I dropped Sarah on the couch. I couldn't stand to touch her. I couldn't stand to look at her. Every time I blinked, I saw her in his arms. Kissing him. Wanting him.

Forgetting me.

I didn't know what she was thinking, but I was also not guarding my own thoughts. I wanted her to know. She *should* know that she crushed me. She should feel my pain.

A clear, crisp image of Ella in my arms stabbed my brain, halting me in place. She had thrown that memory at me, showing me that she understood what I was going through because she had been through the same. She actually believed that this was the same thing! That her kissing Drew was comparable to me having to kiss Ella . . . when Sarah and I weren't even together!

"This is *not* the same thing!" I boomed.

"You don't think so?" she countered, her voice as firm and loud as mine. "You don't think kissing your ex for whatever reasons you have is the same thing as me kissing *my* ex?"

"No, Sarah. No, I don't!"

She tried to stand up to challenge me, but her legs gave out and she fell onto the coffee table. I tried to get there before she fell, but she was fast, and I was preoccupied with angry thoughts. I picked her up and carefully set her back down. Then I uncapped the last bottle of elixir. Her eyes were forced closed as she fought back the crippling pain. I placed the elixir in her hand and closed her fingers around it. She downed it without a word. Her breathing slowly steadied and then she finally opened her eyes.

"Are you okay?" I asked.

"I want you to take me to Etak," she said.

"Why?"

"I want to fight the beast while I'm strong."

"You're not mentally strong."

She stood up and faced me, her eyes a deep black. "I'm mentally stronger than I have ever been before."

"No. You *think* you're mentally stronger because the darkness has a hold of you, Sarah. I'm not taking you."

She *was* strong right now. Stronger than I had seen her before, but she was also wild and unpredictable. The beast would tear her apart.

She threw her hands into my chest. "Damnit, Luke! You know I can do this! I can see it in your eyes. You and me. Come on. Let's do this together."

I grabbed her arms before she could push me again. "I said NO!"

She tried to pull away, but I kept a firm hold. I knew it hurt her, but she wasn't showing signs of defeat as she kept trying to push, pull, and swing.

But then she stopped struggling and her arms dropped to her sides. I was still holding them, not sure of her next move. Our eyes were locked, and suddenly I wanted her. I wanted her so badly that I didn't care how much she hurt me by kissing Drew. I needed her. I grabbed her face and pulled it to mine, and her hands went to my chest, ripping at my shirt. She pulled it over my head, then pushed me toward the wall. I fell into it and she held herself against me, kissing, moaning, and pressing herself into me. Her hands fumbled for my belt and I let her whip it off, then I ripped her shirt off and threw it across the room. I grabbed her thighs and lifted her up, then carried her to the couch where we fell down together. I was kissing her neck when she bit my ear, and suddenly I wasn't sure if this was Sarah. It was how Ella always kissed me—with fury and anger. I jumped off of her and put distance between us.

"What?" she said as she got up from the couch. "I wasn't done with you."

And that was what Ella would have said. She never liked when I stopped it before she got what she wanted. She was forward and persistent, but Sarah never was. Sarah was gentle and sincere. I knew this wasn't Ella in front of me now. But it wasn't Sarah, either.

I turned to the wall and threw my fist into it, creating a large hole that I regretted immediately. Why had I lost control? Why was I letting her affect me like this? I was stronger than this! I had practised for years how to control my anger, my greed, my frustration. Even with Sarah as my temptress, I could do better than this!

"I'm sorry," she said, and I realized she was watching me.

"What did you say?"

"I'm turning you into a monster. I'm so sorry."

"No, you're not. You're not responsible for my actions."

She sat back down on the sofa and put her face in her hands. "I should be trying to control my temper more. I'm relying on you to make me better, and I shouldn't be. I should be fixing myself."

She had just apologized. After going through what she had been through this past week—her body deteriorating, her soul diminishing, trekking through dark worlds and nearly dying at every corner—she was showing compassion, remorse, and concern. How was she doing that? It was hard enough for me, but I at least had the benefit of years of practise.

My anger subsided just a little. Just enough to see the sacrifice in her eyes. The need to make sure I was okay before she went on.

"Sarah," I said, "you still have love left in you."

"Of course I do," she laughed.

"After all that."

"Luke," she said as she stood up and approached me, "I've done a lot, yes, but I can't blame it all on the darkness. I shouldn't have kissed Drew. I knew what I was doing. No one put a gun to my head and made me. I can't explain why I did it or why I didn't have enough strength to stop it, but all I know is I shouldn't have. And I'm so sorry."

"Dark magic makes you do dark things." I understood. All too well.

"Maybe so," she said, "but it's more reason to be prepared for it and stop it before it happens. I should never have left you back there at the river."

"You still love him."

She paused, but I saw the answer on her face so it didn't much matter what she said.

"I'm afraid to lose him," she admitted. "When the enchantment lifts, I want him to remember that he once loved me. I just . . . I don't want to be alone after all of this. If you and I can't be together, Luke, then—"

"Sarah," I said, taking her face in my hands, "we *can* be together. We will make it work."

She kissed my hand. "I love you."

I wanted to tell her I loved her too, and to tell her I forgave her for kissing Drew, and for not being able to trust that our love could withstand the next chapter. I wanted to tell her that I knew how she felt—fighting the darkness wasn't easy and I forgave her for all of the things the darkness made her do. But I couldn't tell her these things. I knew she still had feelings for Drew, and it wasn't fair for any of us to pretend that they weren't there. We just needed to find her key so we could end this impossible, ridiculous mission.

I stood up and found my belt and put it back on while Sarah retrieved her shirt from the floor and turned away while she discreetly replaced it. Just as she finished pulling it into place, a wind blew around the room, and Drew and Maddy appeared.

Drew was carrying Maddy, who was unconscious and burned from head to foot. Her clothes were singed and melted to her body, her hair was blackened and fried. He quickly laid her on the floor and began healing.

"What happened?" Sarah demanded as she fell to Maddy's side.

Drew was concentrating as his hands made their way over Maddy's body, an intense look on his face that I had only seen once before when he was healing Sarah from her fight with the beast.

Slowly, Maddy's burnt, leathery skin lightened and returned to normal, but she didn't wake.

"What happened to her?" Sarah pressed again.

"She slipped on the ledge and fell into the firefall," Drew said, but kept his eyes on Maddy. "She was . . . mad at me."

I nodded, completely understanding. Maddy had just finished telling me, while we walked through the passageway together on our way to find Drew and Sarah, how much she liked Drew and how she thought the feeling was mutual. I could imagine how hurt and betrayed she felt when she found him kissing her best friend.

Sarah picked up Maddy's hand and carefully stroked it. "Will she be okay?"

"She'll be fine," Drew said, his eyes fixated on Maddy's face. "Here," he said, and he pulled out a thin, black box from his back pocket and handed it to Sarah.

"The clue?"

He nodded. "You should've seen her scale the wall. She was amazing."

Sarah watched Drew and studied each eye, his lips as they moved, and then Maddy. A fake smile crossed her lips as she tried to pretend that Drew's affection toward Maddy didn't bother her.

Drew bent over and picked Maddy up. "I'm going to lay her down in my bed."

"I'll stay with her," Sarah offered.

They disappeared into Drew's room, and I couldn't stand to be in the house any longer, watching Drew and Sarah converse, interact, and pretend nothing had just happened between them.

THE COOL SEPTEMBER air was refreshing and my lungs invited it in like a tidal wave. I had wanted to go home, but for whatever reason, I still couldn't bring myself to leave Sarah. Plus I wasn't sure I could trust myself not to go after the beast, and I needed to have a clear mind for that one.

A few minutes later, the patio door opened, then Drew appeared next to me, and we both looked out over the backyard.

"I'm sorry, man. I don't know what came over—"

"Save it, Drew."

"But I really am sorry, Luke. I don't want you to be mad."

"I'm not mad about what you did to me, Drew," I said through clenched teeth. "I'm mad about what you did to *her*."

"What do you mean?"

"You're giving her something to hold onto. Something that's going to hurt when your enchantment lifts and she realizes that it was all one-sided."

Drew shook his head. "I'll always care about her."

"But you won't be drawn to her the same way. If it's possible for you to feel even an inkling of something for Maddy now, then as soon as that enchantment with Sarah is lifted, you won't be thinking of anyone but Maddy."

Drew contorted his brow and looked back onto the yard. "And what about you?" he asked. "You said yourself that you feel the pull to protect her, especially when she's in Etak. So what happens if you've been enchanted too?"

I made a noise of disgust. "First of all, Leah would have no reason to have an enchantment put on Etak's keeper."

"You've thought about this," Drew realized, although he wasn't surprised.

"Of course I have."

"What if she did have a reason," Drew went on. "What if your enchantment was to keep Sarah safe when she was in your world? Because she knew about the beast and needed to know Sarah would be safe there."

My thoughts gathered around yesterday's incident in Etak, and how when the beast found us in the giants' forest, I left my world to bring Sarah to Earth . . . to keep her safe. She had begged me to go back, but I couldn't. I *needed* to protect her. All reason told me to go back, and I couldn't explain the chains that bound me to her in that moment—the *need* to keep her from the beast. It scared me, and I knew it scared her, too, although she was too afraid to admit or talk about it.

"An enchantment on a keeper requires a binding contract," I said. "Both parties have to be in agreement. Your dad signed that contract with Leah, but my dad would never have done that."

My love for Sarah was real. It felt real. It *was* real. And my father could never have been tricked into entering into an enchantment contract. Why would he? What would he gain from protecting Sarah? Even if he knew it would be his son to bare that enchantment one day—

what would be the benefit to Etak?

"Never say never," Drew said. "Your father had good reason to keep Sarah alive. Especially if he knew you were going to be keeper one day."

It was clear what he was implying—that I would be able to seduce Sarah to trust me to help her find her key. Maybe my father was this manipulative—but had he factored in the possibility of me falling in love with her? . . . And what if he *had* factored that in, and he knew that once the enchantment was broken I wouldn't love her anymore? Could that be possible? Would I return to my ruthless heritage and use my knowledge of Sarah to destroy Yelram? That's clearly what he wanted, and what if the darkness was too strong for me to fight?

No! No, I loved Sarah. It was real. It wasn't some enchantment. It couldn't be.

"You okay?" Drew said. "I didn't mean to upset you."

"I'm good," I lied. "Even if I am enchanted, I won't hurt Sarah. I will . . . I will fall in love with her again."

"How are you going to make yourself fall in love with someone?"

"I'll fake it if I have to!" I snapped. "I won't hurt her again! I just *won't*!"

Drew reacted to something out of the corner of his eye and when I turned, I wished I hadn't. Sarah was standing in the doorway, a look of unearthed sadness on her face.

CHAPTER 26

The Puzzle

~ SARAH ~

"SARAH," HE SAID, but it was too late. I heard what he had said. He would fake it. He would fake loving me. How was I ever to trust him now? How could I ever trust that this love was real? I didn't want him to fake it for me. I didn't want to be a burden to someone. I didn't need anyone else sacrificing themselves for me.

How had I not considered this a possibility before? I had been so worried about losing Drew to the enchantment, I never allowed myself to consider the very real possibility that maybe Luke was enchanted too. This made me so physically sick that I could hardly breathe.

My mind raced back to when we were in Etak and Luke turned his back on his own people and took me back to Earth, saying he *needed* to protect me. He couldn't explain it at the time, but . . . if he was enchanted, then it made perfect sense. All of this made perfect sense. How could a guy like Luke fall in love with a girl like me? And I had been so selfish not to see it and appreciate it before. I was too focused on absorbing Drew's love for me while it lasted, that I didn't even consider what life would be like without Luke. My stomach clenched and I struggled to keep myself from throwing up.

Both of them looked worried. Drew was concerned I was going to freak out. But Luke wasn't worried about my breakdown. His concern was surrounding my trust for him. He knew there wasn't anything he could do now to convince me otherwise, and so he chose silence.

I didn't know what I had expected, or wanted. We found our last clue, and soon I would have my key. Soon the enchantments would be lifted and we would all go our separate ways—Drew with Maddy, and Luke . . . well, probably with Ella. Maybe they *were* meant for each other and his enchantment was the only thing keeping them apart. My stomach tightened again.

"Do me a favour," I said, my voice trembling. "If you *are* enchanted, when this is all over, please don't pretend to love me."

Luke looked down, ashamed, I assumed. I didn't have the energy to read him properly. I filled my lungs with air as I tried to stifle the cry that threatened to escape. Then I slowly turned and went back into the house. Neither followed, and I found myself sitting on the living room floor with the black box in my hands. Slowly, I opened it and pulled out the journal pages. I wasn't expecting her to have hidden the key inside the final clue, but I had still hoped. A key meant that I could leave this world, on my own, and go anywhere I wanted. A key meant my freedom. But the key wasn't there, and freedom wasn't mine.

My Darling Girl,

I trust you are home now—safe and healthy. You may need to take a day or two to rest. That world sure knows how to syphon the light right out of a person.

Review all of your clues, Sarah, and you will find something in common with all of them. Once you find that, I know it won't take you long to figure out where the key is hidden.

1

I closed my eyes firmly, wishing I hadn't just read that. Was she serious? I had to review all of the clues and find something in common with them? I wasn't even sure if I had kept them all! That would have been useful information to know in the beginning, mother!

I shuffled the pages around and read the second.

You will be fine, my love. I wish you the most luck in all of the worlds, although I know you won't need it. If you've made it this far, finding the key won't be a challenge at all. If there's one thing I've learned in all of my years discovering the dream worlds, it's that even in the darkest places, you can find faith, hope, and love. And no one can take those things from you. Draw strength from them, my love. These three things are all you need to conquer any fear, obstacle, or demon.

2

There's no beast, creature, demon, monster, or darkness in any of the worlds that can destroy love, take away your faith, or steal your hope. These things are protected in your heart. And darkness can't see inside your heart.

Therefore, whatever is in your heart is protected, safe, and secure.

I love you. Forever.

And that was it. No more words. Nothing.

I tossed the pages into the air, letting them fall down around me.

"She's crazy," I muttered to myself. I sprawled out on the floor and grabbed my hair. "I have no effing idea what she is talking about."

I was barely aware of Luke squatting next to me now.

He gathered the pages and sat down on the couch to read them. When he was finished, he set them on the coffee table. His mind was open, thinking, and I felt his frustration. He knew why the clues had to be cryptic—in case someone ever found one—but why *this* cryptic?

"Well, we know you have to use your gift to retrieve the key."

"Yes, but it would be nice if we knew where *approximately* the key is. We don't even know what *world* it's in! Like, how in the hell did she expect me to go on from here?"

"Maddy kept all the clues," Luke began, "and the answer must be in there somewhere. When she wakes up, we'll get her help. She's good at figuring out puzzles."

MADDY SLEPT ALL night. But when she woke in the morning, she had a clear head and was eager to make up for lost time.

Maddy retrieved the earlier clues from their hiding place, and then laid the pages all out on the floor. The first page of each clue formed the top row, the second pages formed the middle row, and then finally the third pages were at the bottom. Then, with a look of intense examination, she studied the pages for some commonality.

After several long minutes, Maddy spoke. "Okay, so your mother mentions something about a connection with all of the clues, and something about a number. She also says that darkness can't see inside your heart. . . . Now, for every clue, she draws a *heart* around the page number *three* at the bottom of the third page. I think it's a safe bet that three is the number she's referring to."

I craned my neck so I could inspect the third row of pages, and yes, they all had hearts drawn around the number three.

"But then what? If three is the number that connects the clues, what does that mean?" I asked.

Maddy continued scanning the pages. Drew and Luke hovered over us, focused on the pages too.

"Look for a connection in her paragraphs," Maddy directed. "Look at every third line, every third sentence, every third word. See if there's something that can be used."

We studied the pages for several more minutes and then Maddy inhaled sharply and slowly pushed aside the first two rows of pages so that we were only looking at the third row. The third pages.

"Look at the third word on just these pages." She grabbed a pen off the table and circled the words as she read them aloud:

You are the one chosen to rescue the people from harm or danger. My darling Sarah, I believe that...

Yes, the key to remembering the song will lie in your memory of our moments together. The first...

> *Sarah, this **is** not something to take lightly. Do not be hungry for this clue. It will reveal itself in due...*

> *When any hidden thing appears lost, the quest to find it can seem unbearable at times. The next...*

> *Now get inside that memory of yours, and remember when we would play in the grass. ...*

> *These are **the** pieces of armour you will need for protection. Let this belt remind you of the truth,...*

She looked up at me and hesitated before we read the last word together—

> *There's no beast, creature, demon, monster, or darkness in any of the worlds that can destroy...*

"No!" Luke said firmly, standing up. He pointed to the pages, then to me. "No," he said again. "That's not happening." He shook his head back and forth, then began pacing the room.

Drew was quiet, then leaned over closer to study the pages himself. "Maybe that's not it," he said.

I was too busy watching Luke process what this meant, but Maddy answered, "I've checked every other possibility." She looked up at Luke, her eyes sorrowful. "This one makes sense."

Luke knew she wasn't wrong. He knew this was my mother's hidden message. He knew it was the best hiding place for the key—inside a beast that no one could kill, or even get close to.

"This is why the beast could follow you around Etak," Drew realized. "With the key inside him, he could port. We're lucky he didn't follow you to Earth."

"So the key's inside the beast," Maddy said slowly, her eyes focused on the last page of the last clue. "But how?"

How *did* she hide it in the beast? She would have needed the key to go to the worlds to hide the clues, which meant she hadn't hidden the key until the end, until all the clues were in place. She knew all along that the key would end up in the beast.

I gasped. "She meant to die," I said. The others stared at me blankly. "She sacrificed herself to hide the key."

"But why?" Maddy questioned.

"I'll bet that once the beast was created to kill our bloodline, and once she already had one run-in with the beast, she learned that no one was able to get near it but her. She knew that it couldn't be killed, and that one day I, too, would meet the beast. This was why she chose the beast for the key's hiding place."

"Sarah," Luke tried, "if she knew it couldn't be killed, then why would she hide the key there? Why would she send you to fight him?"

"Because she knew of my mindbending powers, and she had faith in me that I could be the one to kill it. And she also knew that until that beast dies, I won't ever be safe. Nor will any of my descendants." I stood up and went to Luke. "And until that beast dies, Yelram can't be reopened. She believed in me. She knew I'd find a way."

"But it can't be killed, Sarah!" Luke argued. "Don't you remember? Maybe she thought you could kill it, but we tried, and it didn't work, remember? It came back to life!"

"We only need it 'dead' for a few minutes. Long enough to slice it open and find the key," I pointed out.

"Wait a second," Drew interjected. "Luke, maybe the beast only resurrected because of the key."

Luke shot an angry look at Drew. "We're not taking her back there!" he roared.

"But this makes sense, Luke," Drew tried again.

"NO!" Luke's face was beat red. I had never seen him that angry about anything. It was unnerving.

"I'll be right back," Luke growled, then backed away from me, pulled his key from his shirt and said, between gritted teeth and a look of rage on his face, "Take me home."

"Luke!" I shouted before he vanished, leaving only a tornado of wind in his wake. "Drew!" I said, turning on him. "Take me to Etak! Now!"

Drew stepped back. "No, Sarah."

"Drew, don't do this!" I warned as I advanced on him.

"Sarah," he said, dodging my grasp, "Luke needs to do this. On his own."

"Does he think he can kill the beast on his own? He can't! Only I can, and you know it! He'll only get himself killed!"

"Then let him!" Drew shouted. "If he's been enchanted to protect you too, then there's nothing you can do to stop him."

His words cut like a sword. My heart cramped at his mention of the enchantment, and I felt my own rage thrashing around inside.

"What did you mean when you said maybe the beast only resurrected because of the key?"

"Yelram's key has the power to heal in any world, not just its own."

"Wait," Maddy said, standing up to join the conversation. "If that's why the beast is still alive, then all we need to do is disarm it long enough to fish the key out, then we should be able to kill it. For good this time." Maddy picked up her sworded belt from the floor and strapped it around her waist. "Drew, take us to Etak."

"Not you, too," Drew groaned. "Guys, we can't do this. Sarah nearly *died* last time."

"But we don't have a choice," Maddy reasoned. "If we don't kill the beast, we don't get the key."

"Luke's working on it," Drew said.

"He can't do it without Sarah," Maddy argued. "And she's stronger now. She knows she's a mindbender. Drew. We need to *try*."

Drew's brow furrowed as he considered Maddy. I didn't know what he had expected Luke to accomplish on his own. Maybe he hoped he had a plan to spare the rest of us from having to face the beast.

Drew nodded slowly, then Maddy and I both took his hand. He picked up his key and said, "Take us to Etak."

Chapter 27

Enemies & Allies

~ Luke ~

"Looking for something?"

I spun around to find Riley standing only about a hundred feet away. He should've still been in prison. How did he escape? And why?

"What are you doing here, Riley?"

"Waiting for you, brother," he said. "Did you miss me?" He began closing the gap between us. "I bet you're wondering how I escaped *your* prison, surrounded by *your* guards and *your* dragons. You see, since you've been running around *betraying* your world, your powers here are draining. The world doesn't recognize you as its keeper anymore, Luke."

My heart beat wildly inside my chest while my palms

burned with a desire to throw him into space. Did he think he could convince me that *my* world no longer recognized me as its keeper?

"And since I am the next living heir, your powers gradually transferred to me," Riley finished.

"You're lying," I challenged. "The key still works for me."

"Which brings me to why I'm here." Riley drew his sword. "I want my key."

I unsheathed my sword too, and pointed it at him. "Come get it, brother."

My inner darkness was ramming against my ribcage, begging me to let it out. I wanted to kill him. I wanted his head on the ground at my feet. For all the trouble he'd caused me, for all the pain he'd caused Sarah, and for all his arrogance and bullshit now.

"Before I come get it from you, Luke," Riley started, "I just have one question." He scanned the area around us, as if looking for something. "Where's the princess?"

"Why do you want to know?" I only let this stall me because I knew the absence of the beast was his doing. He knew where it was, and if I wanted to kill the beast after I killed Riley, then I needed him to tell me.

"I have a gift for her."

"Cut the shit, Riley," I roared. "Where's the beast?"

"Waiting patiently, although he's been getting a little restless. He desperately wants to finish her off, and I think it'll be a much quicker fight this time. He's learned from the last two encounters with her, and he's much stronger now."

This was why the beast was so difficult to restrain with enchantments. He was learning how to fight them. And if he had learned how to fight those, then had he learned also how to shield his mind from Sarah?

"She won't be coming back," I declared. "Ever."

Riley waited for a few seconds. "Such a shame," he said. "I really thought you two were meant to be." The last part was said with a sarcastic sneer that begged me to impale him.

He raised his hand and snapped his fingers, then the horizon was filled with black—black knights, followed by angry giants, and ferocious dragons. He had built his army and was threatening me with it. These were *my* people, this was *my* world, and he dared to threaten me!

"Riley," I growled, "come get your effing key!"

Riley roared as he took a few long strides down the hill toward me, and then leaped into the air. He soared effortlessly through the air but as he got closer, I threw my free hand toward him and sent him off course. He landed only a few feet from me—not nearly as far as I had intended to throw him—and I wondered if he was right, and I was losing my power.

Riley bellowed again and thrust his sword toward me, but I easily blocked it. Then he came at me again, this time grazing my side with his blade. I caught his arm and threw him down. He rolled away from the end of my blade and was on his feet again. Our swords clashed, and I realized he was much stronger than I gave him credit for.

"STOP IT!"

We both froze, our blades pushing against each other, and turned to find Sarah, Drew, and Maddy only twenty feet away.

Riley's army thundered and ran down the hill toward us. I pushed Riley away, ready to protect Sarah, but then Riley turned eagerly to his crowd, raising both his hands.

"HALT!" he roared, extending the word so that they all heard it through their noise. When everyone had stopped, he continued, "The princess belongs to the beast!"

I had Sarah in my arms now. "What the hell are you doing here?" I scolded. "Drew, take her home."

"No," she said, pulling away from me. "What's going on here? Is Riley . . . has he built an army?"

"It doesn't matter," I said. "They're still my people. This is still my world, and I'm telling you to leave . . . *now!*"

"You're wrong, brother!" Riley shouted. "You don't have a home anymore. You abandoned your people, and you have nothing left here. They don't follow you. They follow me!"

The crowd cheered, throwing their sworded fists into the air, gnashing their grizzly teeth, and spitting fire.

"Come on," I said. "We're leaving." I made to grab her arm, but she pulled away.

"What are you doing?" Sarah said. "Challenge him! Tell him he's wrong. Convince them!"

"It's no use. They've been brainwashed. My purpose is to save you, Sarah."

"Your purpose is to save me?"

"Yes."

"You'd rather protect me than take control of your world?"

It occurred to us both at that moment that this was not what a keeper would do. Not unless he was under an enchantment. Was I acting unreasonably? If I weren't enchanted, would I have chosen my world over Sarah?

She pulled from me and turned back to the angry crowd. "Your keeper is under a spell to protect me. Once this enchantment breaks, he will return to power."

The crowd relayed mixed emotions of curiosity and anger.

"So does that mean," Riley began, "that he'll return to full power when you're dead?" A sneer curled his lip. "Because that, my lady, will be sooner than you think."

The ground trembled as the crowd on the hill began to separate, leaving a wide path down the centre of the hill toward us. Riley gave one last smile and disappeared, reappearing a second later on the edge of the crowd, as a spectator now.

"GO!" Sarah screamed at us. "I have to do this myself!"

As she began to run toward the hill, toward the beast, Drew chased after her—Sarah's protector. Maddy drew her sword and followed—Sarah's faithful friend. But as the head of the beast crested the hill, a bright light pierced my head and threw me to the ground. Vibrant flashbacks flooded my memory. Trinity, keeper of Nevaeh's voice was speaking softly into my ear. She was holding my key and I was watching her curiously. "The enchantment binds the keeper of this key—present and future," she explained. "The keeper will be drawn to Princess Sarah, Yelram's rightful heir. The keeper will ensure her protection while in Etak, and the enchantment will only be broken upon the princess' final battle with the beast." The key glowed and Trinity continued, "The terms of this enchantment will be forgotten until it is lifted. Do you agree?" And I heard my father's voice, plainer and calmer than I had ever remembered it before: "Etak's keeper agrees and enters into this binding enchantment for as long as is required, in an effort to restore Yelram."

My body screamed with fury, anger, vengeance, and hatred. Sarah was meeting the beast for their final fight, and my purpose was complete. The enchantment was lifted.

More flashbacks came barrelling through my memory. The first time Sarah came to Etak, and I was drawn to her immediately. I couldn't explain why, but from the moment I saw her, I knew she was special. And every time after that when she came, and I was pulled from whatever I was doing just to be there with her. I always had an intense urge to fight off whatever evil tried to surround her. Like it was my duty. Because it *was* my duty.

I re-lived Sarah's first meeting with the beast when Ella had brought her. I did everything in my power to rescue her. And then again when she met the beast just two days ago, and I abandoned my people to bring her to Earth and protect her. This was all part of the enchantment—to keep her safe until her final battle with the beast.

And today—I hadn't kept her from the beast. I knew she would convince Drew to follow me here, and I knew Drew would listen to her—because his enchantment was to bring her to this moment too. It was engrained in the both of us to bring her here. His enchantment would break soon too. Maybe it already had. But I could see him now that the bright light had subsided. He was fighting alongside Sarah. She had broken down the beast's barrier and the three of them were fighting it. Drew was working hard to protect Sarah. Could his enchantment still be there? Or was it true—was he still in love with her? And why hadn't I rushed in to help now? I wanted to, but even more than that, I wanted revenge.

A low rumble thundered through my bones. The darkness was ceasing every part of my body. The enchantment that was created by light was now gone, and I was left to pick up the pieces of my dark soul and put them back together. Only there was nothing to do—the dark pieces were all finding their places perfectly as my thirst for revenge built, and my need to restore my own world grew.

Sarah, Drew, and Maddy had an audience of hundreds for their battle with the beast, but I only had my eye on one of them—Riley. He felt me coming before he saw me, and when I was close enough, he said, "I always knew the beast inside of you would come back. You can't hide from it, Luke."

"I wasn't hiding," I growled. "Our father entered into a binding enchantment to protect Sarah. It was my duty."

I pushed my sword toward him, and he managed to get out of the way, drawing his own sword at the same time.

"Why the hell would he do that?" Riley accused.

"He knew he'd need her alive," I guessed. "The key was gone, and if he ever wanted to take over Yelram, he'd need her." I pointed my sword at him and narrowed my eyes. "If you were keeper, you would've been the one protecting her."

Riley scoffed. "If being keeper meant I had to betray my world, then I'm fine with being second."

"Maybe that's why you were never chosen," I hissed.

"Enchantment or no, I would *never* have betrayed my world to protect that piece of garbage!"

I sliced my blade through the air, this time grazing him as he fell backward. And then he disappeared, leaving my sword to plummet into the ground where he stood only seconds ago.

His followers looked around desperately for him, unsure what they should do now that he was gone and I was in control again.

"BOW DOWN!" I boomed, and with little hesitation, they all fell to their knees.

I squeezed the air between my fingers, watching as they all gasped for their breaths. I tasted their blood and knew that I only had to finish closing my fist and they would all be dead. Every single one of the traitors would be dead.

You can't heal hurt with hate. Her soft melodic voice played in my head, but my darkness had returned in full force. *Yes, you can.* My fist closed around the air, and as I watched their bodies fall to the ground, I felt the power of my world return to me. This was how was I meant to rule. No one would stand against me. No one would dare challenge me. No one would come into my world and threaten the people I care about.

No one. Not even the beast.

The beast was notably stronger, but so was Sarah. She kept eye contact with the beast, and he swayed, teetering between being confused and docile to angry and vicious.

Even as I stood there, watching their final battle unfold, I wondered how things would've played out if I hadn't been enchanted. Would I have met Sarah? Would I have been drawn to her? Would we have fallen for each other?

What did it matter now, anyway? My full darkness had returned, and with Sarah's failing light, I was the furthest thing from what she needed.

All I could think about now was getting my revenge on the beast for killing the most innocent of giants. The more I thought about that untied blue shoe lying on the forest floor, and the frozen look of fear etched over the giant's young face as it lied cold and still on the ground, the more the blood in my veins pulsed with the need for revenge. I would execute the creature, and deliver its head to the giant's as a promise to never leave them vulnerable again.

CHAPTER 28

Broken & Beaten

~ SARAH ~

MY ARMS BURNED with exhaustion, but I fought on with a revival of energy and determination that I never knew I had. The beast only hungered for me, and its constant advances made it difficult to keep a hold of his mind. I kept slipping, and when I did, he regained control and came at me with more fury than before, and it was harder to gain control again. If it weren't for Drew and Maddy desperately trying to slow the beast down or at least turn its fury in another direction, their lives resting in my hands, I could've just given up and collapsed with exhaustion. And where was Luke? Was he still alive? No. I couldn't think about that right now.

The beast was getting the better of us now. Maddy

had lost her steam, and was mostly just fending off the beast's tail swings.

Drew was pouring everything he had into it, but when the beast swiped its enormous paw toward him, Drew wasn't able to jump out of the way in time. He soared through the air and landed hard against a large rock.

"Drew!" I screamed, and the diversion was enough for the beast to come down hard on me. I raised my sword just as his large jowls opened wide, preparing for the end. But then a ferocious wind came out of nowhere and ripped me away from my doom and into the arms of Luke.

"You're okay!" I gasped, studying his face and body for any measure of defeat.

"I'm okay," he confirmed, but there was a blackness in his eyes that wasn't there before, and it concerned me.

"Look out," he said before throwing me aside. He ran toward the beast, meeting him in mid-air with his sword aimed at the beast's head.

He was more powerful now. Angry. Ferocious. Luke, not the beast. A rich darkness emanated from every fibre of him, and I felt it. It was like a magnetic force that my own darkness couldn't resist. I wanted him. I needed him. And his power brought out my own. As he valiantly fought the beast, I added my newfound strength to his and joined the battle.

Maddy was at Drew's side now. She knew she was no longer needed. She and Drew had exhausted the beast enough for Luke and me to finish him off.

I drove my sword into the beast's throat while Luke flew through the air and attacked him from above, driving his sword deep into its skull. The beast only roared louder, but it gave me a chance to bend his mind.

You're defeated, I screamed at him. *Lay down and accept your loss.*

It wasn't as simple as that, but as he shook his head in confusion and reared up onto his hind legs, I jumped at the blade of my sword, still protruding from his throat, and pulled it down, slicing a long, deep cut right down to his heart. Then I pulled my sword from him and plunged it deep into his heart, bypassing his thick coat of armour and going straight through to the pulsating muscle.

The beast and I collapsed at the same moment—he from death, and me from exhaustion.

Luke jumped from the beast and landed by my side. He helped me to my feet. "You did good," he said.

"You too," I panted. "Thank you."

He just nodded and stepped away, motioning me to finish the job and find my key.

"Heal Drew," I said, and he left my side to attend to this request, while I went to the beast and sliced open its belly.

Blubber and guts poured out around my feet, and I kept slicing until it was all exposed. It stunk of rotting flesh, and I had a vague image of my mother's body being part of that smell. I didn't care now, though. I knew the necklace was in this mound of rot somewhere, and I hadn't come all this way to be turned away by the sickening stench.

Within a few minutes, Drew was on his knees next to me, but Maddy kept her distance, covering her nose and mouth with her hands and periodically emptying the contents of her own stomach onto the grass.

Luke kept his distance, and it killed me to think why. Had he been enchanted after all? Was it now broken and he no longer needed to help me? To protect me? To love me?

But Drew was still there. Helping me. He still fought the beast with me.

"I found something!" Drew finally shouted as he pulled off a long, slimy piece of intestine from a golden object the size of a baseball. He cleaned it off with his shirt and held it up, inspecting it carefully, and I realized it was in the shape of a heart.

Drew handed the golden heart to me, and I twisted the bottom from the top and reached inside. Carefully, I retrieved the folded pages, and then pulled out a chain with a key dangling from the end. Yelram's key.

Luke was the first one I looked to. He wasn't smiling, but I heard his thoughts: *I knew you could do it.*

The key was finally in my hand. Yelram's key. *My* key.

Maddy was next to me now. She wrapped her arms around me. "I'm so proud of you," she said. I hugged her back, full gratitude flowing from me to her. I could not have done this without her.

Drew slowly stood from the mess, and I realized that he had been very quiet since I pulled the key from inside the golden heart. Luke was watching him strangely, and then Drew's eyes met Luke's. He looked scared, but at a realization.

Both were guarding their thoughts, and both looked as though they had let me down.

"What's wrong?" I asked Drew.

He wiped his hands off on his pants. "Nothing. It's all good." He pointed to the key in my hand. "Congrats."

I looked down and realized, in that one moment, that finding this key meant the end of his enchantment.

"It's broken, isn't it?" I asked, the sound quieter than I had intended. Maddy put her arm around me. She saw it too.

"I may not have the *need* to protect you anymore, Sarah," Drew began, "but I still care about you. That will never change."

His face said otherwise. He knew that he didn't love me the same anymore. Or maybe at all. And my heart broke into a million pieces, making it hard to breathe.

Luke was quiet. He hadn't answered. I couldn't look at him. I couldn't hear what he had to say. It was enough to lose Drew in that moment, I couldn't bear to know I had lost him, too. But his mind wasn't as guarded now. And I couldn't feel his love. I only felt his darkness.

I wanted to cry. I wanted to tuck the key back into the golden heart and hide it back inside the beast. If this was what winning felt like, I didn't want to win. I wanted Luke. I wanted Drew.

My eyes fell to the key in my hand. The key that ended our quest. The key that broke the enchantments, finishing Drew's and Luke's love for me. I draped the necklace over my head and tucked the key into my shirt, but the second it made contact with my chest, a bright light blinded me and threw me onto the ground.

My eyes were open, but all I could see were memories from the past. Memories from when I was little. And with my mother. We were in Nevaeh together. Sitting on the same bench that I sat on just last week with Drew and Luke and Maddy. I was sitting on my mother's lap. She was combing my wild, unruly hair with her soft fingers. And Trinity was there, holding my hands and speaking so softly that I barely heard her. "The enchantment binds this child," she explained. "She will accept the protection from the keeper of Earth and allow him access to her life for the purpose of love and protection." Our hands glowed and I realized then that we were holding Yelram's key. Trinity continued, "The terms of this enchantment will be forgotten until it is lifted. Do you agree?" My mother's soft fingers carefully pulled the hair from my face and she kissed my cheek. "We agree," she whispered. "Don't we, darling?" And then my tiny voice answered, "Yes, I agwee."

Maddy was at my side. "Sarah? Sarah, are you okay? What happened?"

My eyes refocused to my surroundings. Drew and Luke kept their distance. They knew what just happened. They had experienced the same. I had been enchanted too, and they knew it. They looked at each other, both wondering what my terms were, and how it affected them. I looked from one to the other—my deep-seeded love for Drew had waned. Yes, he was still one of my best friends and I cared for him deeply, but it no longer hurt to know that he didn't love me. But when my eyes rested on Luke, I realized that I fell in love with him all on my own. And it killed me to know that he didn't feel the same anymore.

"Thank you for helping me get this far," I said as I let Maddy help me up. My legs no longer ached and the bruises and scrapes from the battle were slowly disappearing. "It looks like my key is able to heal my body. Your job is done. I don't need you anymore."

"Sarah," Drew and Maddy both said, but Luke didn't. He held my stare, trying to read my mind.

Does she really not want me? he wondered. He kept a firm face, masking his disappointment. He knew we were no longer a good match. I was a light world keeper trying to restore my goodness; he was a dark world keeper who needed to restore his world.

"Take me to Earth," I said, and the key whisked me away from this world of pain, back to the one place that I always felt free to think by myself.

CHAPTER 29

The Last Letter

~ SARAH ~

THANKFULLY THERE WAS nobody there when I landed on the rock's edge. No one to witness the vortex of wind and a girl randomly appearing out of thin air.

The wind was vicious, ripping at my hair and clothes, so I took shelter in the crevice of the rock where I so often sought refuge before. The ocean was wild, and I noticed every wave, every wash of white, every bubble. It would crash against the rocks, and I heard the sound as loud as if it were inside my head, and then the rushing of the water as it raced back out to sea, and then again as it gained momentum and came back in. The seagulls in the distance sounded as if they were right with me. And I heard their thoughts—their desire for food, and their excitement for the current of air that would challenge their wings.

And I could hear the beating of my own heart—scared but free as it thudded against my chest, beating toward the key that lay near it.

I was still holding the gold heart in my hands. I opened it and pulled out the paper nestled inside. I knew it was from my mother. And I knew it was the last note I would ever receive from her. I didn't want to read it. I didn't want to see the few words. I didn't want to read them and know they were finished.

But I had to.

My Dearest Sarah,

I write this with complete faith that you will one day read it. I know you will be able to defeat the beast. You are meant for great things, and I am so proud of you, baby girl.

The moment you put this necklace around your neck, your enchantment will lift and you will remember the terms. It was important that you allow Earth's keeper into your life so that he could do his job to protect you. I assume that little

Drew Spencer will be Earth's keeper by the time you need protection, and I know how strong-willed you can be. I needed to ensure that you didn't feel threatened by his constant protection and interest in you. For your protection, he has been enchanted too. As his enchantment strengthens through his need to protect you, your connection to him will grow stronger. His enchantment ends when you find your key.

There is one more enchantment in place to ensure your protection. Etak's keeper has agreed to protect you from the beast while you are in Etak until it is time for the final battle where you will reclaim your key. Although Etak's keeper has been less than trustworthy, and his agreement to this enchantment is completely self-serving, it is a risk I had to take. Be careful, my love—dark blood runs deep.

There is one more thing you should know. Because you have both keeper and dreamer blood, there is a very good possibility that you will be gifted with all seven crafts from each dream world. Always remember that great power requires great responsibility. I pray you will be blessed with these crafts, and that they will serve you well when taking back Yelram.

In the event you are pierced by the beast's claws, you will be infected with the darkest poison there is. When you put on the key, it will heal your body, as Yelram's key has the power to heal in any world. However, your soul will still suffer. I know this because I met with the beast once, and am currently enduring this suffering. Trinity is working on finding a cure, and my hope is that by the time you need it, she will have the answer.

I am sure you have figured out by now that my plan is to sacrifice myself to the beast so that I can hide your key inside him where I know it will be well protected. The dark lords all know me. They are determined to get rid of me and use the key for their own agenda. My fear is that if they ever find you, they will be able to use you to torture the key out of me. I hope you will one day understand and forgive me for abandoning you.

And so that is where I am off to today. All of the clues are in place and this is the finale. Trinity will ensure you are kept safe on Earth. Other than Trinity, no one from the dream worlds will know you exist. On your twelfth birthday, however, the enchantment that keeps you from dreaming will be lifted, and then it is up to Earth's keeper to protect you until you are ready to reclaim your throne.

You are a fighter like me, but you have a softness for people and animals like your father. I know you will make the very best keeper of Yelram. I am sure of it.

I love you, my angel.

Mom

I stared at her signature: Mom. It was the first time she referred to herself as "Mom." My "mom" planned this all out. She sacrificed herself. She did all of this. For me. For Yelram.

But I didn't want her to. I wanted my "mom" to raise me. I wanted a normal life.

I was suddenly very angry for where I was and how I got there. My soul was darkening, and I felt it with every angry, jealous, hateful thought.

I was angry that my mother chose this path for me. She could've destroyed the key and we could've lived a normal life on Earth. She wouldn't have had to enchant Drew and Luke, and they wouldn't have had to fall in and out of love with me.

And now my heart was broken. All the love Drew and Luke had for me was just a charade. It wasn't real. Once again, my heart was confused, alone, and completely abandoned.

"There you are."

His voice startled me, and I wasn't immediately sure if it was because I hadn't expected them to find me here, or because I never expected *him* to be the one looking.

"What are you doing here?" I asked while keeping my eyes on the angry waves below.

"We've been looking everywhere for you." Luke jumped down onto the ledge and took a seat next to me. "I'm not sure why it didn't occur to me sooner that you would've come here." He winked. "Penny's Cove."

I smiled half-heartedly, but couldn't ignore the fact that he had avoided my question. "What are you doing here?"

"Trying to find you," he said, as if he was repeating himself.

I shook my head and returned my gaze to the ocean. "You don't need to do this," I said.

"I want to."

"I know you had an enchantment. I know you don't feel the same about me now."

He didn't answer.

"And I get it."

"Because you were enchanted too," he added.

I nodded, letting him assume that my enchantment meant that my feelings for him were just as fake as his were for me.

"Remember when you told Drew that even if you were enchanted, you would fake your love for me?"

"Sarah, I didn't mean—"

"It's okay," I said, saving him from embarrassing me further. "I don't want you to pretend." I picked up a pebble and rotated it in my fingers.

When he didn't respond, I worked at getting into his head. He fought me at first, and I could tell he was trying to put a block up, but he wasn't fast enough, and I felt his emotions—his anger at the enchantment. His realization that the love he felt so strongly wasn't real. The happiness he was once sure of was nothing but a charade. I couldn't bear to feel any more of his pain, so I sucked myself back out of his mind and rested my head against the hard rock wall.

"I'm sorry," he said finally. "I never wanted this to

happen."

"I know," I said. "Me, neither."

"Can I still help you take back Yelram?"

"Your enchantment is lifted, Luke. Just go home. Fix your world. Don't worry about mine."

"I told you I'd help, and I don't break promises."

"You never promised me," I pointed out. "And dark lords break promises all the time."

He was stung by that, I could see it in his eyes. He had once promised that he would always love me. I didn't try to bend his thoughts or feelings, I just wanted to be free. I was a lone wolf now.

I stood up and inhaled the ocean air one last time.

"Where are you going?" Luke asked.

"I need to clear my head."

"Can I go with you?"

"No," I said too quickly. "I need to do this on my own now."

I took my key in my hand, feeling its cool gold against my palm, and thought of the old apple tree. It was the only place I knew I could port into without being seen by anyone. But where I was going after that, I didn't know. I had my key. Yelram was just a short sentence away, but I couldn't bring myself to say the words. The agony in my heart reminded me that I had just suffered two losses, and taking back Yelram would require more strength and perseverance than I had at the moment.

I closed my eyes, tightened my fingers around my key, and whispered, "Apple tree."

CHAPTER 30

Goodbye

~ LUKE ~

AND SHE WAS gone. Just like that. My chest tightened with the pain of losing her. I hated how the enchantment had manipulated her heart. I hated that she kissed Drew, and now that my full darkness was back, I revelled in the cruel emotions that came with these thoughts. Yes, I still loved her—that part of me hadn't changed. But something had changed in her. She no longer needed me. Or wanted me.

Even if I could make her love me again, I was too dark for her now, and she was too weak for me.

Dear Reader,

Thank you for reading *Chasing Light*. I hope you are enjoying this story. There are still more books in this series, so enjoy!

Please consider leaving a review for *Chasing Light* on Amazon and Goodreads. Reviews help other readers decide if a book is worth their investment in time, which, in turn, helps the author. So, in advance, thank you.

And finally, if you would like to be notified of upcoming book releases, please sign up for my newsletter on my website at **www.klhawker.com**.

Thank you so much!

Kimberley

K.L. Hawker
www.KLHawker.com

P.S. Turn the page for a sneak peek at the fourth book in this series, *Eye of Darkness*.

WRECKED WITH BETRAYAL and abandonment, Sarah struggles with her destiny and the love that it cost her. With the help of a new ally—a charismatic dreamer named Keagan—Sarah finally feels ready to unlock her world, drawing from the comfort and security that her new friend offers. But Yelram—a world taken over by monsters—isn't the welcome home Sarah was hoping for. With Keagan distracting her from her misery, and Luke insisting on bringing an army to help, Sarah embarks on a mission to reclaim her world and find the cure that will save her soul and return Yelram to its former glory.

Navigating the cruelties of love is hard enough, but add a destroyed world and impossible odds of survival, and you'll find yourself staring into the *Eye of Darkness* and making choices that could change the fate of your world and everyone in it.

PROLOGUE

A Visit with Luke

~ MADDY ~

THE HALLS WERE dark, but they didn't scare me like they used to. With the dream catcher above my head, I knew nothing *really* bad would happen to me here, and besides, I had to believe that Luke was still my friend.

I turned down the next corridor, running my fingers along the cold stone walls. No one ever guarded these halls, which always seemed strange to me. I guess there weren't many dreamers Luke allowed to enter the castle. I was one of the lucky ones. Or unlucky ones, depending on the mood I found him in.

His door was closed and I hesitated before knocking, remembering the time I walked in on him and Ella when I thought he was lying to Sarah. I took a deep breath. That was in the past. I had to do this again. For Sarah. I knocked hard on the door and waited. A minute later the door opened and Luke stood in the doorway wearing nothing but an old pair of jogging pants that hung low on his hips. I looked down, averting my eyes from his chiseled abs and rippled pecs. I swallowed.

"What are you doing here?" he asked, his voice low and dark. "Is something wrong?"

"I . . . uh," I said, looking from the floor to the fireplace behind him and back to the window. "Can . . . we talk?"

He pushed the door open further and stepped back to let me in. I turned my head away from him and walked in as he shut the door behind me.

"What's wrong?" he asked. "Is it Sarah?" There was concern in his voice, which I couldn't quite understand given his hiatus.

"Can you please put a shirt on?" I blurted.

"Really?"

"Yes," I said. "I find it hard to . . . *focus* when you're half naked."

"It's your dream," he said. "Maybe I did have a shirt on before you got here." He chuckled, but I knew this wasn't true.

"Maybe," I said. "It very well could be a nightmare."

I took a seat on the sofa next to the fireplace. There was a glass on the coffee table that was half full of a clear brown liquid and ice cubes.

He returned to the fire a minute later wearing a white v-neck t-shirt and grinning. "Better?"

"Yes," I said.

"So why are you here?" He took a seat in the chair next to me, in front of the glass.

"Well, we haven't seen you in a while, and . . . I was wondering if you planned on ever coming back?"

"Is there a reason to? Is everything okay?"

"You mean with Sarah?"

He reached for the glass and took a drink. "Or whatever."

"You still love her, don't you?"

"And why would you think that?"

"Because I saw the way you looked at her after her enchantment broke. You thought she didn't love you anymore and it hurt you."

He was silent.

"Why are you pretending it doesn't hurt?"

"Because it doesn't."

"Why are you lying?"

"Because I don't feel hurt, Maddy. Pain empowers me because I'm a dark lord and that's just how it goes."

"But you're not happy."

"Of course I'm not happy."

"Then why are you doing this? Why are you staying away?"

"Because I *have* to, Maddy, okay? Because Sarah is better off without me."

"How can you say that?"

"Look at me, Maddy!" he shouted, and his eyes were blacker now. They were sunken into a paler face than I remembered. "I'm no good for her." He downed the rest of his drink and set the glass abruptly on the table.

"What's happening to you?"

"Being around Sarah made me a better person. I was taking light from her."

"Well, then you should definitely see her again. You look like shit."

He ignored my joke. "And guess what happens when I take her light? . . . She becomes darker."

I considered the impact of that statement. "And that's why you've been avoiding her."

He nodded. "Until she finds that cure, she can't surround herself with someone like me."

I went to him and took his colds hands. His eyebrows puckered and I could tell he didn't enjoy my touch.

"Luke," I said, keeping my hands on his, "she's been a mess. She won't open her world. She just sleeps all day and stays up all night. She needs you."

He pulled his hands from mine and turned away. "That's where you're wrong. She needs Drew."

"What?"

"She kissed him. Did you forget about that?"

"I know." I flinched, the pain of this memory was like a slap in the face. If he thought he was the only one tortured by that kiss, he was wrong. "But that was a mistake, Luke, and it was their enchantments that connected them. That's over now."

"But now she has the darkness in her, which fills her with a greed and need that she won't be able to control, and that darkness gets stronger when she's around me, so why would I subject myself and her to that?"

I took a deep breath and exhaled slowly. "Fine," I said. "Suit yourself. But just so you know, she's miserable right now."

"I can't fix that."

"Maybe not, but you could help us find the cure."

"As soon as that world is open, Maddy, what the hell do you think I'll be doing?"

"What do you mean?"

"The minute she crosses over into Yelram, she unlocks her world for the rest of us." He took his necklace donning his keeper key and said, "Take me to Yelram." Nothing happened. "See? She hasn't opened her world yet."

"Then you do care."

"Of course I care. I want her to find the cure, but I don't want to be the reason she turns before she does."

"That's not going to happen," I said, dismissing his concern without a second thought. But of course I had thought about it. So had Drew, which was why we had been trying so hard to convince her to open the world so we could start the search for the cure.

"What is she waiting for?"

"Why don't you ask her yourself?"

"Maddy," he began, "I can't be around her. If she hasn't turned already, it won't take much to send her to the dark side."

"Luke," I tried one last time as I felt myself waking, being sent from his world, "you're our last hope."

ABOUT THE AUTHOR

K.L. HAWKER grew up in Nova Scotia, Canada, where she spent her childhood writing stores that took her imagination all over the world. All grown up, Hawker is still an avid daydreamer and writer, and enjoys travelling the globe with her family, visiting all the places she once only dreamed about.

For more information, please visit:

WWW.KLHAWKER.COM

ABOUT THE DAISIES

SEVENTEEN-YEAR-OLD Alexis Fletcher is the artist and creator of this beautiful trio of daisies that you will find at every chapter heading in this book series. In December 2015, after an unforgiving struggle with mental illness, Alexis ended her life. A close friend of my son's, Alexis was a beautiful, caring, outgoing, funny, smart and very talented girl. She is loved by all who knew her. As light and delicate as a daisy, Alexis's spirit now blooms freely and without suffering.

MY HOPE IS that you will consider educating yourself on mental illness and suicide prevention. If not for yourself, then for someone you care about, because we all struggle at one point or another. Alexis's family started a non-profit foundation in Alexis's memory wherein they help to provide much-needed support for other young people like Alexis. You can find out more about this foundation by following the link below. You can also purchase a piece of jewellery for just $20CDN and wear this trio of daisies proudly in support of mental health. All proceeds will go to the foundation to ensure youth get the help they need.

WWW.BELIEVEINHOPEFORALEXIS.COM

ACKNOWLEDGMENTS

I wouldn't be where I am today without the continued love and support of:

My superstar husband, Stuart, who believes in my dreams and encourages me daily.

My three amazing kids—Austin, Kate, and Marley. I love you more than you'll ever know.

My amazing mother, Linda, who inspires me daily to be a better version of myself. If I'm half the woman she is, I'm pretty incredible.

My big sister, Krista, who is always there for me. She has the biggest heart, and I love having her in my corner.

My amazing friends, for their encouragement, support, and invaluable feedback.

My faith, my God. For giving me a place to run to when I'm afraid, for being a listening ear when I'm down, and for helping me to believe in myself and my God-given talents.

And all my faithful readers. Always.